Siblings

INTRIGUE AND DECEPTION

A story of love, sacrifice, secrets, and espionage

R.D. Ellis

Australian Self Publishing Group
P.O. Box 159, Calwell, ACT Australia 2905
Email: publishaspg@gmail.com
http://www.inspiringpublishers.com

 A catalogue record for this book is available from the National Library of Australia

National Library of Australia The Prepublication Data Service

Author: R.D. Ellis
Title: Siblings
Genre: Fiction

Paperback ISBN: 978-1-923449-74-9

To Roslyn, Lyn, and Michele
for all their love, support, and encouragement.

PART ONE

Eva

CHAPTER ONE

1959

"The wrong decisions will haunt you until the day you die." These were the words of wisdom my twin sister Eloise and I received the day we started school. I don't recall who said it, but I wish we had remembered this advice when we were older. Our lives may have turned out very differently.

Our father, Ben Carter, was the only parent my sister and I knew. He worked two jobs to make ends meet. During the day he repaired cars, and three nights a week he worked at an all-night gas station. Although Dad always worked hard, when we were together, we had the best time.

The only other family Dad had was his younger brother and best friend, Mike. Uncle Mike adored us girls and wanted to be part of our lives so, when we were only a few weeks old, he moved into our tiny house outside of Denver. My grandfather had been cruel to his sons, especially Mike, so when Mary, their loving mother, passed away, they cut all ties with their father. It was easier to think he had died too.

Dad was a tall, slender man with dark curly hair, brown eyes, a winning smile, and a dimple on his chin. When he was eighteen, he joined the Air Force as a mechanic and was discharged at age twenty-six, the same day he met our mother, Emily. They instantly fell in love. His face always lit up when he spoke of her and their time together. He would tell us about her flowing auburn curls, her red lips and green eyes, her gentle touch, and how she loved to dance.

Eloise and I would only ever hear about Dad's good times with Mom and the beautiful spring day in 1953 when we were born. If we asked anything else about her, he would abruptly change the subject. We could see how painful it was for him to try to explain why she left, so we never asked.

When we were seven, Eloise and I were snooping around for our Christmas presents when we discovered a box at the back of Dad's closet. It was filled with different documents, including our birth certificates, and a photo of him with our mother when she was pregnant. She had been captured looking sad. There was also a note:

> *Ben,*
>
> *I never wanted to be a mother. The twins are all yours. Don't ever search for me.*
>
> *Emily.*

We waited until Dad was at work and asked Uncle Mike. He told us our mother had abandoned us the night we were born, and no one had heard from her since.

"Some people are not meant to be parents," he said.

Later, I realized he was also talking about his father.

Uncle Mike was a quiet, kindhearted man with fair hair and sad green eyes. He was slender, the same as Dad, but a little shorter. His face would change completely when he smiled, and when he laughed his shoulders shook up and down, making my sister and I giggle. Uncle Mike was a professor at the nearby university, and he came alive when he read adventure stories to us at night. He had such a fantastic way of telling them.

Dad and Uncle Mike may have been brothers, but they were very different, like Eloise and me. Although my sister and I were twins and had the same brown hair, we were not identical, and our personalities were opposites.

Uncle Mike and Eloise were the quiet ones. She had Mom's green eyes and was artistic. She always wore dresses, skirts, and girly things and hated wearing overalls. Her dream was to play the piano all over the world.

She often asked Dad, "Do you think I could take piano lessons one day?"

"One day, kiddo," he would say and hug her.

I was loud, athletic, and a tomboy. Dad said I had his brown eyes and a touch of Mom's auburn hair. I enjoyed playing soccer and would run around the field and yell as loud as I could. I wore overalls, long pants, and shorts—getting me into a dress was a battle.

One year for our birthday, when money was tight, Dad gave me a new soccer ball and Eloise a plastic keyboard. We were both thrilled with our gifts. I would go outside and kick the ball around with Dad while my sister and uncle would sit on our tiny patio— Uncle Mike reading a book and Eloise playing her keyboard and humming along to the music.

We didn't need a lot of money. The four of us were happy. Although we were all different, it worked, and we adored each other.

One cold fall night, when we were only eight, Dad was working at the gas station when two young men, high on drugs, entered the station intending to rob it. Dad, the ex-soldier, tried to stop them, and they shot him. He was dead before he hit the floor. After all those years defending his country, two drugged-out teenagers took his life without a single thought.

I only remember snippets of that night, but those stayed with me forever.

I woke up to blue-and-red lights flashing outside the bedroom window. I quickly got out of bed, rushed to my sister, and woke her. We went into the living room together and found two police officers with Uncle Mike.

He was sitting on the couch, his face buried in his hands, sobbing. It was the first time I had seen my uncle cry. I pulled his hands away and sat on his lap. He looked at me with the saddest eyes.

"Uncle Mike, it's okay," I said. "Whatever it is, Daddy will fix it when he gets home."

"Oh, sweet Eva, your daddy died tonight. He's never coming home."

My sister fell to the floor and cried in despair. I stared at my uncle momentarily, not understanding what was happening, and put my arms around his neck. He was distraught, and all I could say was, "There, there, it will be okay," while he hugged me tightly.

I don't remember much else about that night, but I do remember Eloise and I staying very close to each other for weeks after, barely letting go of each other's hands.

CHAPTER TWO

The following day, an older man, tall and slender with gray hair and a grubby mustache, was in our house on the telephone.

We found out he was our grandfather. Neither Dad nor Uncle Mike had ever spoken about him.

He put the phone down and introduced himself as "the Colonel." Jacob Carter had been in the military, and everyone, including his family, still addressed him as Colonel.

The Colonel picked both of us up together, just as Dad used to, and said he had everything under control. I remember him smelling of tobacco with a hint of mothballs.

The day of Dad's funeral was cold and gray. The icy-cold south winds blew and chilled us to the bone. The Colonel had supplied Eloise and me with identical black dresses, black shoes, and white socks. I didn't fight this time about wearing a dress, but the Colonel also insisted we wear identical black bows pinned on the left side of our hair, and though my sister didn't mind, I hated bows. I remember the Colonel telling me many times to stop touching it and to leave it alone.

Uncle Mike wore a white shirt with a black suit, which was too big for him. He wouldn't let go of our hands during the service. I remember him sitting between Eloise and me on a wooden bench in a small church. There was a large photo of Dad in his military uniform beside the closed coffin, which was dark timber with the flag on top instead of flowers.

Not many people were at the funeral—some from Dad's work, our uncle's school, and a few neighbors. People from his work stood beside his coffin, saying kind things, but I wasn't listening. Instead, I studied Dad's photo. I couldn't take my eyes off it. I had never seen my father in this uniform before. It didn't look anything like him.

Years later, I discovered the Colonel had insisted on the photo. It was not what the three of us, who knew him, would have chosen.

There was no money left for a wake after the cremation, so the generous ladies of the church committee prepared coffee and cakes in the adjoining small community center. My sister, uncle, and I sat in chairs facing the door. Part of me kept waiting for Dad to come in and say, "Come on, time to go to the playground," but he never appeared. People tried speaking to Uncle Mike, but he had trouble finding words as he was grief-stricken. Uncle Mike had not only lost his big brother but also his best friend.

I didn't cry at the funeral. I knew I had to be brave for Uncle Mike and Eloise. Dad used to say to me, "I love you and Eloise the same, but you, Eva, you and I are alike, and we must be brave for the other two." And I was.

When we got home, with the Colonel in tow, I pulled the stupid bow out of my hair, threw it onto the floor, and ran into my bedroom. There were muffled sounds behind me, but I didn't care what they said. I took off the black dress and tossed it in the corner of the room, along with the shoes, and changed into my pajamas, got into bed, buried my face in my pillow, and cried.

Eloise came into our room and saw my dress and shoes dumped on the floor in the corner, and without a word, she did the same thing. She then climbed into bed next to me and rubbed my back.

I turned and faced her and said, "Dad's not coming back, is he?"

"No," she softly answered.

We put our foreheads together, sobbed, and did what we called our twin chant. It was our secret. No other person knew about it. We would say this over and over until we fell asleep in each other's arms.

"We were born together, and together we will always be."

* * *

The Colonel's loud voice from the kitchen woke me the following morning. I carefully got out of bed, not wanting to wake Eloise.

My uncle was sitting on the kitchen chair, looking down at his cup of coffee, and the Colonel was standing over him, saying, "This is how it has to be. You can't support yourself, let alone two children. I don't know what your brother thought when he made you the guardian of those girls."

Uncle Mike continued to stare into his coffee.

Why isn't he telling him to shut up? I thought. But my uncle sat there, appearing broken.

The Colonel saw me in the doorway, came over, picked me up, and said with a broad smile, "Well, granddaughter, it's been decided. You girls and your uncle are coming to live with me. It's the only way."

My uncle finally spoke up, still looking at his coffee. "You know Ben didn't want this for his girls."

"Well, Ben didn't want to be murdered either, but he's gone, so this is how it has to be."

With his head still lowered, Uncle Mike stood up, went to his bedroom, and closed his door.

Still holding me in his arms, the Colonel joyfully announced, "You, little lady, go get your sister. We must pack."

"But I don't want to leave our home," I said.

His face turned from joy to anger, as if I had flicked a switch. "From now on, you, your sister, and your uncle will do what I say, and no one will question it. Got it?" he snarled.

I cringed in his arms, suddenly afraid.

He put me down and patted me on top of my head. The smile returned to his face. "You'll see, little miss, it's for the best."

I felt sad about leaving our home. We grew up there, and our dad had lived here, but if Uncle Mike wasn't going to stop his father from making us move, what chance did we have?

The Colonel left and returned within the hour with boxes for us to start packing up our lives. It only took a day and a half to do so, and before we knew it, we were on the road to the Colonel's house.

Eloise and I drove with Uncle Mike in his car. Our grandfather drove alone, always behind us in his car. I think it was to make sure we didn't make a run for it. During the three-hour drive, no one spoke. Eloise and I sat in the back, me peering out the left window and her peering out the right, our hands joined in the middle. Uncle Mike drove in silence with the same sad expression he'd had since Dad died; the same sad face that stayed with him for the rest of his life.

The Colonel had been widowed eleven years ago and lived in a relatively large, slightly rundown farmhouse in the country. His property had a barn and a few chickens, and behind the barn were woods. They looked inviting, and I couldn't wait to explore them.

When we walked into the house, we entered straight into the living room, where a piano was next to the bay windows.

Eloise gasped. She turned to the Colonel and softly asked, "Can I please touch it?"

He gazed at the piano and said, "It was my Mary's, your grandmother. I guess it would be okay. Don't damage it."

Uncle Mike finally spoke. "She won't damage it. She has always wanted to play the piano."

"Well then, we'll have to consider getting you girls some lessons."

"Not me," I said. "Only Eloise plays."

"Well, I will decide later. Now go unpack your things, and I'll get dinner started. I'll tell you girls in a little while to set the table. That's going to be one of your jobs from now on. Setting the table, doing dishes, and collecting eggs. We will go over the rules at dinner."

Rules. The Colonel said *rules*, not chores. We didn't mind doing chores, we had always done those, but *rules* sounded very strict.

Uncle Mike moved into his old bedroom. When I passed his room, the door was ajar, and I saw him sitting on the edge of his bed with his head in his hands. I think he was crying.

Eloise and I shared a room. We could have had separate rooms if we had wanted, we didn't. The bedroom assigned to us had bunk beds and blue walls. I quickly claimed the top bunk.

As we unpacked, Eloise asked me, "Do you think he will let me take piano lessons?"

I hugged her. "I hope so."

* * *

After a week of living at the Colonel's house, he took the two of us out into the woods to teach us how to shoot a rifle. He told us it was the same gun he had taught his boys to shoot with.

Eloise was not pleased about the idea, but I couldn't wait. It was exhilarating creeping through the woods, the Colonel showing us how to move among the trees and shrubs quietly.

He handed Eloise the rifle first and set her up to shoot a rabbit.

No, I can't do it," she cried, dropping the rifle and running back to the house.

"All right, girl," he said to me. "We know what your sister is made of. Let's see what *you're* made of."

I took the rifle, stood the way he told me, and carefully, silently, waited for the next rabbit.

There was a slight rustle in the undergrowth, and the Colonel whispered instructions in my ear. The rabbit hopped across the clearing, and I took aim and fired.

I got it in a single shot.

"That's my girl, a natural, the same as your daddy."

I observed the poor rabbit I had killed, realizing I had taken a life, wondering if this was how I was supposed to feel: simultaneously excited and guilty.

"What you must remember, girl, is this is life. You'll know what to do when you're hungry or need to protect your family. One thing is for sure, we can't rely on your sister or uncle to protect or feed us." The Colonel came over and picked up the rabbit by its back legs. "You've put dinner on the table tonight. You should be very proud of yourself."

And I was.

When we returned to the barn, the Colonel showed me how to skin and prepare my first kill. I found it fascinating, but I knew Eloise would be horrified.

Before going back inside, I asked the Colonel, "Can we go hunting again?"

He laughed. "Of course we can, little darling." He put his arm around my shoulders and explained how he would cook the rabbit.

When we got inside the house, Eloise was sitting on the couch beside Uncle Mike, who had his arm around her. I could tell she was distressed.

The Colonel approached Eloise, grabbed her by her arm, and pulled her up. "You, missy, show respect when you have a gun. You hear me? Don't ever drop a gun again." He yelled at her.

"Yes, sir," she said quietly, unable to look him in the eye.

Uncle Mike tried to defend her. "She's not like that, Colonel."

"Hell, that's all I need, another you." He let go of her arm and headed to the kitchen, calling over his shoulder at me, "Come on, girl, you and I have some cooking to do."

My sister seemed scared as she rubbed her arm, tears running down her face. I hugged her and told her it was okay, as the Colonel called me again to come help with the rabbit.

The following week, the Colonel purchased me a new rifle and announced that Eloise could start piano lessons. We were both shocked. I was thrilled with my new rifle, and Eloise was ecstatic to be finally playing a real piano.

As time passed, we stopped doing many things together as a family. By the time I realized this, it was too late.

The Colonel became a little mellower over time. He was caring toward Eloise and me, but he was hard and unkind to Uncle Mike. The Colonel's stories about his son's earlier life showed that Dad had been his favorite. The Colonel had always thought Uncle Mike was a failure, as he had never wanted to join the military.

Uncle Mike's views on life differed from his father's, but he put all of it aside, stayed quiet, and lived in his world of work and books. It was easier to let his father make all the decisions. There was no confrontation that way, as he knew he would never get his father to agree with him.

When Eloise and I started at a new school, Uncle Mike became a professor at the nearby college, and he would drive us to and from school most days. We were put in the same class and got the same grades. We stuck together and ate lunch together. We didn't have any other friends, only each other, and we were happy.

Our weekends were mainly spent with the Colonel teaching me hunting and survival in the woods, and Eloise playing the piano. Uncle Mike would prepare lessons and sometimes do private tutoring. He never went out with friends. He stayed home but mostly worked late at the university. I realize now what Uncle Mike meant when he said, "This is not what Ben would have wanted for his girls." He was right.

CHAPTER THREE

It was 1970, and Eloise and I had just finished our senior year of high school. Things had changed since elementary school. We attended separate classes—I joined the track and field team, and Eloise joined the music group. My sister had a gift, and her music teacher believed that, with the proper teaching, she would go far. We both excelled in our studies, and our career adviser encouraged us to apply to colleges. We had always thought we would attend the same college, but it didn't work out that way. Eloise received a scholarship from the San Francisco Conservatory for Music and, to my surprise, Arizona State University offered me one.

We discussed not going away and attending the local university together, but I knew all Eloise wanted in life was to play the piano professionally, and I would never have forgiven myself if I stopped her from going after her dream. So, I encouraged her to go, and we told each other that if we were miserable being apart, we would change colleges and move somewhere together after a year.

One evening, as we were going through college information packages, I asked my sister a question I had been putting off for years.

"Do you ever think about finding our mother?"

"No," she snapped back at me. "Remember what Uncle Mike said? She abandoned us. Why would we want to find someone who never wanted us? She never loved or tried to get to know you or me, and I'll never forgive her for breaking Dad's heart. Besides, in her note, she said, 'Don't find me.' We're better off without her."

Eloise was upset, and I was stunned by her rant. But the more we debated it, the more heated things got.

"Eva, you have to promise me you won't go and find her. Nothing good will come of it. Please, promise me," she demanded.

Eventually, I gave in and agreed.

When Eloise finally calmed down, she said, "I'm never going to fall in love or have children. I couldn't bear disappointing anyone."

Her words didn't shock me as I had similar feelings.

The Colonel died in his sleep three weeks before we were to leave for college. He had organized and paid for his funeral with instructions to bury him next to his wife. He had left Uncle Mike his property "so he wouldn't be homeless." He actually said it in his will. I couldn't decide if the old man was having the last word or if, deep down, he cared for his only living child. He also left Eloise and me enough money to attend college with our scholarships.

The funeral was quick as only the three of us were at the graveside. I was the only one who shed tears for the Colonel. He had burned many bridges throughout his life, including those with his son and Eloise.

After the burial, we went home and silently ate dinner. No words could explain how we were feeling. It wasn't sadness. It may have been pity.

Before we knew it, Eloise and I had to leave for college. I was worried about leaving our uncle alone and being separated from my twin.

Uncle Mike took us out for the fanciest dinner in town the evening before we left. He told us how proud he was of us and how proud our dad would have been to see his two girls attend college. At the end of the meal, after he had paid the bill, he pulled two identical black velvet boxes out of his jacket pockets. Inside each box was a single strand of pearls. It must have taken him a long time to save up for these on a professor's salary; you could tell they were expensive. We both gasped with delight, hugged him, and told him we would cherish them forever.

"Every young lady must have a strand of pearls," he said with a tear in his eye before pulling himself together. "Best we get going. You girls have a big day tomorrow." He stood up and headed for the door.

That night, after Eloise and I had finished our last bit of packing, the two of us decided, for old times' sake, we would share a bed, as we had when we were little. We spent the night crying, laughing, making plans, and sharing our hopes and dreams. We got about two hours of sleep, but it was a night I will never forget. We both had mixed emotions—hating the idea of leaving each other and Uncle Mike, but also wanting to experience the excitement of the unknown.

We recited our secret twin chant to each other. *"We were born together, and together we shall always be."*

The morning came quickly, and we had to leave early to get to the airport, so there was no time to be sad. Uncle Mike drove us and waited until we left. Our flights were an hour and fifteen minutes apart, and Eloise's was first. After a tearful, drawn-out goodbye, Uncle Mike and I watched Eloise walk across the tarmac to the stairs of her aircraft. My heart skipped a beat, and the hairs on my body stood on end. Something made me feel afraid. I couldn't put my finger on it, but I knew something bigger than both of us was on its way.

I think Eloise sensed it too as she suddenly stopped, turned, and looked back at me, frightened. Then she smiled and nodded her head as if to say it was okay. And she turned and disappeared up the stairs and onto the aircraft.

I wanted to run after her, pull her back, and tell her we should stay together, but I knew we had to take this journey apart.

CHAPTER FOUR

Once settled into our dorms, Eloise and I tried to telephone each other every second day, and we would talk a mile a minute at the same time. Oh, how I missed her.

About two months after we started college, Uncle Mike sent us a letter to tell us he had sold the farmhouse and moved into a three-bedroom apartment closer to work. He'd had no desire to stay in the house as it held too many bad memories.

He told us he had placed the piano, rifles, and our other belongings into storage for when we were ready for them. He also made it clear that his home would be ours as well, and we would always have a room there.

Eloise was passionate about her music and excelled at it; she always had part-time work playing for orchestras and theater productions.

My career counselor, Mr. Gerald, thought a behavioral and criminal investigation degree would suit me. After the first lecture, I felt inspired and decided it was what I wanted to do. I excelled in the course and aced every exam. I still did well in the athletic department to keep my scholarship, but criminal investigation inspired me.

When I told Eloise, she didn't seem surprised.

"I always knew you had the brains," she said.

* * *

My first year at college went by faster than I thought it would. I was doing great in my subjects and even made friends. Although my sister and I missed each other a lot, being apart forced us to create other friendships, something we hadn't needed to do in the past as we always had each other.

Eloise and I met at Uncle Mike's place for our summer break. After spending a few weeks with him, we decided to take a road trip together. We borrowed Uncle Mike's car and drove without a plan. We stayed in a little beach town and, although we didn't do much, reconnecting with my sister was fun. Before we knew it, we returned to college for our second year.

After a few months back at school, Uncle Mike sent us both another letter. He wrote to say he had an inoperable brain tumor. He didn't want us to rush home or telephone as he would see us both at Christmas. We would all discuss it then.

Eloise phoned me as I had finished reading the letter. We were both stunned by the news and his request not to visit, and as much as we wanted to rush to his side, it was more important to follow his wishes.

A week later, he called me to say he was entering a care facility as he didn't want us coming home and care for him. I told him I loved him and that he was a wonderful uncle.

There was silence on the other end of the phone, then he said something I didn't understand.

"Eva, your world can change quickly. Think very carefully before you make decisions about your future."

I was a little taken aback by his comment. What on earth did he mean?

Then he said, "Keep this conversation to yourself. I need your promise."

He sounded like the Colonel.

Maybe it was the medication or the brain tumor talking, but I wanted to make him happy, so I promised. After I hung up, I phoned Eloise and asked if he had called her as well. She said he had told her about us not coming home and how he was entering a care facility. I asked her if he'd sounded strange, and she said he was a little odd, but she thought, as I did, that it was his medication.

I put the promise I had made in the back of my mind. Besides, maybe Uncle Mike had asked Eloise to keep the same promise.

Eighteen days later, we received a message from our uncle's lawyer. Uncle Mike had passed away, and he had already been cremated and placed next to his brother and best friend, our father. His lawyer had strict instructions not to contact us until it was over, as our uncle hadn't wanted us to go through any more funerals.

Poor Uncle Mike. He'd died alone.

His apartment would be kept while we were in college for us to use. Once we had graduated, it would be sold, with the money to be split between the two of us, his only living relatives. Uncle Mike had also paid for the storage unit holding our childhood items for another five years.

Our family had been small, and now it was only the two of us.

I lay awake thinking of my uncle taking his last breath with no family around him, and it was the first time I realized it had been the same for Dad.

The news of Uncle Mike made me very sad. Not only for him but for Dad as well.

I was crying when the phone rang. I knew straight away it was my sister.

"He died alone, just as Dad did," she said, crying.

We often shared the same thoughts.

We stayed on the line together for a long time, listening to each other cry, and decided to meet up at the apartment for Christmas.

Two months after I received the news about Uncle Mike, my career counselor, Mr. Gerald, called me into his office. When I arrived, a tall man in a dark suit was talking to him.

Mr. Gerald said, "Eva, are you comfortable if I leave you two alone?"

I said yes, curious about what this man wanted.

"I'll be outside if you need me," Mr. Gerald said.

"Please sit," the tall man said. He sat in Mr. Gerald's chair behind his desk, facing me.

I sat down. "What's this about?" I asked.

"My name is Mr. Nichols." He opened the file on the desk and studied it. "Let's see, Eva Carter, twin sister to Eloise Carter, is currently studying at the San Francisco Conservatory for Music. Your father, Benjamin Carter, served his country in the Air Force, then died in a shooting when you and your sister were eight years and two months old. Your mother, Emily Sawyer, left after giving birth and was never seen again." He stopped and stared at me with dark-brown eyes and a straight face.

Although I was intimidated by him, I didn't flinch.

He continued. "Grandfather, Colonel Jacob Carter, who also served in the military, died two years and seven months ago from natural causes, and your uncle … hmm, your uncle Michael Carter died very recently from a brain tumor." He closed the file and glared at me again. "Can you tell me what your uncle did for a living?"

I was caught off-guard by the question. "You seem to be the expert on my family, you tell me," I said, challenging him.

The expression on his face didn't change, and a few seconds passed with us staring at each other.

I broke the silence. "A college professor." Then I got concerned. "Did my uncle do something wrong? Is my sister all right?"

"Yes, your sister is fine and doing extremely well," he stated. "Miss Carter, you seem to be excelling in your studies. You're also doing very well at all your track and field events. You have been brought to our attention because of these things, along with some other attributes you possess, and a high recommendation from the college." Then he paused, reviewed the file again, and looked up at me. "Miss Carter, you're the type of person we consider inviting to join our organization."

I sat there with my mouth open before I finally said, "Are you offering me a job?"

"It's a possibility. However, there are some very strict conditions."

My curiosity took over. "What kind of conditions?"

"Miss Carter, what I am about to tell you is extremely confidential, and you must not repeat it to anyone." He took a piece of paper from the file and handed it to me. "To continue this conversation, I first need you to read this confidentiality agreement carefully and sign it. Please take your time."

Is he for real? Is someone pranking me? I gingerly took the paper and noticed it bore a government seal. I looked at Mr. Nichols as he crossed his arms and settled back into Mr. Gerald's chair.

The first time I read the page, my brain didn't absorb any of it. I took a moment to calm my mind and reread it. I had to do this several times before it all sank in.

Wow, this guy was serious.

"If I sign this," I said, looking for his confirmation, "it doesn't mean I accept the job. It's so we can discuss it. And I can't tell anyone about it, ever, or I and whoever I tell could go to jail."

"Correct. Signing the confidentiality agreement gives me the authority to discuss the position with you. It doesn't mean you will accept any position, or that we will accept you into the organization. Do you understand?"

I reread the agreement one more time. Infatuated by the mystery and intrigue, I said "yes," signed the document, and handed it back.

"Very well, now we can begin. Miss Carter, you are being considered as an operations officer for the government's Illegal Arms and Counterterrorism Agency. Our agency is highly confidential, dealing with terrorists and illegal cartels worldwide. You would be helping to keep our country safe."

Our meeting lasted nearly two hours. Mr. Gerald knocked on the door once to see if I was okay, and I assured him everything was fine. When I left the office, pure exhilaration ran through my body. As Christmas was not far away, I had until after the holidays to decide, but I knew deep down what I wanted to do. The hard part was going to be lying to my sister.

For the next twenty-four hours, I weighed the pros and cons of all my options. There were more cons than pros, but there was no doubt I was ecstatic about the job.

I knew what I wanted to do when I left to meet with Eloise at Uncle Mike's place for Christmas. I wished I could talk to my sister about it, but I couldn't. It would be too dangerous for both of us if I did.

CHAPTER FIVE

Our Christmas together was wonderful but sad. Uncle Mike had thought of everything. Cleaners had been in and the refrigerator filled, all organized by Uncle Mike's lawyer as per his instructions. They also arranged for a Christmas tree, ready for us to decorate. It was clear he must have known he wouldn't be there for Christmas but still wanted us to enjoy ourselves.

The days with Eloise leading up to Christmas and the New Year were wonderful. After a few glasses of wine one night, she told me about all the male suitors who had asked her out and how she turned them away.

"I'm in love with my music. It's the only thing that won't betray or lie to me, apart from you. So, no serious relationships for me, just my career and you," she informed me.

Her statement made me feel guilty about keeping my news from her, but the excitement about my prospects was greater than my guilt.

On our last night together, we were in the kitchen doing the dishes when Eloise said, "You're daydreaming again."

Her words snapped me out of it. "No, I'm not."

She stopped wiping the dishes. "Yes, you are. Why do I feel you're keeping something from me? What aren't you telling me?"

I tried not to get flustered by her questions. "I was thinking about poor Uncle Mike."

"Eva, you have never lied to me before, and I know you're doing it now."

Damn her. Eloise could always sense these things.

I stopped washing up, wiped my hands, and turned and hugged her. "I'm not, sis, truly I'm not. It's strange being in this place surrounded by Uncle Mike's things. I was wondering how this Christmas would have been if Dad and Uncle Mike had been with us. I didn't want to say anything because I didn't want to upset you."

She stared into my eyes, as if she were trying to read my mind, then hugged me back. "I'm sorry. I didn't mean to say you were lying to me. It *is* strange being here, and now we have to go back to school and not see each other again for a while. Hey, how about we do something this summer? Maybe a trip overseas. We could use the money Uncle Mike left us." Eloise was thrilled at the idea.

I couldn't tell her I didn't know where I would be in the summer, so I lied again. "It would be great."

"We could do Europe. I've always wanted to go to the Theater an der Wien or the Musikverein concert hall in Vienna."

Eloise hugged me again. I felt ashamed for stringing her along, but I knew I had no choice.

The next day, we said our teary goodbyes at the airport. I cried a little more than my sister, as I didn't know when I would see her again.

"I'll talk to you next week, and we can start planning our trip," she said.

I hugged her again and told her I loved her, and even though we were grown up, we still recited our twin chant before we left each other.

The whole trip back to college, my guilt grew, and I started to have second thoughts about my decision. But the day after I returned to college, Mr. Nichols was back in Mr. Gerald's office, sitting behind the desk, and I came right out and said, "Yes, I want this. I feel I was born for this." I had no hesitation.

"Excellent. Now there are more confidentiality agreements to look over and sign. You understand it is illegal for you to speak to anyone regarding your position or anything about it. Your contract will be for five years. After that time, if you do not wish to renew your contract, you will still be legally unable to disclose any information about your time with the agency. Have you considered this?"

"Yes. I have considered everything and still want it," I said.

"Once you have signed, we'll discuss the training. You will also need to get your affairs in order." He handed me the documents, and I signed them without wavering.

Mr. Nichols checked them over and handed me an envelope. "This contains your cover story—what you tell people about who you are and what you do—and there will be consequences if there are any deviations from the script. Memorize it ASAP, then dispose of it." He glared straight at me. "Do you understand?"

I pulled my shoulders back in confidence. "Yes, I understand."

Mr. Nichols told me I would be reporting to the training center as soon as next week for rigorous psychological and physical testing. "After you have passed them, you will start your training. It will cover the complexities of handling foreign assets and retrieving the most closely guarded information across multiple scenarios, preparing you to handle anything that may go wrong. It will be physically, mentally, and emotionally challenging, and not everyone makes it."

The more he explained, the more excited I got.

After carefully studying my cover story and the training requirements, I knew I had to make the phone call I didn't want to make.

Eloise picked up the telephone on the first ring. "What's wrong?" She didn't even say hello. It creeps me out when she does it.

"Nothing's wrong. I want to tell you I was offered a great opportunity. It's overseas, and I have decided to take it."

At first, nothing but silence.

"What?"

"There's a private organization that allows you to get a teacher degree while teaching kids English in villages and a few of us signed up and we're going to Southeast Asia. As I said, it's a wonderful opportunity."

"Where in Southeast Asia?" she asked.

"Thailand, at first."

"Are you kidding? Why can't you do this when you graduate? Wait, this is what was wrong with you at Christmas, right?"

She sounded betrayed, and I didn't blame her. I would have felt the same if the shoe were on the other foot.

Throughout our lives, my sister and I barely argued. But this argument made up for it. We fought for nearly an hour.

In the end, Eloise said, "So how will I be able to contact you?"

"We'll find a way, we always do," I reassured her. "Anyway, there will be holidays, and I can come and visit."

There was another silence on the other end of the phone.

"I guess we won't be going to Europe this summer," she said. "Do I get to see you before you go?"

"I have about four to five months of preparation at their corporate headquarters first, then I don't know."

"When do you leave?" she asked. I could tell she was crying.

"In a few days."

"You're leaving that soon? Can you at least phone me while you're at their headquarters?" Eloise asked.

"Yes. When I find out the number, I will let you know. I promise. I'll always keep in touch with you. Cross my heart."

More silence, then, "I have a bad feeling about this, Eva. Are you sure you want to do this?"

"This is what I want to do. It feels right."

"Well, I guess there's nothing more I can say if this is what you want." Eloise sounded hurt. "Make sure you keep your word," she said.

"I will," I assured her, not knowing it would be over a month before I would speak to her again and years until we would reunite.

CHAPTER SIX

Seven years had passed since joining the agency. Seven long years, and I had only seen my sister twice and telephoned her about four times a year. Each time we spoke, we acted more like distant relatives than twins.

As each year passed, I tried to ignore the guilt that consumed me. I hadn't kept my promises as I was either in some remote location or deep undercover. I couldn't contact my sister, and I couldn't explain why I had been absent when I eventually got to speak with her. That was the hard part.

I did, however, keep track of her career. She had accomplished what she had set out to do when she was a little girl: becoming a concert pianist and traveling the world playing in famous concert halls. She had fulfilled her dream, breaking hearts along the way (or so it was said in the music press).

I prayed she was happy. I missed her.

I was thinking of Eloise the day my cover was exposed. After eight successful assignments, two commendations, and finishing my teacher's diploma in preparation for my assignment, I had been deployed to the Philippines to go undercover for several months as an English tutor to Jacob Cruz's six-year-old daughter Sofia. Cruz was the head of a cartel illegally transporting weapons to the Middle East. My assignment was to gather intel on their strengths and weaknesses, and any terrorist activities in which they were involved.

At the time, another operative, Cole, was on Cruz's security detail. We had each other's backs, but it was forbidden for lower-level staff to talk together in the compound, so we didn't interact much.

I had been getting information to our people, but someone blew my cover. One minute I was tidying Sofia's room while she was out with her parents, and the next I was hit from behind, waking up later in a warehouse tied to a chair, blood dripping down my face and guns pointing at me.

An ugly man with no hair, a red scar running from his left eye to his chin, and foul breath that lingered in my nostrils would randomly punch me. You could tell he enjoyed it. When I passed out, he would throw a bucket of icy water in my face. Then the questioning and threats would start again.

"Tell me what you know, and you can live," he would say in his thick Filipino accent.

I knew that if I told the truth, my life would be over.

The man's face was constantly in front of me, yelling. I tried to act as the innocent victim, but it didn't work. Someone had told them who I was.

I kept slipping in and out of consciousness and didn't know how long I had been held captive. At times, I could see a man's figure in the shadows through my bloody eyes. He seemed familiar, but I couldn't quite recognize him.

The pain of the torture made me want to give up, but I mustered enough energy when the ugly man was close to my face to headbutt him. I don't know who it hurt more, but he retaliated by plunging his knife into my right side.

"I know how far to put it in again and again without it killing you."

His venomous words frightened me. Then the burning pain in my side took over. It was unbearable as blood soaked my dress, pooling on the floor. Between the loss of blood, the swollen eyes, and the injuries to my head and face, I knew it was only a matter of time before I succumbed to my torture.

It didn't take long for the hallucinations to start. I saw Dad's coffin with the draped flag, the first rabbit I killed, the Colonel laughing as he skinned it, and Uncle Mike saying, "Think carefully before you make any decisions." I also heard Eloise playing the piano and us giggling as little girls.

But it was Eloise's voice saying our chant that brought me back from the brink of death. I pleaded with God to let me live so I could see my sister again. The worst pain of all was the thought of Eloise never knowing what had happened to me.

More icy water was thrown in my face. The shock of it hitting me felt like thousands of tiny needles. I came around with such a start that it was hard to catch my breath. Weak, cold, and in pain, I was convinced my head had split open.

Suddenly, the warehouse doors blew apart, and Navy SEAL teams were shooting at my captors as the team ran toward me, asking for my code name.

They were here to rescue me. I managed to answer them before blacking out again.

CHAPTER SEVEN

I remember flashes of being transported onto a helicopter and Cole being restrained by two Navy SEALs in the back of the aircraft.

I regained consciousness briefly as they wheeled me into a hospital. Doctors were yelling orders, and a nurse was cutting off my bloody clothes.

Drifting in and out of consciousness for a week, the hospital staff buzzing around me, tending to my painful head and side wounds, I realized I was in an English-speaking hospital. When I finally came to, my handler told me the agency had airlifted me to a military base hospital.

Three high-level senior agents entered my room the next day and debriefed me for over two hours. After the debriefing, they informed me that Cole, my colleague on the mission, was a double agent and had orchestrated my capture. They explained that they had only recently uncovered evidence that he was a sadist and enjoyed watching young women being tortured. He was the one in the shadows watching, and I wasn't his first victim.

The agency was embarrassed for not detecting his *behaviors* earlier and wanted him in jail, never to be seen again.

I had let my guard down, and he had betrayed me.

They had caught him when the Navy SEAL team stormed the warehouse. With my testimony, the government could legally charge Cole with treason.

Good. Treason came with the death penalty.

I was still in the hospital nearly a month later when the hearing started, so they set up a camera and recorded my testimony. I told them everything I could about Cole's involvement in the mission.

A few days later, the agency informed me Cole had made a deal with the federal prosecutors. He took life in solitary confinement for a list of names. The death penalty was taken off the table. Cole had sworn he would search for me if he ever got the chance, but I wasn't afraid. He would never see the outside world again.

The whole time I was in the hospital, I only thought of Eloise and how I desperately wanted to talk to her. But I knew if I called her, she would know something was wrong, and I would probably tell her the truth about everything. I couldn't risk it.

But I had placed conditions on my testifying in Cole's trial. I was to be released from my contract immediately and relocated to a suitable location with a job away from anything to do with the agency. I had had enough and wanted an everyday life. I wanted the kind of life my father wanted for me and to reconnect with my sister. I needed to start over.

It didn't take long for my conditions to be approved. The agency had organized a little cottage in Oahu, Hawaii, near the beach, and since I had my diploma, a job as a schoolteacher, and a cover story for the past seven years, I had my fresh start where no one knew me.

The first thing I did when I reached the island was contact Eloise in San Francisco.

CHAPTER EIGHT

During the first two weeks of my new life, I took long, soothing walks along the beach nearly every day and slept as if I hadn't slept for a long time.

When I began teaching, I would go to the beach and swim after work. I enjoyed being in the water; it was calming and helped me to forget the last seven years of always looking over my shoulder and never being in the same place for more than a few months.

I kept to myself for the first six months. The other teachers would ask me to go out after work, but I would decline. Eloise visited for a few weeks. She had stopped touring and taken up a teacher's position at a university in San Francisco.

At first, we didn't know how to interact with each other; we were more like strangers. She had been furious with me for a long time because I pulled away, and I understood this. But Eloise could never stay mad at me for long, and, after a while, our relationship slowly became strong again.

Unable to tell her what I had been doing for those seven years, I stuck to my official cover story of teaching English in Asia. I didn't want to risk anything. But before she left, we committed ourselves to being in each other's lives more. Although we didn't visit together often, we spoke regularly.

One day in my first year in Oahu, Anne, a colleague, was having a birthday party and begged me to come. I said yes.

It was a warm spring Saturday night, and I was riddled with nerves as I approached Anne's front door. I hadn't felt this way in ages, and it took me by surprise. I stood at the door, trying to decide whether to go in, when I heard a male voice behind me.

"You know, I heard it helps if you ring the bell."

Turning around to give a smart reply, I had trouble speaking when I saw a tall, slender man smiling at me. He had sparkling green eyes and a flawless tan face. With those eyes on me and still smiling, he reached over my shoulder and rang the bell.

Anne answered the door straight away.

"Welcome." She said, laughing. "We've already started drinking."

I handed her a gift of scented candles, and she thanked me. Then we moved toward the people gathered on the back veranda. The man was still behind me. He kissed Anne on the cheek, gave her a bottle of champagne, and wished her a happy birthday.

"Charlie, Glad you could make it. Wait, did you two arrive together?" she asked.

"No," I quickly answered.

"We met at the door," he replied.

Anne introduced us to each other. "Eva works with me," Anne explained, "and Charlie works with Henry at the same firehouse."

We greeted each other and shook hands. As our hands pulled apart, there was a small zap of electricity.

"Henry, Henry!" Anne shouted, "Charlie and Eva are here." Henry appeared, and he and Charlie shook hands. "Nice to see you both. What can I get you both to drink?"

I asked for a glass of white wine, and Charlie wanted a beer.

"So, do you know many people here?" Charlie asked me.

"A few," I said.

"Me too."

Henry arrived with our drinks. I sipped my wine and noticed Charlie still staring at me.

"Is there something on my face?" I asked.

He laughed. His laugh was warm and charming. He took me gently by the arm and led me to two chairs at the side of the veranda. I was staring at Charlie as well. There was something about *him* that made *me* smile. I had never experienced such a strong connection with a stranger before, and we had only known each other for ten minutes.

"I apologize for staring," he said, "but this is the first time I've been here where Henry's had such a beautiful guest."

"How many times have you used that line?"

Charlie laughed. "I may have used the line before, but I can honestly tell you that this is the first time I meant it."

We sat together for hours. He had lived on Oahu his entire life. His Scottish mother, Olivia, fell in love with a young Hawaiian firefighter named Alika, Hawaiian for Alex. Charlie was an only child. Not long after he graduated from the fire academy, his father died in a fire. His mother died two years later from cancer, but Charlie knew she died from a broken heart.

After he told me about his parents, he lowered his head as if to pay respect to them.

It had been a long time since I had talked with anyone with so much passion for life. I could tell what kind of man he was in those few short hours. He would often gently put his hand on mine, and every time he did, my heart skipped a beat.

"So that's my story. Now I want to hear everything about you."

I told him about my father, uncle, and twin sister. I didn't, however, mention my work with the agency, instead giving him the same story I had told Eloise.

Henry and Anne kept bringing drinks and food and dropping in to chat, but Charlie listened as closely to my story as I had to his.

Before we knew it, Anne was blowing out birthday candles, and people were starting to leave.

"Oh, look at the time," I said. "I can't believe we talked for so long."

Charlie leaned over, gave me a gentle kiss on my cheek, and softly said, "I could talk to you until the end of time. Please say you'll meet me tomorrow. We can go on a picnic or whatever you want. I want to show you my island."

I nodded. "That would be wonderful."

"Good," he said, grinning from ear to ear. "I'll organize everything. Give me your number, and I'll phone you in the morning."

I smiled, got up, and went into Anne's kitchen to get paper and a pen.

Anne looked at me. "You and Charlie seemed to hit it off. He's a fabulous guy. You two would make a great couple."

"He wants my number," I said with a giggle. I hadn't giggled since I was young. Dating was all very new to me. Sure, guys had asked me out before, but there was something very different about this man.

Anne quickly found a piece of paper and a pen, and I gave my number to Charlie.

I didn't want to say goodnight to him as he walked me to my car. When he kissed me, shivers flooded my body.

* * *

Charlie phoned me at six the following morning, sounding very eager. He asked if he could pick me up at eight and start our day with breakfast at a little diner he knew. I couldn't wait. It took me trying on four outfits before I decided which one to wear, something I had never done before.

He arrived at 8 o'clock sharp. When I opened the door, he presented me with a round crystal vase full of white flowers. "I hope you like lilies," he said.

"They're one of my favorites."

"All right then, this day is getting off to a great start."

I had never laughed or smiled as much as I did that day. We began with breakfast at his favorite diner, then he took me all around the island, showed me his firehouse, and we finished back at the diner for an early dinner.

When he finally took me home, we were exhausted and happy. I asked him in, but he declined, stating he would be a gentleman and that he had to prepare for the night shift. We made plans for his next rostered day off. He was going to teach me how to surf; I couldn't wait.

How could I be falling for a guy after one day?

As Charlie reached his car, he called back to me, "Hey, beautiful, do you believe in soulmates?"

Surprised by his question, I replied, "I don't know. I've never thought about it."

A smile came over his face. "After today, I definitely do." And, still smiling, he got into his car and drove off.

Half an hour later my phone rang. It was Charlie. "Good night and sweet dreams," he said.

"Be careful tonight, okay, and no heroics," I said.

"For you, I'll be extra careful."

CHAPTER NINE

When neither of us were working, Charlie and I were together, and it felt right. After a month, I told my sister about him.

Charlie tried to get me to move in with him, but although we had already made love after our second date, in the seventies it wasn't proper for a single young lady to move in with a man.

One afternoon, after only six months of dating, we walked along the beach and saw a single-story house up for sale. Charlie immediately fell in love with the place and couldn't contain his excitement. He ran to the back door and knocked.

An elderly couple answered, and Charlie introduced us. He asked the couple if we could look around and, to my surprise, they said yes and offered to give us a tour. It was a sizable house with a spacious open-floorplan kitchen, dining room, and living room painted in a warm cream. Charlie commented the place was cozy like his parents' home, and it took me back to the loving feeling of my home before Dad died.

The kitchen windows were large and looked out onto the backyard and beach. The back door opened straight onto a deck, leading to a grassy area before reaching the sand and ocean. Off the living area was a long hallway and four bedrooms in total.

Charlie asked if I liked the house, and I did. He turned to the elderly couple and announced he wanted to buy it. When they agreed, Charlie got down on one knee, pulled out a diamond ring, and asked me to marry him. The couple stood there in amazement.

I surprised myself by saying yes to his proposal. I would never have thought I would agree to marriage after a short time of meeting someone. I started to cry as he placed the ring on my finger, then he picked me up and kissed me.

We had our dream home.

* * *

We didn't want a fancy wedding. We just wanted to get married.

I phoned Eloise the morning after we got engaged and told her we were getting married in a few days. I would have loved for her to be at my wedding, but she was in the middle of exams at the university and couldn't get away for some time. She said she was disappointed but understood and accepted my invitation to spend Christmas with us.

We called Anne and Henry, and two days later, after we got the marriage license, the four of us went to the city hall. Within a few hours, we were married. I wore a pastel blue dress and carried white lilies and white roses with a touch of Hawaiian tree fern, and Charlie was handsome in his uniform.

Before we entered the courtroom, he presented me with a velvet box. Inside was a single-diamond-drop necklace.

"I wanted you to have this on our wedding day," he said as he took the necklace out of the box and placed it around my neck.

I was wearing my pearls from Uncle Mike, and the diamond drop hung a little below them. The new and old parts of my life together.

The ceremony was quick and, before we knew it, the four of us celebrated at a restaurant on the beach with dinner and dancing.

CHAPTER TEN

The purchase of the house went through fast, and we were in it the week before Christmas. I was exhausted but wanted to get the house ready before Eloise arrived. I wanted her to feel welcome.

Charlie was working a twelve-hour shift, and I was unpacking and arranging the kitchen when a sudden wave of nausea hit me. I ran to the bathroom and threw up.

Eloise is arriving in a few days, and I'm coming down with stomach flu, I thought. I placed a cold washcloth on my face and lay on the bed.

Suddenly, I was overwhelmed with fear. I was pregnant.

No, this couldn't be happening. Eight months ago, I didn't have a boyfriend, and now I was married and pregnant. It was the first time since I had left the agency that I had the urge to run.

I calmed myself and decided I wouldn't tell Charlie until I saw the doctor and knew my options. I was scared. A baby. I didn't know anything about babies. I had never had any maternal role models; what if I had the same feelings as my mother and didn't want kids?

Charlie had talked about having children, but I had gone along with him, thinking I would deal with it if it happened. Well, it had happened.

I called the doctor's office and was lucky to get an appointment that afternoon. I needed to keep it together until I got the results.

The doctor took a blood test and examined me. He said he would get back to me as quickly as possible, but he was fairly positive I was pregnant. What was I going to do? Could I handle this? Did I *want* to handle this? My mind was racing. I thought of my mother and how trapped she must have felt to leave the way she did.

Charlie came home tired from his shift. "Are you okay, honey? You look a little pale."

"Just a bit tired from getting things ready." I didn't want to tell him the news because there was no turning back once it was out there.

A few days after my appointment, the doctor phoned and congratulated me. We were having a baby.

I paced the floor for nearly an hour after I got off the phone. It was Christmas Eve, and Charlie was due home soon before we picked up Eloise at the airport. What was I going to do? My emotions were all over the place, and I had many scenarios playing in my head.

The drive to the airport was mostly in silence.

"Are you alright?" Charlie asked, his voice full of care.

"Yes, a bit anxious to see Eloise. We haven't seen each other in a while," I said.

"Ah, you girls will have fun," he said as we parked the car and headed for the busy baggage claim area.

Looking around, I noticed babies everywhere. Was this a sign? But a sign for what? One mother was holding her baby protectively to her chest. You could see her love for her child as she gently kissed the top of its head. I put my hands to my stomach and suddenly experienced the bond everyone talked about.

Eloise arrived, and I wrapped my arms around her. We hugged as if we were little again.

"Well, what a great welcome," she said.

"Hi, I'm your brother Charlie." He also gave her a huge hug.

"I'm glad to be here."

"Let's get out of this chaos," he said as he grabbed her bags.

I took hold of her arm as we followed Charlie to the car.

We stopped at Charlie's favorite diner on the way home for dinner. He told Eloise all about his job and how we met. The two of them talked up a storm. I was relieved they were doing most of the talking as my mind was still racing about the pregnancy.

When we got home and opened the front door, all the Christmas decorations were lit up in the room. The tree was in the corner with its lights twinkling, and as I looked around, I saw how warm and cozy we had made our home. 'Home.' I hadn't had a loving home like this since Dad died.

I gave Eloise a tour of the house, and as I was helping her unpack, she stopped and held my hands.

"I can see why you fell in love with Charlie so quickly," she said. "You seem very content." She peered at me as if she knew something was up but couldn't quite put her finger on it. "I've never seen you like this."

I quickly changed the subject and picked up some of her clothes to put in the closet. I knew she would guess my secret if she stared at me any longer, and I wasn't ready to tell anyone.

"How about some cocoa around the Christmas tree? We can open one present," I said.

As if Charlie had read my mind, he was already making the cocoa when we entered the living room. The three of us sat around the tree, handing out presents, when a calmness came over me. I studied the only two people I loved, and without thinking it through, said, "I want to give you both a Christmas present, but you have to wait."

They both gazed at me.

"You have to wait about seven months." I turned to Charlie. "We're having a baby."

They were both stunned, and I thought I had made a mistake in telling them. Then, before I knew it, Charlie scooped me into his arms, and Eloise laughed and cried simultaneously.

"Really? Really?" Charlie kept asking.

"I thought there was something different about you. I can't wait to be an aunt." Eloise was hugging me. "I promise I will be the best aunt ever."

Later, when Charlie and I went to bed, Eloise poked her head around the doorway to say goodnight. Charlie got up and told her to stay, saying he would catch up on football while "you girls talk."

Eloise climbed onto the bed, and we faced each other.

"Are you happy about being pregnant?" she asked.

I thought for a second, knowing what she was getting at. "Yes, and I won't run as our mother did."

"Dad and Uncle Mike would have been ecstatic. You know I will be visiting a lot, and I will be as hands-on as possible," she said.

"I wish I could take back the last seven years and not have taken the job and stayed in college," I confessed. "We lost a lot of time together."

"Hey," she said. "No looking back. We have each other now. And a baby on the way."

We smiled at each other, and for the first time in years, we whispered our twin chant. Then we curled up together as if we were still young girls and fell asleep.

PART TWO

Ohana (Family)

CHAPTER ELEVEN

Ally

I was the firstborn child of Charlie and Eva Kane. Charles Adamu Kane was a well-respected fire chief for the Hawaiian Fire Department, and Eva was a much-loved elementary schoolteacher. They met at a party and instantly fell in love. Eight months later, they were married, and nine months after that, I came along.

During Mom's pregnancy, Dad was sure I was a boy and that my name would be Alex, after his father. He would tell his friends and colleagues, "his boy Alex" would be very handsome like his dad.

Well, to his surprise, I was a girl.

Dad fell in love with me the first time the nurse placed me in his arms. I was screaming, and when we gazed into each other's eyes, I stopped. I had him. I was his little girl. I had dark-brown hair, green eyes, and the fair skin of my Scottish grandmother.

He still wanted to name me Alex but settled for Alexandria, intending to shorten it to Alex. Yet, for some reason, everyone called me Ally unless I was in trouble—then I got my full name, Alexandria Leilani Kane.

Dad took me everywhere, mainly carrying me on his shoulders. He taught me how to swim, surf, and ride a bike.

At age four, my neighbor Cassie, my lifelong best friend, and her mother, Trudy, signed her up for dance classes. Cassie looked like a dancer with long legs, olive skin, and dark curly hair. Mom decided I needed some girly activities and signed me up as well.

After my first lesson, I immediately fell in love with dancing. I danced anywhere to any music. I danced in every room of the house, on the sand, along the beach, in the water, everywhere. I drove my mother crazy, leaping and twirling around the house and banging into things.

When Cassie and I were seven, we tried dancing on a surfboard. It didn't go well, and I ended up with a trip to the hospital, but it didn't stop us from trying again and again until we achieved it with screams of delight everyone could hear along the beach.

My parents came along to every performance, and Dad videotaped them. He was proud of everything his family did. We had a hall closet full of family videos. One time when Dad couldn't change his shift to attend a recital, the whole squad stopped at the concert hall on the way back from a job. They stood in the back and watched, loudly clapping when I finished. Dad proudly told his squad, "My daughter's up there, and one day she'll be the lead dancer." When I eventually got the lead role and did my first solo, Dad had tears in his eyes.

When I was eight years old, my mother gave birth to Adam Charles Kane. My dad now had his son. At first, I was a little put out that someone else was taking their attention, but I soon got over it. He was a cute baby with Mom's hair color and brown eyes. I adored my little brother. After a week of him being home, I became very protective of this little bundle that made a lot of noise and spat up.

When Adam was older, Dad and I taught him to swim, but Mom was the one who taught us both how to paddleboard. I have a lot of happy memories of my brother and me swimming with Mom and Dad. We had many dinners in our backyard near the beach as we watched the sun set.

Cassie and I had decided halfway through high school we wanted dancing careers. We researched and found a Bachelor of Fine Arts dance program at the University of Hawaii. One afternoon, while dancing on our surfboards, we decided to approach our parents and convince them this was what we wanted to do. We decided to talk to Auntie Ell first, hoping she could give us some advice. She had always been in my life, and I had an incredible bond with her. Aunty Ell visited as often as possible and made it for nearly every Christmas. She always wanted to hear about my dancing. After listening to Cassie and me, my auntie suggested we make a good presentation with solid facts and have answers ready for our parents' questions.

It took a week to gather all the information we needed, then we invited Cassie's family for dinner. While our parents were finishing their dessert, we pitched our presentation. We explained the BFA program and how it was designed for students who wanted to pursue professional careers as dancers, dance teachers, or choreographers, and one of the requirements for admission to the program was by audition.

Both sets of parents stared at us throughout. You could see they were stunned that their daughters had been giving this a lot of thought and research, and were pleased we wanted to go to university. When we finally finished and answered all their questions, they informed us they would talk about it and let us know in a few days. It was the longest few days of our lives.

After school one day, our parents called us to Cassie's place. They all agreed we could go ahead with the applications; however, we would need to keep our grades up and apply for partial scholarships. Over the next twelve months, we did everything we could to get good grades, practise dancing, and stay in good terms with our parents. We had never worked this hard in our lives, but in the end, the gods looked down on us both. Not only did we get into the university with partial scholarships, but we also aced our audition for the BFA program and started reaching for our dreams.

CHAPTER TWELVE

At the end of summer in 1997, Cassie and I moved into a dorm together. We both decided to live at UH even though our homes were only twenty minutes away. We could concentrate on dancing and come home when we needed laundry or a decent meal.

In our first week at college, Cassie and I met Donna, who was also doing her BFA. Donna Kono was tall and slender with a beautiful Hawaiian complexion and gorgeous dark hair. Like Cassie, she was a wonderful dancer, and the three of us became fast friends.

My first year at UH went by fast and was nearing the end, and even though it was backbreaking work, I loved it. I knew this was what I was born to do.

Students had to perform in at least one production in the first year. The three of us had already been in two performances, but when a two-act performance of *Sleeping Beauty* came up, I knew I had to audition. Donna and Cassie wanted to concentrate on their exams, but the role spoke to me. I needed to audition, and if I auditioned, I was going for the lead role. I had to try.

When the morning of the audition finally arrived, I wasn't nervous. I had nothing to lose and everything to gain. It felt very natural for me to perform, and even if I didn't get the role, I would know I had given it everything.

As I walked on stage, I was in my zone. It was just me, the music, the dance moves, and the sound of my ballet shoes' leather soles against the wooden floor. It all flowed. It was a ten-minute audition, and I noticed the judges for the first time when the music finished.

"That will be all. You may go." Their stony faces didn't give anything away. I thanked them for their time.

Offstage, I took a long drink from my water bottle and lay on the floor in the wings, panting for about five minutes.

I watched the next girl perform and thought she was better than me. I decided I had to leave for my mental health. I needed to find my friends.

Cassie and Donna met me outside the dance hall under a monkey tree, and I collapsed into the cool grass. We were all physically and mentally exhausted. The girls had finished their exams, and we told each other about the mistakes we thought we had made.

The performance results would be announced on the bulletin board the following morning. Eighteen long hours of waiting.

After fifteen minutes of complaining to each other, Cassie and Donna went to class, and I had a few hours off. As they were leaving, Mom phoned me and asked if we could have lunch. I didn't want to as I was exhausted, and I also didn't want to tell my family about the audition in case I jinxed myself and didn't get the part.

"I have a class in two hours," I said.

But Mom was insistent. "Well, I'm in the area and want to have lunch with my daughter. Can't you take an hour out of your day?" The guilt trip. "I can be there in ten minutes. We'll make it a quick lunch."

"Okay," I said and told her where I was.

When Mom met me at the monkey tree, she was wearing navy pants and a navy-and-white blouse, and she had on the diamond-drop necklace Dad had given her on their wedding day.

"Mom," I said, "is everything okay?"

"Does something have to be wrong for me to have lunch with my daughter?"

"No," I said, hugging her. "Do you want to eat at the café off campus we went to last time?"

A smile appeared across her face. "That would be wonderful."

When we got to the café, we sat at a quiet little table in the corner and ordered a Diet Coke and a green salad.

"You know," she said, "we're more alike than you think."

I cocked my head to one side, unsure of what she was trying to say.

She leaned over the table and gently touched my arm. "You know, my darling daughter, you and your father may think you're two peas in a pod, but always remember you also have your mother's genes."

I gazed at my mother's soft, loving face and smiled. "I know I was lucky to take after you both. Poor Adam," I joked with a giggle.

We ate our lunch and chatted about Adam and Dad and what they were up to, then it was time to head back to the university. I was dying to tell her about the role I was up for, but I restrained myself.

"Come home for dinner tomorrow night," Mom said.

"Sure. Any special reason?" I asked.

"No, just dinner."

Hopefully, I would have good news tomorrow night.

We said our goodbyes with kisses and hugs, and I promised I would come for dinner.

For the rest of the afternoon, it was hard to concentrate on my remaining classes. By evening, the excitement of waiting for the announcements had driven me crazy. I couldn't sleep. I got Cassie and Donna up, and we did a slow jog around the campus to tire me out. When I finally got to bed, I kept going over my audition in my head until I eventually fell asleep.

CHAPTER THIRTEEN

The following morning, I woke up to banging on my door. Someone was running down the hall and shouting out that the call sheets were up. I grabbed a T-shirt and shorts and put them on over my nightie, not realizing my T-shirt was inside out, and ran barefoot along the hall. I didn't know where Cassie or Donna were, but I knew they would be nearby.

Students were surrounding the bulletin board, and I couldn't get close. Please, please, at least let me be in the performance, I prayed.

Some students screamed with excitement while others cried. Then, I saw Donna push her way out of the crowd.

"You did it. You got the lead." She threw her arms around me.

I was shocked. "I got it? Are you sure?" I asked pushing in through the crowd.

And there it was:

Performance 2

Lead: Aurora—Alexandria Kane

We jumped and screamed with joy. Oh my God. I couldn't believe what I was reading. If I pulled this off, it could be the start of an amazing career.

Miss Richards, the strictest and most disliked dance teacher, appeared at the end of the hallway and clapped her hands several times to get everyone's attention. "You all know what your parts are. Please be at the assigned practice halls within the hour. We start today."

Miss Richards always had her nose in the air as if there was a bad smell. Donna gave an excellent impression of her, but there would be hell to pay if she got caught.

I was thrilled, but then the fear took over. Maybe the instructors would take one look at my dancing and change their minds. We had been told many times that everyone is replaceable.

I quickly showered, changed, and got to the practice hall early. The rehearsals were strenuous, but I loved them. The only time we stopped was for lunch. Rehearsals finished late in the afternoon, and I quickly returned to my room and changed, eager to get home to tell my family about the fantastic role I had landed.

* * *

Mom was setting the table, and Dad was helping my ten-year-old brother with his homework when I finally got home. Everything smelled great. Adam got up and hugged me, followed by Dad.

"Here's our beautiful ballerina. How's it all going?" Dad asked.

All I could say was, "It's going well." I kissed Mom on the cheek and asked if I could help.

"No, dinner is ready," she said to me. "Everyone, come to the table," she yelled out to the others.

Dad sat at the head of the table at one end and Mom at the other, with Adam and me sitting on either side.

As we ate our delicious pot roast dinner, Dad asked, "You've been smiling since you arrived. What's up?"

I put down my knife and fork. "Well, I have some good news." They all stopped eating and stared at me.

I blurted out, "I got the lead role in *Sleeping Beauty* for the end-of-year performance," then squealed.

Mom jumped up and threw her arms around me, saying congratulations, and Dad banged his hands on the table.

"Well, if that isn't the best news … Congratulations, darling. I'm proud of you. When is it?"

"In three weeks. You guys must come." I couldn't contain my excitement any longer. I told my family about the two-act performance and how much work I would need to do. "Mom, could you tell Auntie Ell when you talk to her next?" I asked.

"We wouldn't miss it for the world, and I'll phone your aunt tomorrow," she said.

After dinner, Dad and Adam left the table to finish Adam's homework, and I helped Mom clean up. Mom had gone back to part-time teaching when Adam started school. She liked the school she was at, and working part-time suited her. She told me her colleagues were having dinner next Friday evening and asked if I could take care of Adam for her, as Dad was working.

At first, I wanted to say, "Didn't you listen to what I said about all the work I had to do?" But I stopped myself. Mom didn't get out much with her friends, and she always put her family first, so I agreed.

"Sure, you go and have fun. Adam and I haven't hung out together for a long time, and we can go for pizza."

"He'd enjoy that. He misses you," Mom said.

"I know."

When I said my goodbyes, Mom walked me to my car.

"No Cassie tonight?" she asked.

"No, she wanted to stay at school and study."

Cassie and I would often drive home together, our families only next door to each other. We had our own cars, but it was easier to take one.

"Will you be home on the weekend?" Mom asked.

"I don't know," I said. "It depends on how things go at rehearsals. I'm scared I'll screw it up. I want to do as much practice as possible."

Mom reached over and pulled me into her arms. "You won't 'screw it up,' my darling. You're talented, and you're going to be great at everything you do. You must believe in yourself."

"Thanks, Mom. Love you," I said as I got into my car.

* * *

I spent most of the weekend practicing. The following week, I was busy with rehearsals and fell into bed exhausted by the end of each day. There were many times I thought I wasn't going to make it.

You need to develop a tough skin when dancing. So many people with their eyes on you, whispering, waiting for you to make a mistake, while teachers, sometimes two simultaneously, yelling at you. But if you want to be in this business, you can't show any weakness.

I was frustrated when Mom called to remind me about taking care of Adam, but I thought it would probably do me good to get away for the evening. A night with my little bro would help recharge my batteries. I asked Cassie if she wanted to come, but she had a date with a guy she had met the week before. She made me swear not to tell my parents as they would only tell hers, and she didn't want them to find out, yet. None of us had had time to date this year, and I was pleased for my friend. I knew the guy, and she had my approval. At half-past five, I raced out of the dorm room, wishing Cassie luck as I left for home.

When I got to the house, Mom was in the kitchen staring out the window. She turned and looked at me. My mother, who hardly ever wore dresses, was stunning in her pink-and-brown dress and beige shoes. Her slightly curled hair rested above her shoulders, and she wore her single-diamond-drop necklace. She had applied a light powder to her face with a bit of blush, which showed off her fabulous high cheekbones.

I did my best wolf whistle. "Wow, don't you look incredible?"

"Mahalo," she said as she ran her hands over her dress, as if to smooth it out.

"You don't have a boyfriend on the side, do you?" I joked.

"No, darling. Your father is and will always be the only man for me," she said as she gently touched my face.

Adam came running. "Are we going for pizza?" he asked.

"You bet, and probably ice cream. Well, you can have the pizza and ice cream, I'd better stick to a salad, or the prince won't be able to lift me tomorrow." I said, then laughed.

Mom bent down and kissed him on the cheek. "Love you buddy, be good for your sister."

He wiggled out of her grasp. "Okay, bye, Mom, have fun," he called back as he ran to my car.

"I guess he's in a hurry." I laughed. "You have a good time, Mom, and don't worry, I've got this."

"I won't be late home," she said as she waved goodbye.

CHAPTER FOURTEEN

Adam and I dined at a little family restaurant near home. They catered for kids, which was great as he ate a whole pizza for himself. I wanted to take a slice but stuck to my boring salad. After he finished two bowls of ice cream, something we both decided not to tell Mom about, we went home, curled up on the couch, and watched a kid-friendly movie. Adam was lying at one end of the couch, and I was at the other. Before I knew it, we both fell asleep.

I was dreaming I was in my dance costume, struggling to swim in the ocean, when a gentle stroke on my face woke me.

"Honey, I need you to wake up." It was my dad's voice.

I stirred, opened my eyes, and looked up at him. Still half asleep, I said, "Hi, what time …?"

"Shh, don't wake your brother. Honey, I have something to tell you." He seemed distraught.

I realized Uncle Henry was behind him.

"What happened?" I was scared.

"Your mother was in a car accident." It was clear he was trying not to cry.

"An accident. Is Mom okay?" I said, unraveling myself from the blanket to stand.

Uncle Henry put his hand on Dad's shoulder for support.

"She's gone, honey. Mom died."

I fell into his arms.

Adam woke up and was immediately scared to see his father and sister crying. "What's going on?"

"Buddy, I have something to tell you," Dad said.

I sat next to Adam and put my arm around him, bracing him for the news no ten-year-old kid should hear.

Dad took a second to steady himself. "Your mom had a bad car accident tonight and didn't make it. She died."

"No, you're wrong. Mom wouldn't die."

"I'm sorry, buddy," he whispered.

Adam turned and buried his face into my lap and cried. I rubbed his back to try and soothe him, but it didn't work. Dad tried to hold him, but Adam shrugged him off. Dad sat next to me on the couch, and I put my head on his shoulder and cried, while Adam sat with his head still buried in my lap, sobbing.

After about an hour, Adam drifted off to sleep, emotionally drained. Uncle Henry gently lifted him up and carried him to bed. I followed to ensure he didn't wake, and I draped a blanket over him. When I returned to the living room, more people arrived, all shocked by the news.

I tightly hugged my dad. "What are we going to do?" I asked him.

"We have to tell Ell," he said. "I don't know how … there's a lot to do, and I don't know where to start."

Dad seemed broken and confused. I knew I had to find the strength to help him. My instincts immediately took over. "I'll tell her. I'll do it now," I said. I went into my parents' room for privacy and dialed my aunt's number.

She answered straight away.

"What happened?"

I don't know if it was the lateness of the call, but she knew something was wrong.

"It's Mom. She was in a car accident, and—" I started to cry. "She died."

There was silence.

"Auntie Ell?"

"It's going to be okay, darling. I'll be on a plane first thing in the morning. Don't worry about picking me up. I'll get a cab."

CHAPTER FIFTEEN

The investigation into the accident found it involved a single car. Mom lost control around the bend on Canyon Road after she swerved to miss what they thought was an animal crossing the road. Her vehicle skidded, broke through the barrier, and burst into flames as it hit the rocky sides of the canyon. The two witnesses who saw her car go over the cliff stopped their vehicles and ran to help, but there was nothing anyone could do.

As Mom's body was burned beyond recognition, she could only be identified by her dental records, wedding rings, and the single-diamond-drop necklace she was wearing. Dad assured us it happened so fast that she had no time to be scared.

He had the worst job—dealing with the medical examiner and the identifying process—but would only let Uncle Henry help him. What he had to deal with after the accident nearly broke him.

So, when it came to making decisions for the funeral, Auntie Ell and I took over. I think Dad was relieved we did. He kept saying, "I trust you two."

Two nights after the accident, I phoned my college counselor and explained I couldn't perform in *Sleeping Beauty*, and they replaced me. I had fantasized about them saying how they couldn't possibly go on without me, but deep down, I knew the show must go on. I wish I could say it didn't hurt, but it did. It felt as though a knife had plunged into my chest.

I didn't tell my father or aunt. I couldn't handle their sad faces over a dance. Besides, they had forgotten about it with everything that was going on. Part of me was hurt, but I was also ashamed of my feelings.

I lay on top of my bed fully dressed, staring at my ceiling fan going around and around while the music to the dance, my dance, played in my head as I drifted off to sleep. I dreamt I was performing on stage. Someone was talking as I danced, then my legs buckled from under me, and every time I tried to get up, I fell.

There was a sudden sharp pain in my leg, and I woke with a start. Adam was next to me and had kicked me in his sleep. I looked at the clock and saw it was after midnight. The house was quiet, and my head was aching, so I decided to get some aspirin from the kitchen.

The house was in darkness except for a small lamp at the end of the hallway that we always had on at night. Auntie Ell's bedroom door was closed; I guess she had turned in for the evening. Passing my parents' bedroom, I noticed, once again, Dad was not in bed. He hadn't slept in there since the accident. One of the bedside lamps was on, sending off a soft, warm glow, and I tiptoed in. I don't know why. It wasn't as if there was anyone to disturb.

I walked up to my parents' bed and slowly ran my hand over the bedspread. Mom's blue cotton dressing gown was still lying at the end of the bed where she had left it. I moved over to her dressing table and picked up her hairbrush, touching the strands of her hair. I softly touched the photos Mom had put in their mirror of her and Dad's wedding, the four of us together, and a photo of her and Auntie Ell as little girls. Some of her jewelry was lying on the dressing table, and next to it was her perfume bottle. I picked it up, and my heart hurt at the scent. My eyes filled with tears, and I put the perfume and hairbrush back in their places and quickly left the room.

As I entered the living room, Dad was in his chair, snoring with a blanket falling off him. I crept over and gently re-covered him. I only remembered my dad being happy, and now, even in his sleep, he looked sad.

I grabbed a glass of water and a few aspirin. I needed to change my clothes. As I returned to my room, I kicked my dance bag, and my rose-pink ballet shoes for the performance fell out. I stood staring at them first, then slowly picked them up and ran my hands over the soft satin. I gazed at a sleeping Adam, who seemed so small. Then I thought of my father sleeping in the chair, and I knew I couldn't leave them.

I hadn't wanted to face the fact that I wouldn't be returning to the dorm and performing the dance I imagined would be my big break, but reality had caught up with me. I felt angry and selfish at the same time. With my ballet shoes clutched to my chest, I ran into my bathroom, shut the door, grabbed a washcloth and stuffed it into my mouth to stop myself from screaming, then I slid to the floor and sobbed.

Loneliness overcame me, even with three other people in the house. I missed my mother, but I was also furious at her for leaving us, even though it wasn't her fault. I lay on the bathroom floor with a towel under my head, sobbing until I fell asleep.

It was my aunt softly knocking on the bathroom door that woke me.

"Ally, darling, breakfast is ready. Are you okay?"

"I'm fine. I'll be out in a minute," I answered.

I got up and glared at myself in the mirror. My eyes were red and puffy from crying, and my head still ached. I told myself to pull it together, knowing what I had to do.

I took a few controlling breaths, put drops in my eyes, showered, and dressed. I quietly phoned Cassie and asked if she and Donna could pack up my dorm room, as I would be living at home from then on. Decision made; I didn't see the need to tell my family yet.

CHAPTER SIXTEEN

The days leading to the funeral were hard, and I was grateful my auntie was with us. Cassie and Donna were always helping out too: putting food away people had brought by, packing up my dorm room, taking Adam off my hands when I needed to make difficult decisions, and coming with me when I had to buy him a suit. I was glad they were there.

The funeral was held six days after the accident. That morning, Dad came out of his room wearing his dress uniform.

I was struggling to put on Adam's tie. Dad took over and said, "Let me, honey. This is a man's job."

I was relieved when he took over. I could only smile as Dad explained to Adam how to tie a tie.

When Dad finished the tie, the two men in my life stood beside each other, facing me.

"Well, do we pass inspection?" Dad asked, trying to smile.

"Very handsome, both of you," I replied.

"You don't look too bad yourself."

I had found a black dress of Mom's in the back of her closet. I didn't know how long it had been there, and I didn't remember ever seeing her wear it. It was a simple black A-line dress with a sweetheart neckline, and it came slightly below my knees.

Dad reached into his pocket. "You need something else, though." He pulled out the strand of pearls Uncle Mike had given Mom when she was about my age. "Your mom would have wanted you to have these," he said as he put them around my neck.

I couldn't speak; I was trying not to cry. I turned and hugged Dad, and he kissed me on top of my head.

"I'm proud of you. You're the lady of the house now," he said.

His words stunned me. I didn't think I could live up to all the responsibilities that came with the title or Mom's standards.

Auntie Ell was watching, also trying hard not to cry.

"Well, don't you all look nice," she said.

Dad extended his arms to her, and he embraced us all.

"Okay," he said, choking back the tears, "we need to go. I want to be there before people arrive."

Mom and Auntie Ell had told me the story of Uncle Mike giving the twins their pearls many times, and when I noticed my auntie was wearing hers, I asked, "Do you mind me having these?"

She gently ran her fingers over the pearls and cupped my face. "My darling girl, you are the only one who should have them." She kissed my cheek.

As we walked to the door, I turned to look around the room. People would be in to prepare for the wake, but I wasn't worried about that. I was worried that when we arrived back, our life, *my life*, would change forever.

* * *

Mom's urn was placed next to a large picture of her sitting on the beach, smiling with the wind in her hair. She had been cremated before her funeral, and her ashes would later be buried in the plot Mom and Dad had picked out years ago. They had wanted to make sure they would be together for all eternity.

The sun shone as people arrived at the gravesite, and a slightly warm sea breeze crept through the gathering, carrying a hint of hibiscus. The end of spring and the beginning of summer, Mom's favorite time of year.

Dad stood next to Mom's framed picture as he delivered the eulogy. His words made people cry and laugh. He spoke of how they met, her love for her children and sister, and how people who met her admired her. I was proud of the way he held himself together.

Auntie Ell and I were too emotional to speak, but Auntie Anne and Uncle Henry gave a heartwarming speech about their friend. Adam was trying hard to be brave, taking a tight hold of my hand the minute we arrived at the cemetery and never letting it go. He sat there, staring at the ground, and didn't cry.

After the eulogies had finished, Auntie Ell placed a white rose next to Mom's picture and whispered something softly; no one else heard it. It was a sister moment for only the two of them.

Then it was our turn. Adam and I approached her photo with Dad by our side and placed two red roses next to her picture. Dad then added a single white lily. He had told me earlier that lilies were the first flowers he had given her. As people started to leave and give their condolences, Dad asked me to take Adam and my aunt back to the car. He wanted a final moment alone with Mom. Fifteen minutes later, Dad joined us, and we drove home in silence.

Friends from the firehouse had set up all the food and beverages for the wake. I was grateful they took it out of our hands. Adam was still next to me, hardly ever letting go of my hand. He had barely left my side since the accident, clinging to me most of the time. He had even taken to sleeping in my bed or on the floor beside me. Sometimes I wanted to yell at him to leave me alone, I needed time too, but when he looked at me with such sad, scared eyes, I feared he would break into thousands of pieces if I pushed him away even a little.

Uncle Henry was talking to Adam about helicopters, a great distraction. They went and sat on the back step together, and I was relieved. I entered the kitchen to get a drink when Auntie Ell approached me.

"It was today, wasn't it?" she asked.

"What was?" I asked, pretending I didn't know what she was talking about.

"Your performance. It was today."

I couldn't answer her.

"Your mother called me about it. I was going to surprise you and come over." She hugged me, and I silently cried into her shoulder. "It's okay, darling. You have a right to cry. Your whole world has been turned upside down," she said. "But please don't get so busy with your father and brother that you lose yourself."

I hugged her tighter as she said the words I had been afraid of thinking. I thought I had always known my future, but now I wasn't sure.

For two weeks after the funeral, Dad was home on leave. Auntie Ell had returned to San Francisco, and Adam and I were on school vacation. The three of us hung around the house for the first week. But at the start of the second week, Dad said, "Enough. We have to get out of the house and do something. We're going swimming. Go change, and I won't take no for an answer."

It was the last thing I wanted to do, but Dad was right. We had to get out of the house. I slowly followed them out the back door and into the ocean.

We spent the rest of the day swimming and paddleboarding, ending with dinner on the back porch. At times we caught ourselves laughing and would quickly fall silent.

"No guilt," Dad said. "This is what your mother would want us to do—enjoy our lives and get on with living."

Dad was right. That night, he took his own advice and stopped sleeping in the chair.

CHAPTER SEVENTEEN

When Dad returned to work, it was just Adam and me, and I was concerned about my brother. He would go into rages quickly and pulled away from his friends. He couldn't hang around me forever. We had to get back to our own lives.

I organized a picnic and a swim with two of Adam's friends, Zac and Brendan, and I also asked Cassie and Donna. He could play with his friends, and I could finally hang out with the girls. Running a household was hard work, not just physically but mentally as well. All the planning and organizing made me crazy. It was like being thrown into the ocean with your hands tied and struggling to swim. It was the same feeling from the dream I'd had the night of Mom's accident.

I knew I would work it out eventually, but getting there would be difficult. I tried working out a schedule for doing the laundry on certain days, but it didn't seem to work when Dad needed uniforms washed and ironed. After the first few weeks, he had no clean work clothes and told me I had enough to do without his uniforms being a concern and took them to the dry cleaners near the fire station. I was a little hurt at first, but when all the shopping, cleaning, supervising, and running around after Adam started to take hold, I was relieved he took that particular job off my hands.

When I got the university schedule for the year, we realized we had a problem. Who would be around for Adam when he returned to school? Dad's shifts were twelve hours long, and there was no guarantee he would be off when Adam needed collecting. My classes began at eight o'clock and sometimes finished at four-thirty, and that was without practice time before or after class.

The three of us sat around the table and discussed how it could work. Adam wanted to stay home by himself, which was never going to happen. We decided I would drop Adam off at school a bit earlier than usual on my way to class, then Dad would pick him up from after-school care on his way home from work on the days I had a late class. Cassie's mother offered to pick him up on the days neither of us could.

Adam ran late on the first day of school, despite my yelling at him to hurry up. This, in turn, made me late for class. Every day, my first dance class was with Miss Richards, the most hated teacher. It was not the most accessible room, and it was impossible to sneak in without being noticed. For a week, we ran late, and each morning I got sarcastic comments from Miss Richards. "So nice of you to join us, Miss Kane." I had heard she wasn't pleased I had backed out of the performance at the last moment. Miss Richards had no empathy for anyone, and I knew she would make things difficult for me.

By the time Friday afternoon of the first week came, I was exhausted. I hadn't had any practice time, I was in the bad books with my dance teacher for always being late, and Adam had been in a bad mood. Dinner was always late, and the laundry was piling up. I thought I would catch up on the weekend, but by Sunday afternoon, I hadn't even taken my ballet shoes out of my bag or studied my assignments.

Monday had come back fast, and both Adam and I were miserable. My brother woke up in another bad mood and was even slower than usual, and once again, I was late.

When I arrived at the class, Miss Richards clapped her hands together to stop the lesson and yelled, "Miss Kane, once again, you are late. If you are late again, don't bother attending my class."

My cheeks burned with embarrassment. "I apologize, Miss Richards."

"Now apologize to the class, as it is them who you are consistently interrupting with your tardiness."

I wanted the ground to open up and swallow me. I turned to the class and said, "I apologize." I wanted to add, "But you try and get a ten-year-old boy ready for school," but I didn't. I took my place at the end of the barre, hoping to lose myself in the group.

My counselor, Mrs. Baxter, arrived at the door an hour into the class.

"Miss Richards, may I have a word with Ally, please."

"Take her. She's wasting my time."

Ouch, her words hurt. My face turned red again. I excused myself and left the room.

Mrs. Baxter was the opposite of Miss Richards. She was kind, caring, and easy to talk to.

"I know I've been late, but we are trying to get—"

She put her hand on my shoulder before I could finish. "Your brother's school phoned. He's had a small accident, and they think he may require stitches in his head. They tried ringing your father but couldn't get hold of him."

I began to panic. "Is my brother alright? Where is he?"

"He's okay. One of the teachers has taken him to the hospital," she explained.

I ran to my locker, grabbed my gear, changed my shoes, and threw a sweater over my leotard and ballet skirt.

"Just drive safely," Mrs. Baxter said.

I ran toward the door, stopped, and turned back to her. "I think I need to drop out, maybe for a little while until things settle down." I shocked myself with my own words.

She put her arm around my shoulders. "Let me investigate some options. Maybe you can take fewer classes or defer for a little while. Don't worry about it now, and go to your brother," she said calmly.

"Cassie and Donna are going to be worried. Please let them know and tell them I'll speak to them later."

"Of course." she said. "Slow down, take a breath, and it will work out."

CHAPTER EIGHTEEN

I don't remember driving to the hospital. I didn't have trouble parking and ran straight into the ER to the nurses' station.

"Please, my brother, Adam Kane, was brought in from school. Can you please take me to him?" I blurted out. Then I heard Adam yelling, and I followed his voice. The poor guy was lying on the hospital bed with blood on his face.

"I want Ally. Where's Ally?" he cried.

I ran to his side. "It's okay, buddy. I'm here. What happened?"

There was a young woman next to him. "Hi, I'm Louisa Denny, the teacher's aide. He fought with Zac, and neither will say what it was about."

"A fight? Adam. You know better than to fight." I started to scold him, but he hung his head in shame, and I knew not to push him at the moment. "Don't worry about it now," I said calmly, "we'll talk about it later. Is Zac okay?" I asked Louisa.

"Yes. I think Zac's more upset Adam was hurt," the aide said. "Anyway, now you're here, I should go. Please let the school know how he gets on. I think the principal will contact you later."

Great, I thought, *something to look forward to.*

"What happened?" I asked Adam when Louisa had left. "I thought you and Zac were friends."

"We are."

I was about to ask more questions when the doctor came in. He explained Adam would need a few stitches and might have a slight concussion, but he would be fine.

"I'll give him some antibiotics for the gash in his head to ensure there's no infection," the doctor explained. "When was the last time he had a tetanus shot?"

I had no idea. I didn't know these things about my brother.

"I'm not sure. My mother always handled those things, but I know she would have been up to date." I didn't have the energy to go into the whole dead-mom explanation.

The cute doctor glanced at me, then at Adam. "It's okay. We can give him a booster, which will be perfectly safe." He must have seen the relief on my face. "It's okay, sis. He is going to be fine. He'll have to stay quiet this week. You, however, look like you need to sit down."

The doctor gently took hold of my arm, ensuring I sat on the chair next to Adam. He must have seen my legs shaking and didn't want to end up with another patient. I was still in my dance gear and must have appeared ridiculous, but I didn't care.

As everything seemed to be under control with Adam, I left a message for Dad not to worry, all was okay, and to contact me when he got back. Something else for me to worry about—Dad attending a massive fire. What if something happened to Dad? How would we cope? I forced myself to shake off that horrifying thought.

We were finally at home when Dad called. I was relieved he was safely back at the fire station.

We had been at the hospital nearly all day, so I told Adam he could have anything for dinner, and he decided on pizza. At that time of night, it would take at least fifty minutes. The poor kid hadn't eaten since breakfast and was already half asleep. I had to get some food into him before he took his medication.

"Okay, I'll order, but how about a grilled cheese sandwich before it arrives?"

I didn't think he would still be awake when the pizza arrived—I was right. He was fast asleep seconds after he finished his grilled cheese.

Adam was sleeping peacefully in the chair, and I was curled up on the couch, watching him, when Cassie and Donna phoned.

They told me Miss Richards was less than impressed with me, but I didn't care. What mattered was that Adam and Dad were safe.

I had to work out how to coordinate my life with Adam's. How did my mom make all of this look easy? Dad couldn't help not being home by a particular hour. It had always been what the job entailed, and we had all accepted it long ago. We always knew he would do his best to get home on time.

Adam would be out of school for the rest of the week, and although I could pass him on to other people, I didn't want to leave him. This was the first time he was sick without his mom. I may have wanted to kill him sometimes, but he was still my little brother.

I was deep in thought when Dad came in. I didn't hear him at first, and he startled me. He came over, kissed the top of my head, and checked on Adam, stroking his hair gently.

"How is he?" he asked. I saw the exhaustion on Dad's face.

"He's going to be fine. Four stitches and a slight concussion. His principal rang, but neither boy would tell what the fight was about, so they let them off with a warning," I whispered.

Dad smiled and turned to me. "Boys fight. I'm not worried," he said, pulling two beers out of the fridge, and handed me one.

I was still just under the drinking age and looked at him with my eyebrow raised.

"Go ahead. I know this isn't your first drink. Besides, you deserve this. We've both had a rough day," he said as he sat beside me on the couch. Though he had showered at the station, you could still smell smoke on him.

"Bad fire?" I asked.

He slowly nodded, sipped his beer, and quietly said, "Yeah. An old warehouse caught fire. Arson."

"Anyone hurt?" I asked.

"Some homeless people didn't make it."

I knew from experience he didn't want to talk about certain fires, especially when people died. I interlocked my arm with his and put my head on his shoulder.

"Have you eaten? There's pizza," I said.

"Thanks, honey. I grabbed a couple of sandwiches at the station." Then he said, "I don't know what I would have done if you weren't with Adam today. I was relieved to hear you were there." Then he asked, "School was okay with you leaving early?"

Now was no time to tell him how much trouble I was in with my dance teacher.

"Sure, I didn't have much on today."

"Good," he said with a sigh. "Because of the arson and lost lives, I have a lot of meetings this week at headquarters, and I have to figure out who we can leave Adam with. Maybe Cassie's mom could watch him for a while."

I knew Dad would have a stressful week ahead going over everything with the arson investigators.

"It's okay," I reassured him, "I've spoken to my instructors, and Cassie is bringing work home for me." It was a white lie. "I don't want to leave him while he's sick. It's the first time without Mom and …" I choked back the tears.

Dad put his arm around my shoulders. "Well, as long as it's okay with your instructors. I don't want you to get behind."

I decided to talk to Mrs. Baxter the next day and consider what she suggested—changing some classes or deferring for a while. When I had arranged it, I would tell Dad.

We both sat in silence watching TV, sipping our beers.

After nearly an hour had passed, Dad said, "I need to get this guy to bed and have another shower." He gently picked up Adam, who stirred a little. "It's okay, buddy," Dad said softly.

"Put him in my bed," I told him.

"You sure?" he asked.

"The doctor wants me to check him every couple of hours, so he might as well sleep with me."

I wasn't going to tell him I didn't want Adam out of my sight at the moment.

"You're a good sister. Gosh, he's getting heavy. Won't be long before I can't lift him."

"I'll be there in a minute. I want to tidy up the kitchen first."

When I entered my bedroom, Adam was curled up under the covers on the left side of my bed. Quietly slipping into my bathroom, I changed and washed my face. I was worn out.

I got into bed very carefully and watched Adam sleeping. Although he was only ten and growing fast, he reminded me of when he was little, nestled in Mom's arms.

Throughout the night, I checked on him every couple of hours. He woke every time, and I let out a sigh of relief.

"Ally, Alllllly, wake up."

I woke with a jolt.

"What, are you okay?"

"Can I have the pizza now?" he asked.

"What?" I looked at the clock and saw it was 8:19 a.m. "How long have you been awake?"

"A little while. I talked to Dad before he left, and I watched TV. Dad said to let you sleep a little, but I'm hungry."

"How's your head?" I put the back of my hand to his forehead to check for a fever.

"I have a bit of a headache, but nothing pizza can't fix."

I thought for a moment. Adam was okay, I was tired, and we did have a perfectly good pizza in the fridge.

"Just this once, you can have it for breakfast if you stay on the couch today. Deal?"

"Deal," he said.

Going into the living room, Adam lay on the couch while I heated a few slices and poured him a glass of milk, then we both dozed on and off all morning.

By midday, I decided I needed to make an appointment with Mrs. Baxter to discuss my future. I called her, and she had an appointment the next day around two o'clock. I asked Donna or Cassie if they could stay with Adam but told him I would be doing some shopping. I didn't want him to say anything to Dad before I could figure things out.

Donna called to say she was free and could watch Adam. Now I only had to work out what I wanted to do. I thought of my mom once more and tried to work out what she would have done in this situation—how she managed to combine her home duties and work as a teacher.

Wait. Maybe that was an option. If I attended teachers' college, the same as Mom, I would be doing regular school hours and the same holidays as Adam.

I had never considered being a schoolteacher, but I didn't hate the idea. I could always go back and get my dance qualifications, and having a teacher's degree wouldn't hurt achieving the final goal of being a dance teacher once I had finished my dancing career. I kept reassuring myself I was still going to be a dancer. It would take a little longer than I hoped, a slight detour was all.

I found the teachers' college number, spoke to them, and explained my situation. I could start next week. Having already done a year at university helped me get in, and I would have only missed a week of class. All I had to do was have my transcripts transferred from the university, apply, and pay a tuition fee, and I would be in teacher's college.

In an hour, I changed my career path. It may not have been the one I had started or wanted, but it would be good for now. Besides, Mom enjoyed teaching, and I would be taking after her.

My only problem would be telling Dad and my friends. I didn't know who was going to accept the news worse.

I met with Mrs. Baxter and told her my plans. She understood and assured me that a degree from there would help me return to university when I was ready. It was done. Mrs. Baxter was going to set the wheels in motion.

* * *

The next afternoon, when I was home with Adam, the front door opened and slammed shut. It was my dad.

"Alexandria Leilani Kane, where are you?" he yelled. I had only heard my father call me by my full name a few times.

"You're in trouble," Adam said with a slight giggle, and he got out of the way fast, sinking into a corner of the couch to watch the action.

"Hi, Daddy, is something wrong?" I said sweetly.

"Don't you 'hi Daddy' me. Did you think I wouldn't find out about you dropping out of university? When were you going to tell me this important bit of information?"

"How did you find out?" I was flabbergasted at how quickly it had happened.

"The university phoned me wanting to discuss refunding your tuition. When I asked them why, imagine my surprise when they told me." He continued to rage. "Please explain why you want to throw your dance career away, the career you begged us to have?"

I had never seen him this angry. He was red in the face and kept pacing in front of me. The pacing was a new habit he had developed since Mom had died.

"Dad, calm down, let me explain." This was not how I wanted the conversation to go. I moved over to the dining table, hoping he would follow so we could talk. "Daddy, please, come and sit down."

He stopped pacing and stood beside the table. The expression on his face flustered me, and I couldn't remember my argument for dropping out. But I had to say something.

I lied. "Dad, I couldn't cut it. I wasn't doing well."

"You're going with that?" His face was getting redder, and he started pacing again. "The university told me, 'We're sorry to see someone so talented leave the program.' Alexandria, you have never lied like this to me before, so tell me the truth."

"Okay, but stop pacing and sit down so we can talk," I said.

He stopped pacing, went to the fridge, and got a beer. I was about to ask for one too but thought better of it.

"Okay, talk."

"I think it would be better if I attend teachers' college and be a teacher, the same as Mom." I thought mentioning Mom might soften the blow.

But Dad was waiting for more.

"So, when I go back to university," I continued, "and I *will* go back, I'll go back with a teacher's degree, and in the meantime …" I tried to pick my words very carefully.

"In the meantime, what?" he barked.

"I can still dance on the weekends. You see, teachers' college has better hours to fit in everything else and—"

"No," he said. "You are not giving up university for '*better hours.*' I won't have it."

Now I was starting to get my back up. I was nineteen and could make my own decisions. "Well, I'm sorry, but I have decided. I've already enrolled, and my transcripts have been sent. I want this."

I thought he was going to blow. He got up and began pacing again.

"You made all these decisions without even discussing them with me?"

"Dad, I love you, and I know you want the best for me, but this is what I want." I hoped I was convincing.

"So you're changing your life for better hours? I'm furious you didn't discuss this with me first. Your mother would be appalled at you throwing your dreams away."

His words were like a slap to the face. "I'm not throwing anything away, and I think Mom would be proud I'm taking after her. What's the difference between you wanting Adam to take after you and me wanting to be like Mom?" I abruptly replied.

"Well, daughter, there's nothing wrong with being a teacher, but *you* have made the decision to leave your dreams behind, and *you* will have to live with it." He sounded disappointed with me. Couldn't he see I was doing this for him and Adam?

A tightness formed in my chest. I got up and hugged him, hoping it would stop the fighting. "Daddy, I want to do this. I really do. I'm sorry I didn't talk to you first. I should have, but I'd thought about it and talked to my advisers." I pushed ahead with my argument. "My BFA has only been deferred for a while, and in the meantime, I'll get a teacher's degree. You'll see. It will all be okay." I kissed him on the cheek.

Eventually, he put his arms around me. "I worry you will regret your decision," he gently said.

"I won't," I assured him.

He held me at arm's length and glared at me. Then a cheeky smile came over his face. "Well, you're going to have to tell your aunt. Good luck," he said, walking away.

I stood there, stuck to the floor. Oh my God, my auntie will probably give me a bigger lecture than Dad. I need to think of a way to sweet-talk her.

Suddenly, I heard my father on the phone saying, "Hi, Ell, how are you? Alexandria has something to tell you." He handed me the phone.

I didn't have time to think of what to say to her. Dad was still mad, as he was still calling me by my full name. He stood there and watched me squirm while I repeated the same explanation, then gave him the evil eye as Auntie Ell also started to call me Alexandria.

I had made a big decision, and they were both disappointed about it, but things would settle down once everything was in play. Now the only person I had to convince was me.

Things did calm down after a week or so. Dad threw in a few "Alexandrias" occasionally, but he eventually came around. We had agreed I would take Adam to and from school, and Dad would take him to practice and football games in the evenings and on weekends. After two months, our family finally got into a rhythm. Adam wasn't in any more fights, Dad seemed calmer, I still danced on most weekends, and every Monday morning, I convinced myself I loved teaching.

CHAPTER NINETEEN

After three years rolled by, I had graduated from college and was teaching at a private school. Adam began high school, and Cassie and Donna graduated from university.

Four years after graduation, Donna married a fellow dancer, Anton. He was hot property in the ballet community and traveled worldwide, performing all over Europe.

Donna didn't want to travel. She was close to her family and had always wanted to teach ballet rather than perform. She danced with Cassie for two years on stage, and when she had enough money for a deposit, she left the theater and opened her own studio. Anton grew tired of touring and missed Donna, so he left the dance company and became a freelance choreographer. Although he still did some touring, he could pick and choose and stay with Donna more.

Donna's dance studio was a success from the start, and she asked me if I could teach a ballet class on Saturday mornings for four-and-five-year-olds. It also meant I got to dance for free. I had never returned for my BFA, and as my dreams to perform became less and less, teaching little ones was a compromise.

Cassie continued dancing on stage for a while, but what she enjoyed most was acting as a dance captain. The excitement, chaos, and organization of the production were an adrenaline rush for her. Cassie became very popular with performance companies; she could select any job she wanted around the country, although after two years of traveling, she tended to spend most of her time closer to home.

I transferred to the Llewellyn Elementary Private School and became good friends with the principal, Bernadette Gear, a kindhearted woman who held her ground as principal. Bernie was tall with curly auburn hair and olive skin and always looked classy. She was married to Michael Gear, a high-profile prosecutor in the District Attorney's office.

My life may not have turned out how I had imagined it would when I was a teenager, but I had great friends and a loving family, and there was much to be grateful for.

When Adam was halfway through high school, he told me he wanted to join the Air Force and not the fire service as Dad had hoped he would. From an early age, Adam was obsessed with all aircraft, especially helicopters. But Dad always tried to steer him more toward being a firefighter, and Adam was worried Dad would be disappointed. He had forgotten I had always wanted to be a dancer. He had forgotten a lot of things from around the time Mom died.

I explained Dad wouldn't be mad and, taking Auntie Ell's advice to me and Cassie years before, I advised Adam to find all the information he needed to explain how he could get into the Air Force and present it to Dad.

It only took him a week to find all the requirements and the cost. I was impressed. Adam wanted this, and I told him I would back him. If he kept going on the path he was on with his grades, he wouldn't have a problem.

We picked a time and approached Dad. He listened carefully, asked a few questions, and told Adam he had his full support. We would miss him, but Dad wouldn't stop him. I was surprised Adam got off easily compared to me, but I was glad for my brother.

The plan was, when Adam graduated from high school, he would be off to the Air Force Academy, and Dad would retire.

The following two years flew by. Adam never doubted his choice of what he wanted to do, and when he was old enough, he started flying lessons at the local airfield. He graduated from high school with honors, and Dad and I were very proud. As promised, Dad retired from the fire department, and we threw a big, combined party for father and son.

At the beginning of the summer, I told Dad I wanted to visit Auntie Ell. He thought it was a good idea and booked me on a flight the day Adam was also leaving. He seemed content with being alone in the house, and I was eager to visit my aunt. The afternoon before we left, Adam was out saying goodbye to his friends, again, so Dad and I took our usual calming afternoon stroll along the beach. It had become a father–daughter activity we did a few times a week. We had only gone about four houses up when I saw the McGregor house had a "For Sale" sign.

"I've always liked this house. It always felt cozy, like ours."

Dad told me Mrs. McGregor was leaving to live with her daughter on the other side of the island. Her daughter was a single mom and needed help caring for her three children. What was a grandmother supposed to do? We both stood staring at the house.

"Dad, are you sure about being alone while I'm away?"

He put his arm around me. "Stop worrying. I'll be fine. Go, visit your aunt and have fun. I know you miss her, and she misses you."

I hugged him, and we continued our walk.

When we got back, Adam was in a panic. "Where have you been? I can't fit everything into my duffel bag."

Dad chuckled. "I'll order dinner; you help him."

We ate on the deck when the food arrived, watching the sunset. I wondered if this would be the last time we would do this together, and a sadness washed over me. Dad noticed and put his arm around my shoulders.

"Everything will be fine, honey. Wait and see."

The next day, Adam and I walked to our gates at the airport after saying a tearful goodbye to Dad. It was harder than I thought to leave Dad and even harder to leave Adam.

CHAPTER TWENTY

Auntie Ell had met a charming lawyer, Frank Ronan. He was around the same age as her and very handsome. He was tall with silver hair and brown eyes; very distinguished. After leaving a meeting two years ago, Frank was walking past the piano bar where she worked and heard her playing. He was instantly enchanted and waited around until she finished her set then asked her out.

Like Auntie Ell, Frank had never married and never wanted his own family. Apart from spending time with his younger brother Sean, who was married with two boys, Frank buried himself in the law and his firm until he saw Ell. Then he realized it wasn't too late to change his views on relationships and wouldn't let her go.

Auntie Ell was equally enchanted with Frank. She had brought him to visit us the previous Christmas, and he had immediately got the family's approval. It didn't take long before they moved in together.

Frank was still involved with his law firm but had cut back on his hours. Ell still took pleasure playing piano a few nights a week, and Frank went with her every time as her biggest fan, listening to every note she played.

On their last visit, as the two of us were walking along the beach, Auntie Ell told me a little about Frank's past. His parents had left Ireland when Frank was eight and his brother was three. Not long after arriving in the States, Frank's mother got a job as a secretary and had an affair with the wealthy owner. Soon after the affair began, his mother ran off with the owner, never seeing her family again, and Frank watched his father turn into a bitter, angry man. A few years after starting his law firm—Ronan and Ronan & Associates—with his brother, Frank had the pleasure of bankrupting the man who ran off with his mother.

Frank and Auntie Ell picked me up from the airport and took me to their new townhouse. It was the perfect size for them. The walls and furniture were in fresh pastel colors, and they had family photos on her grandmother's piano, including pictures of their last visit to the island. I picked up the photo of her and Mom together as young girls with two men behind them, smiling.

She came up behind me. "That's your mother and me with our father and Uncle Mike. Dad died not long after. I still miss them," she said.

I looked at the picture and saw a bit of my grandfather in Adam, then carefully put the photo back on the piano.

"What do you want to do first, my darling?" she asked as she showed me to my room. "Frank has cooked an Irish stew for dinner, his father's recipe. Alright with you? We thought you'd prefer an easy night after a day of traveling."

It had been a long day, emotionally more than anything, and I was exhausted.

"I would like a shower, a glass of wine, dinner, and a good night's sleep."

"Done," she said. "I must say, Frank does make a great stew." Then she sat on the bed. "Now, don't get mad, but your father told me you haven't been dancing much lately. I've found a few classes in the area. Your father and I discussed it—he even put your ballet shoes in your case."

"What, how …?" I was surprised.

"We both knew this holiday must be about you, and I insist you do what you want. If you would rather not attend the classes, then that's okay too."

I smiled at her. "Let me think about it."

"I'll get your glass of wine while you shower and unpack."

She left the room. As I continued unpacking, I found my ballet shoes with a note from Dad.

In case you need them. Love you.

I was touched by such a wonderful gesture.

Looking around the blue pastel room, I knew I couldn't start to relax until I checked on my brother and father. Adam was first.

"Yes, I arrived safely. I'm in the barracks now, and my bunkmate is Mitch. He has a bit of an attitude."

"Well, you two should get on great then," I joked.

"Nice. Anyway, sis, I must go. There's an introduction gathering I have to attend. Love you and give my love to Ell and Frank."

He hung up before I could answer him.

Although I felt a little dismissed, I knew my little brother was okay. I called Dad next.

"Hey, kiddo, good flight?"

"Yes. What are you up to?" I could hear noises in the background.

"The boys came over for some poker and beer. How's Ell's new place?"

"It's great. Have you spoken to Adam?"

"Yes, he sounds good."

"I found my ballet shoes."

"Well, kiddo, it's up to you. But I think getting some dancing in would do you good."

Before I could say anything else, I heard yelling in the background.

"Honey, I've got to go. Your Uncle Henry has tried to cheat and got caught. Love you, have a good time. I'll talk to you tomorrow."

The line went dead again.

As I sat on the bed, my tiredness increased. I grabbed my sweats and an oversized T-shirt, picked up my toiletry bag, and showered, letting the warm water run over me. When I came out, a glass of wine sat on the bedside table, and I picked it up and joined Ell and Frank in the living area. The aroma of dinner cooking filled the room.

"The stew smells great," I said, sinking into their comfortable couch.

"I'm sorry I have to work while you're here," Frank said. "My firm is in the middle of a big case, and it's all hands-on deck."

"Frank's lead counsel," Ell chimed in, very proud.

"Are you able to talk about it?" I asked.

"Not really. The government is involved and wants it kept out of the media."

"Wow." It sounded interesting.

"I would rather spend my time with you girls than in some courtroom … well, I've said enough. How about dinner?"

As promised, dinner was great, and they wouldn't let me help them with the dishes, so I excused myself and went to bed. When my head hit the pillow, I was asleep almost immediately. My Auntie woke me the following day around ten o'clock.

While Frank was at work, we checked out dance classes, shopped, and got our nails done. I had decided it would be nice to do a bit of dancing while I was here. It had always made me feel alive.

Though my holiday quickly came to an end, I was refreshed. My time away was filled with dancing, going with Frank to listen to Ell play, visiting people, shopping, and sleeping. I hadn't slept like that in years. I had only heard from Adam a few times, but he loved the academy, and Dad seemed to be coping well on his own, even if I got a few calls from him wanting to know where things were.

I was looking forward to getting home and thinking about getting my own place.

CHAPTER TWENTY-ONE

When I returned home, Dad met me at the airport. I could tell he was up to something as he was making small talk and seemed distracted.

He stopped a few doors from home as we reached our street. He turned off the engine and faced me.

"I want to say this, and I don't want you to interrupt." He was serious. "I am very proud and grateful for all you have done for your brother and me since your mother died." He stopped to steady his voice. "You gave up a great deal to look after us, and I don't think we could have done it without you. Now, I don't want you to take this the wrong way, but it's time for you to move out."

I was shocked. I had barely been back for an hour, and Dad was kicking me out of the home. I had been thinking of moving out, but this took me by surprise.

Then he held up a set of keys.

I stared at him, baffled.

"You told me before you left how you felt about this house."

I turned and saw we were outside the McGregor house.

"I bought it for you."

I sat there with my mouth open. All I could say was, "You bought me a house? But how? Why?"

Then he said. "There was insurance money after your mother died, and I invested it as I didn't want to spend it on just anything. We wanted to do this for you and I know your mother would have approved."

"But Dad, I can't accept a house."

"You can. Your friends and I have already moved in most of your things. You have their approval. Mrs. McGregor was pleased to hear it was going to someone she knew, and because she couldn't take all her furniture with her, she left a few things behind. You can replace them when you're able."

"Dad, I don't know what to say."

"Well, let's go in and look at your house." He smiled. "And don't think you're getting rid of me that easily. I'm only a few doors away."

"What about Adam? He should get some of the money."

"I've discussed it with your brother, and he thought it was a good idea. Adam will be getting our house when I go. I thought it was fair, and so does he."

"He's really okay with it?"

"Of course he is. He loves you very much. We both want this for you."

I threw my arms around my dad and told him how much I love and appreciate him. Then I grabbed the keys and ran into my new home.

My little house was adorable. It was a single-story home with three bedrooms, two bathrooms, and a porch that backed on to one of the Pacific Ocean's many beaches. It was only four doors from Dad, and it was all mine.

CHAPTER TWENTY-TWO

Adam met Mitch Simon on his first day at the Air Force Academy, and they became best friends. They were both young, full of energy, and loved to fly helicopters—they were a team. No one in their unit worked as well together as those two, although you wouldn't know it to listen to them speak to each other.

Mitch had next to no family. His stepfather Carl was from Germany and had planned to move back to "the homeland" when Mitch graduated from high school. Carl disapproved of anything military. When Mitch announced he was joining the Air Force, his parents disowned him and moved to Germany without him. What hurt Mitch the most was his mother going along with whatever Carl demanded.

Mitch's stepbrother Alfred was eighteen years older than him and took Mitch in out of a sense of duty until he entered the academy, then he too left for Germany. When the first holiday break from the academy came along, Adam invited Mitch home with him, and he was with us for every holiday and vacation from then on.

After six years in the Air Force and traveling the world, they returned home and partnered in a helicopter business. They shared a place on the other side of town, despite Dad wanting them to move in with him—they wanted their own space.

Dad and I spoke with Adam and Mitch once a week, and one weekend a month they both came over for a beach BBQ along with our other friends.

I could tell from the first time Mitch met Cassie that he was smitten. She was older than him and called him "kid," but he didn't care. His face always lit up whenever she was near. Initially, Cassie never really came out and admitted she felt the same toward Mitch, as she thought she was too grown-up to show she cared for a younger man. But around the same time, she also decided not to travel as much and stay closer to home. With all their silly banter and teasing and the nights out "as friends" over the years, they didn't fool anyone. We all knew one day they would end up together.

Adam was dating Megan Cartwright, a law clerk for a federal judge. Megan was tall and very attractive, with blonde hair and blue eyes. She was Adam's opposite in a good way and would always pull him up on his crap, which was one of the many things I liked about her. They were a perfect couple, and it only took three months of dating before they got their own apartment and moved in together.

Life continued until one day, two years later in the fall of 2012, Dad died unexpectedly from a heart attack in his sleep.

I was picking him up for an appointment and found him sitting in his favorite chair with the TV on. At first, I thought he was asleep.

My heart broke for the second time in my life. Calling Adam to let him know was one of the hardest things I had ever had to do.

I struggled that week leading up to the funeral as my grief had nearly crippled me. Surrounded by couples, the loneliness I didn't know I had, mingled with my sadness, causing my body to ache. But I knew I had to hold it together once again until after his funeral.

The fire department gave Dad the traditional send-off for retired firefighters. At his funeral, my chest was filled with pride as his friends spoke of his leadership, courage, and friendship.

After Auntie Ell left, I wept like I had never wept before. I wept for the loss of my parents, the loss of my dance career, and I wept in fear, knowing I was suddenly alone.

Living down the beach from Dad had been wonderful. Often, I would come home and find him fixing something in my house. He would say, "Honey, I noticed your light globe was out," or "the back door was squeaking." Some days after work, I would walk along the beach with two beers to where Dad was fishing. I would sit on the sand beside him, watch him fish, and chat.

"Catch anything yet, or are we eating takeout again?" I would ask.

Most of the time, it was takeout. However, when we did have fresh fish, it was courtesy of Dad's fishing skills.

He told me stories of his days in the fire department and life with Mom before and after marriage. It was calming listening to him. I missed our talks, the sound of his laugh, his big hugs, the smell of his aftershave, his dad jokes, everything. They say time heals, but how much time does it take?

As promised, Adam and Megan took over Dad's house and started to make it theirs.

I remember my brother and I running out the back door straight into the ocean as young kids. I could still hear the sound of the screen door banging shut as we ran out. I was thrilled they decided to move in. I don't think I could have coped with strangers living there.

CHAPTER TWENTY-THREE

Some school days seemed longer than others, and this one was no different. It was two in the afternoon, with only an hour left before the home bell rang. I had given my fourth-graders a quiz earlier, which hadn't gone well. Oh, how I hated these days when the kids were restless. It was hard to get them to focus, and there seemed to be more arguments over little things. Maybe the trade winds were affecting everyone, including me.

I wanted to go home and have a simple dinner and a glass of wine, but after I got these little darlings out of my classroom, I had a staff meeting, which could be two hours long—if I was lucky—and then I had to mark the quiz papers.

Damn, I also need to go to the market. There was no food for my cat Blossom, or me. I could survive on the crackers in the cupboard and the wine, but Blossom would not be happy.

I thought the best way to get through the last hour of the day was to get some artwork going. The kids could take out their restlessness on paper. Most students settled down as I moved around the room to observe their artwork. Coloring is known to be calming, and I was thankful when we finally heard the school bell. They hurried to put their things away, then they sat waiting for me to say, "You're excused." With those two words, there was a stampede for the door.

The kids and I exchanged goodbyes as my friend Bernadette entered the room, dodging the children.

As the last kid left, I told Bernie, "You know, I think they're as pleased to see the back of me as I am to see them leave."

Bernie gave a little laugh. "I know how you feel. My class drove me crazy today."

"I thought today would never end," I said.

"So you're ready for the staff meeting?" Her tone was sarcastic.

"Not unless you can write me a note to get out of it." I was almost pleading.

"Ah, no. If I have to attend, *you* have to attend also. I've got to have at least one friend there."

"So why do you plan these meetings if you don't want to go?" I asked.

"School board," she said as she grabbed my arm and pulled me out of my chair.

"Please don't let Ethel drag this out. You know how she brings up every little thing. Last time we spent half an hour on dirty cups left in the staff lounge."

"There, my friend, is the silver lining. Ethel had to leave early today."

"Oh, thank God," I said with a sigh.

When we got to the staff lounge, Brett, one of two male teachers, flopped onto the couch. "Was today long or was it just me?"

"No, it was a long day," Vince replied.

"Right," said Bernie, "let's get this meeting started so we can all go home."

Luckily, the meeting only lasted an hour. We discussed rosters and the next school excursion. No one was in the mood to go over things, and there wasn't anything important to discuss. After the meeting, I returned to my classroom to mark the papers. If I did it now, I wouldn't have to think about it when I got home. It didn't take long, and I was impressed with the marks they all earned. Wow, they must be listening.

As I headed out the door, Bernie was also leaving her office, and we walked to our cars together. We chatted about the meeting and how there was only one more day before the weekend, and school break wasn't far away. We said our goodbyes and got into our cars.

My car had a little trouble starting. Adam had promised that if I got the new parts, he would fix it a month ago. My car was nine years old, but up until a month ago, I had never had any problems with it. Dad had helped me choose it, and it always made me smile when I thought of that day.

I drove to the market nearest my home, driving the back way to avoid most of the traffic. Fifteen minutes later, I pulled into the market's parking lot. Thank God there weren't many cars around.

Entering the market, I grabbed a cart and started walking up the aisle. Not knowing what I wanted for dinner, I eventually settled on a frozen pizza. How original. I grabbed the milk and two bottles of wine and stood in the pet food aisle for six minutes, deciding what Blossom would eat. Cats could be very fussy. If you got the wrong food, you would be back the next day getting something else as they would rather starve than eat what they didn't want. I finally saw the brand she preferred and put it in the cart.

At the checkout, an older woman in front of me took longer than I liked, but I kept reminding myself to be patient. Finally, I went through the checkout, put the groceries in the back seat of my car, and turned the key in the ignition.

Nothing happened.

I tried it again.

Nothing happened.

"No, no, don't do this." I tried it once more. Still nothing. I hit the steering wheel with the palm of my hand. "No, no, no." The car wouldn't turn over. "Shit! I'm going to kill Adam," I yelled. Opening and propping up the car's hood, I stared into the engine. "Now, what are you going to do? Work, you stupid thing," I yelled at the car as if it would make a difference.

I wiggled some wires, hit a few things with my hand, sat back in the driver's seat, and turned the key again. Still, nothing happened.

Okay, Adam is going to have to come and fix this now. I reached for my cell to dial his number and noticed my battery was completely flat.

"Great," I said aloud. "Now what?"

I saw a man leaving the market and walking past my car, and I started running after him.

"Excuse me. Excuse me," I called.

The man slowed down, then stopped and turned.

"Sorry to trouble you. I was hoping I could use your phone."

He looked at me. "Excuse me?"

"Can I use your phone, please? My car won't start, and I need to contact my brother to come and get it started."

"Oh, I've heard about this. A lady in distress who wants to use your phone, and next thing you know, a gang comes and robs you," he said.

"A gang? What, are you for real? You can see my car's hood is up. Please, it's one call." I pleaded. "I have to phone my brother."

"Is he a mechanic?"

"No, he's a helicopter pilot." I was getting frustrated. "I tell you what, so you don't have to worry about a schoolteacher robbing you …"

"I thought you said he was a helicopter pilot?"

"He is. I'm a schoolteacher." I let out a big sigh. "Since you're not very trusting, why don't I give you his number and you telephone him?"

"Ah, but once again," he said, "how do I know this is for real?"

"Fine, ring Kane and Simon Helicopter Services and tell them Adam's sister needs assistance and wants to talk to him urgently."

"Okay, what's the number?"

"Seriously? You're the one who's not trusting. Look it up."

"Before I make this call, can I at least know your name?"

"Of course, it's Ally, Ally Kane."

"Erick Morgan." He put out his right hand, and I shook it. He leaned back against his car, searched for the number, and dialed. "They're putting me through." He seemed surprised.

"See!"

I noticed he seemed to be trying not to smile. I looked him over as he was waiting to be put through to Adam. He was tall and lean, and I could tell he worked out. He wore dark-blue pants with a button-down gray shirt tucked into them. He had dark wavy hair, a bit of facial hair on his chiseled square jaw, and his eyes were brown with flecks of gold. When he smiled, he had the cutest half-moon dimples.

As I was admiring him, I noticed he was also looking me over too. My cheeks started to heat up as I blushed, and I turned away, trying hard not to smile.

"Hi, I'm Erick. No, your sister's fine; I'll put her on," he said, handing me his cell.

"My car won't start, Adam, and I'm stuck at the market, and my cell battery's dead."

"Are you okay?" Adam asked.

"Yes, *but my car won't start. I am stranded*," I yelled at him.

"Get a taxi home." Adam's answer to everything.

"No, you were supposed to fix it a month ago, and now I'm stuck. You come. Now."

"Okay, we'll be there in about ten minutes," he said.

"Fine." I hung up.

Erick was still leaning against his car, his arms crossed, smiling at me.

"He's on his way. Thank you for your assistance. I won't hold you up any longer."

"It's okay. I want to see this pilot-slash-mechanic."

I gave a bit of a laugh and slightly bit my lower lip. "You don't have to stay." Secretly, I was hoping he would.

Smiling, he said, "No, I'll stay until he comes." Oh my God, his smile was infectious. I felt the need to make small talk. "So, Erick, do you live nearby?"

"Not far. What about you?" he asked.

"Only ten minutes away."

"What school do you teach at?" he asked.

"How did you know I was a schoolteacher?" I questioned.

"You told me."

"Oh, yes, I did." I was distracted. "I teach fourth grade at Llewellyn Elementary Private School."

"Ahh, a private-school teacher. Do you come from here, or did you move from the mainland?"

"I was born and bred here," I stated with pride. "What about yourself?"

"Here on business for a while," he said.

"Nice," I said, nodding my head.

"Well, I'm still trying to get my bearings. You're the first person I've had a conversation with that has lasted for more than fifteen minutes that doesn't involve my job," he stated.

"You know, most of the people on the island are very friendly."

"Yeah, I was told that after they called me a 'howley.' Is that right, *howley*?"

"A haole. It's a term for individuals who aren't native Hawaiian."

"Wow," he said, acting a little offended.

I crossed my arms. "Oh, I see we've failed to make a good impression. Look, I know some great places you can go."

"Well, you owe me a drink for using my phone, and maybe we can have dinner at one of these great places you're talking about," he said.

I was a little taken aback by his forwardness.

"Alright, I'll buy you a drink, but we'll see about dinner," I said. It was unusual for me to go out with someone I didn't know, but there was something about Erick I felt a connection with.

"Fair," he said. "Give me a call and let me know the details."

Our eyes locked. Oh my God, was he flirting with me?

He grabbed a business card from his shirt pocket and handed it to me. "Here's my number."

Before I could read it, Adam, along with Mitch, came speeding into the car lot in his white truck. *Great timing, as always*, I thought.

"Hi, I'm Adam."

"Erick."

The two men shook hands.

Adam turned toward me. "Are you okay?"

"I want my car to work."

"I told you to buy the parts."

"I did. Over a month ago."

"You didn't tell me."

"I did. Over a month ago. I even texted you so you couldn't say I didn't tell you."

"Oh, I remember now. I'm sorry," Adam said, hugging me. "Let me look at it and get it started. I promise I'll fix it on the weekend."

"Just get it started." I had trouble staying mad at him. After all, he was my little brother, even though he towered over me.

Adam walked to my car and disappeared under the hood.

Mitch approached Erick. "Hi, I'm Mitch."

"Erick."

They also shook hands.

Mitch turned to me and put his arm around my shoulders. "You know what I don't get? You're a brilliant woman, so why would you let this guy"—he pointed to Adam—"fix your car is unbelievable to me."

"Lapse of judgment, I guess," I said, shrugging my shoulders.

"Hear from Cassie today?"

"Yes, she's busy at the theater and waiting for you to phone," I said.

He nodded his head and smiled. "Good, really good."

I wish he and Cassie would get their acts together. They had been playing this game forever, and it was time to make it official.

Erick was still smiling. "Well, I can see you're in good hands, so I'll leave you and wait for your call about that drink."

"Mahalo. I do appreciate your help," I said.

"Mahalo?" he asked.

"It means thank you," I replied.

"You're very welcome," he said as he got into his car. Before I could think of anything to say, he drove off.

"A drink? Is this how you're picking up guys now?" Mitch joked.

I laughed and pushed him away. "Don't say anything to Adam," I threatened him.

Within ten minutes, Adam had my car started.

"It'll get you home, but don't drive until after I fix it." He kissed me on the cheek, then he and Mitch drove off.

When I got home, I called Bernie and asked if she could give me a ride to work in the morning. I briefly told her what happened and said I would explain the rest tomorrow.

CHAPTER TWENTY-FOUR

The following morning, Bernie arrived to drive me to work.

"Okay," she said before I had the car door closed. "You promised to tell me everything about this mystery man."

I laughed and told her the whole story about the car and meeting Erick Morgan. I finished my story as Bernie was pulling into her parking space.

"You were flirting," she said.

I turned to her. "No, I wasn't. He was."

She laughed. "Oh, my dear friend, *you* were also flirting. If you weren't, why didn't you go back into the store, use their phone, and tell him to get lost?"

I opened my mouth to answer her, but no words came out. I thought back to the previous afternoon, and she was right.

"Oh my God, I *was* flirting," I said, shocked. "I did it and didn't know."

Bernie and I looked at each other and burst out laughing.

There was a knock on the car's side window, which startled us both.

Ethel put her head through the open window. "Are you ladies coming or are you going to sit there talking all day?" she scolded us before walking off.

"I think Ethel was a nun in a past life," I said.

"So, will you see him again?" Bernie asked. She wasn't going to move until I gave her an answer.

"I do have his number." I pulled his business card out of my purse, showed it to her, and placed it in my dress pocket. "I told him I would buy him a drink because he helped me, but I don't know."

Bernie rolled her eyes and opened her door. "Don't start this again."

"You know what I mean. 'That type of guy' isn't usually interested in me. I only seem to attract the deadbeats."

"Then go have a drink with him. It's only one drink. Pick a place. One of us will drive you, and you can get a taxi home. I'll even phone with a pretend emergency if you want to leave."

I laughed. "I feel like we're back in high school." I stopped walking. "Should I? I mean, should I be considering this?"

"If you don't contact him," Bernie said as she took the card from my pocket, "I'll do it for you and set it up."

Snatching the card from her, I put it back in my pocket. "Okay, I'll do it later." Was I a bit excited, or was it anxiety?

The school bell sounded, and kids ran everywhere to get to class. As I headed to my classroom, Bernie mouthed the words "Phone him."

* * *

By the time lunch came around, I was looking forward to getting outside. I was on playground duty, and it was nice in the sun and fresh air.

After thirty minutes out there, Bernie came and stood next to me. "So?"

"I haven't done it yet."

"Okay, but can I ask, will it happen this year?"

I nudged her with my elbow.

We were chatting away, and all seemed as normal as it could be in the playground when Louise and Lilah, pretty twin sisters, came running up to me, a pink rose in Lilah's hand.

"Ms. Kane, there's a man at the gate and he said to give you this," Louise said as Lilah handed me the pink rose.

I was confused as I took it from her.

Bernie replied in her strong principal voice, "Girls, you know not to talk to strangers. Where is this man?"

They both turned and pointed to the gate where Erick was standing on the other side, smiling.

"Oh no," I said.

"What? Is that him?" she asked.

I nodded.

"Thank you, girls. You can go," said Bernie. Once they had left, she asked again, "Is it him? He's gorgeous. Go talk to him."

Erick was waving at me, and I automatically waved back.

"I can't." I was suddenly terrified.

"Then I will," said Bernie.

"No, you won't. I'll go." I turned to face her. "Do I look okay?"

"Yes, go," she said eagerly.

As I slowly approached the closed gate, under my breath, I told myself, "Be cool. Don't act anxious."

"Hi," he said as I got close. He was showing his perfect smile.

"Hi. How did you know where I worked?"

"You told me yesterday, remember."

I quickly thought back. *You idiot, you did.* "Thank you for the rose. Pink roses are my favorite."

"You know, I sensed that. Can you open the gate?" he asked as he peered through the iron bars.

"Do you have a child at this school?" I teased.

"No."

"Do you have school business here?"

"No."

"Then I'm sorry, I can't open the gate. Against the rules," I said. We both smiled.

"Why are you here?" I asked.

"Well, I thought you might have forgotten about your promise to buy me a drink, or your cell battery was still dead, and I wanted to remind you."

Is he flirting with me? God, I hope so.

"I hadn't forgotten. I was going to call you later today." I pulled his business card from my pocket to show him.

"Great. Then I'll save you a call. I'm free tonight."

I gazed into his amazing brown eyes and saw those dimples in his cheeks. Without hesitation, I replied, "I'm free tonight also. How about seven? I'll text you the location."

"Can I pick you up?"

"It's okay, I'll meet you there." His smile may have got me to say yes, but I was still going to be a little cautious.

"Okay. I'll see you at seven. Don't stand me up."

"I won't."

The bell to end the lunch period sounded.

"I must go. Thanks again for the rose."

"See you tonight, Ms. Kane. I'm looking forward to it. And don't forget to text me the address."

I walked off, but as I got halfway back across the playground, I turned and glanced at the gate. Erick was still there watching me, and I gave a final wave. As I reached the top of the stairs, Bernie was waiting for me.

"Your cheeks are red," she pointed out.

I put my hands to my face, and it was hot. "It's from the sun," I tried to convince her.

"So, are you going out?"

"Tonight at seven."

We both let out a little giggle. Then panic set in.

"Tonight. Holly cow, I have nothing to wear. I can't do this."

"Don't worry." She put her arm around my shoulders. "I'll phone the girls, and we'll pick something out for you. I'm sure you have something in the back of your closet."

CHAPTER TWENTY-FIVE

After an hour of the girls and me going through my closet, I settled for my green sleeveless dress with the gold buckle and put on my mother's pearls for luck. I was nervous. It had been a long time since any guy had made me feel this way. Cassie dropped me at the restaurant with strict instructions to phone her if I needed a reason to bail.

I was a little late on purpose as I didn't want to get there first and wait to see if he arrived. I got to the door and hesitated. *Maybe I shouldn't go in*, I thought. *I could tell the girls it didn't work out.*

Taking a deep breath, I decided to be brave and go inside. Looking around the room, I saw Erick sitting at the bar, smiling at me.

He stood up, kissed the back of my hand, and said, "Madame." Still holding on to my hand, he led me to a small table in a quiet corner of the bar area. He was very attractive in his black pants and an open-neck light-blue shirt. His hair was perfect, his face freshly shaved, and his cologne was intoxicating.

Before we sat down, he said, "*Wow*, you look beautiful."

"Mahalo, and may I say you look very nice yourself."

He blushed a little. "Well, thank you, ma'am."

The waiter approached us and asked us for our drink order. Erick said a beer, and I asked for a glass of white wine.

Erick smiled when we were alone again. "So, you come here a lot?"

"I've only been a few times."

"With your boyfriends?"

Ah, he's fishing. Two could play this game.

"Not always," I said, being a little coy. "What type of place would you take your girlfriend?" I asked.

"Well, I don't know. Where would you enjoy going?" He stared into my eyes.

This time it was me who was blushing. I didn't know what to say. The waiter arrived with our drinks, and I gratefully took a sip of mine.

"So, you said your company transferred you from …"

"Washington DC," he said.

"How long are you here for?"

"Not sure. It can vary, and it depends on how well I do."

"So, if you do well, you stay longer?"

"Something like that."

"We'll have to make sure you do well then."

His face lit up. "I'll be trying extra hard."

My heartbeat quickened, and, as if he knew, he reached out and put his hand on mine, calming me.

"I think we need to get to know each other better over dinner," he said.

I smiled back at him, finished my wine, and said, "I would love to."

"Marvelous. I took the liberty to book a table here."

Before I could reply, my cell phone rang. It was Cassie.

"Excuse me a moment. I have to take this call."

Cassie was on the phone and quickly asked. "Do you have an emergency?"

I glanced at Erick and said, "I'm pleased with my current provider. Thank you."

"Ring me later, don't care what time." She hung up.

"That was your friend from the school checking up on you, right?" Erick chuckled.

I cocked my head to the side. "No," I said, "it was another friend."

He threw his head back with laughter, then stood up. Like a true gentleman, he walked around to the back of my chair and slightly pulled it out for me then whispered, in my ear, "If I had a friend as lovely as you, I would also want you to be protected."

Blushing again, I stood up, Erick gently took my hand, which fitted perfectly into his, and we entered the restaurant area. A waiter showed us to another quiet table, and on it was a single pink rose.

"You were so sure I would say yes to dinner," I said.

The waiter pulled out my chair for me as we sat down.

Erick looked at me with a serious expression on his face. "I would never take you for granted. I was *hoping* you would say yes."

We ordered more drinks as the waiter handed us menus. I skimmed mine, but I couldn't concentrate on it. Erick had some great lines, but did he mean them?

"What do you enjoy eating?" I asked.

"Most anything."

"Me too."

We both ordered steaks with baked potatoes.

"Tell me about your family," he said.

I told him about my brother and aunt, my parents' deaths and friends, and how I cherished teaching little kids to dance on a Saturday at Donna's studio. Erick listened carefully and said he would like to see me teach dance one weekend.

"So, tell me about your family," I asked.

He told me his parents had also died and that he had no siblings. He also didn't have close friends because he traveled a lot. When the opportunity arose to work in Hawaii, he thought it would be a new and exciting time. He explained he was an investment analyst for a private equity firm and was traveling around the islands visiting various clients. The apartment he was staying in was small, with very little furniture, which didn't bother him as he was hardly there.

We talked through dinner, dessert, and brandy, telling each other stories about our lives. He was very easy to talk to, and we were comfortable with each other. We didn't notice the restaurant was nearly empty when the waiter came up with the bill.

"I got this," Erick said.

"I owe you, remember."

"Your company is my payment," he said sincerely.

"At least let me go half," I insisted.

"You can get it next time. Hoping there is a next time."

We both reached over the table and held hands.

After paying the waiter, Erick said, "I had such a great time tonight."

"Me too." I picked up my flower and smelled it. "Thank you for dinner. And the rose."

"Thank you for asking me to use my phone."

We held hands as we left the restaurant. I'm not sure if it was the wine, but I felt happy. When we stepped outside, you could smell a mix of sea breeze and jasmine in the warm night air.

I inhaled deeply. "God, I love that smell."

He looked at me.

"Go ahead. Try it," I encouraged him.

Erick inhaled slowly. "You're right. It does smell good. I think I'll like this place after all." He squeezed my hand. "Let me drive you home."

"It's okay. There are taxi cabs over there." I pointed to a line of waiting taxis. I was tempted to let him take me home, but I had promised the girls I wouldn't let him on the first date.

He squeezed my hand again and walked me over to the cabs. "Is it okay if I contact you tomorrow? Can we get together again in, say, the next twenty-four hours?" he said with a smile.

"That would be lovely."

He opened the back door of the cab, and as I was about to get in, he very softly kissed me. My body tingled, and I stopped breathing for a second.

I sat in the back, and Erick closed the door, smiled at me, and reached into the driver's window and handed him money.

"A little extra, sir, for taking her home safely."

My cab driver gave him a wave of thanks, then drove off.

Peering back, I saw Erick watching the cab leave. I gave the driver my address, wondering what was happening to me. Could this be for real? Was I going to hear from him again?

Within seconds, I received Erick's text message.

Good night. I'll talk to you tomorrow.

My body tingled again with excitement.

CHAPTER TWENTY-SIX

The cab arrived at my place in ten minutes. As I walked up my front path, I noticed the light in my carport was on, and my car hood was up.

"Adam, is that you?" I yelled out.

"Yeah, just fixing your car."

"At this time? It's late."

"I know, sorry. I couldn't sleep."

"Tough day?" I asked.

"Oh yeah, you need more beer. This was your last one," he said, holding up the bottle.

"How many have you drunk?"

"Only three. This is the fourth."

"Okay, put the tools down and go home," I ordered him.

"No, I'm fine," he replied. "Hey, why are you getting home at this hour? Where did you get the rose?"

"I had a date," I said. Even I could hear how happy I sounded.

"No way. Really? Who? You know, I should meet any guy before he takes you out." He sounded like Dad.

"You've met him," I reminded him.

"Who?"

I hesitated for a moment. "The guy from the market. The one who lent me his phone to call you."

"Seriously?" he said, sounding stunned.

"Don't sound surprised someone would want to take your sister out."

"No, I think it's great. Did you have a good time?"

"Yes, He was a perfect gentleman," I assured him.

"He'd better have been." He was trying to sound tough.

I took the beer from Adam's hand.

"Okay, I'll go home and finish your car in the morning."

"Thank you," I said.

"Hey, you want to come over for a BBQ tomorrow night? All the guys will be there."

"I'll see. I may be busy," I said.

"Oh, you may, may you? You know you could bring him. Give us a chance to check him out."

"Ah, no, not yet. I'm perfectly capable of scaring him away all by myself."

Adam put his arm around my shoulders carefully, trying not to get grease on me. "Any guy who dates you, sis, would be very lucky." He kissed me on the cheek.

"Thanks, bro, but you're not meeting him yet. Good night," I said, walking around to the back door.

Blossom came to greet me.

"Hello, beautiful." I picked her up. "You know, Blossom, I met a wonderful guy tonight. Do you think he'll call?"

She meowed.

"I hope so too."

As I got comfortable in bed, my head was still spinning from my evening.

My cell phone pinged. It was another text message from Erick. *I hope you arrived home safely.*

Giggling, I texted back. *Yes, I did thank you, good night.*

Blossom curled up in her usual position, and I couldn't stop smiling.

CHAPTER TWENTY-SEVEN

Y alarm clock startled me. I quickly turned it off and stretched. *Did last night happen, or did I dream it? I* asked myself.

I had to teach a dance class this morning, so I showered and got dressed, but then remembered I didn't have a car. I phoned Adam and asked if I could borrow his truck for a few hours.

I always ensured I arrived at the studio well before anyone else to warm up and get in a bit of dancing for myself. I loved stepping onto the dance floor with no one around, the sound of my ballet slippers' leather soles on the wooden floor, the music—everything about it.

First, I put on some classical music to stretch and warm up. After about fifteen minutes, I played music from the ballet *Sleeping Beauty*. After all those years, I still remembered all the moves and was still light on my feet.

I was lost in my dancing when I realized my cell phone was ringing. I answered with a breathless hello. It was Erick.

"You sound out of breath. I hope you're not in the middle of a class?"

I couldn't help smiling. "No, not yet. I have a little time before the kids arrive," I replied.

"I was hoping we could catch up today."

"That would be great." I blushed, remembering his gentle kiss last night.

"Good. I'll ring you when you finish and arrange a time to meet, or do you want me to pick you up at the studio or maybe from home?" He sounded a bit flustered, which made me giggle again and smile even more.

Before answering him, I realized I had an audience.

"Woo, Miss Ally has a date." The words came from little Kelly, making me blush even more as I told Erick I would call him in a few hours.

Kelly's mom sidled up to me, winked and said, "Miss Ally, who's the lucky guy?"

I didn't think my face could go any redder, but it did. I grabbed my water bottle and took a drink, hoping the redness in my face would calm down. Then I faced the children as if nothing had happened, clapped my hands, and called out to the class, "Children, come and line up and we'll get started."

I have always loved teaching these kids, though focusing was challenging at first. However, as the little ones warmed up and danced around the room like butterflies, it allowed me to set aside thoughts of Erick.

After class, I returned Adam's truck, and he told me my car was fixed. He asked me again if I was coming to his BBQ that evening. He mentioned that "What's his name" could come and promised he wouldn't ask him too many questions, although he couldn't guarantee what Mitch would say. I thanked him and sarcastically said I would think about it.

Strolling up the beach to my house, my cell phone rang. It was Erick again.

"Hello," I said.

"Hi, beautiful ballerina."

Oh God, there I go again, blushing.

"Have you finished for the day?" he asked.

I didn't hesitate. "Yes, I'm home."

"Great. I'll pick you up in ten minutes." He sounded eager.

"Can you give me twenty?" I replied.

"How about fifteen, and you give me your address."

Not wanting to be out-bargained, I said, "Give me *eighteen* minutes, and I'll text you the address."

"Deal," he said, "see you in seventeen minutes."

I couldn't help but laugh as I hung up and sent him my details.

I chose my floral skirt and black top. I had just finished putting on my lipstick when the doorbell rang. Giggling, I took a moment and reminded myself to act my age.

Erick was wearing black jeans, sneakers, and a silver-gray polo shirt. He looked and smelled great, and he seemed to be more handsome than last night. He handed me four pink roses.

"Four roses for our fourth meeting," he stated.

He was keeping count.

"Thank you, come in. I'll put these in a vase."

He followed me to the kitchen. "Nice house."

Walking toward the back door, he looked out onto the beach. "Great view."

"Thanks. We like it."

"We?" He asked.

"Blossom and I."

He stared at me for a moment. "That's right. You said you have a cat."

I took a vase from the cabinet. It was the same crystal vase Dad gave Mom on their first date. After arranging the roses and positioning the vase in the center of my dining table, I looked at Erick and asked, "Shall we go?"

"After you, my lady."

I decided we would skip Adam's invitation because I wanted Erick all to myself.

CHAPTER TWENTY-EIGHT

After our second date, we spoke at least twice daily and saw each other every second day. After two weeks, I slowly introduced Erick to my friends, as well as Adam. They all liked him and thought we were good together.

Erick didn't have any friends or colleagues for me to meet, being new in town, but he seemed to be making friends with my family, friends, and their partners. He made me happier than I ever thought I could be.

I taught him paddleboarding, and afterwards, we would relax on the inflatable mattress in the grass outside my back door, watching the sunset. Erick had a passion for dancing. Many evenings were spent with me barefoot, my arms wrapped around his neck, swaying to a slow song. No matter the location, he would often hear a song and pull me into his embrace.

One day, we were in the grocery aisle when the song "Save the Last Dance for Me" started playing over the intercom. Erick grabbed me, and we began dancing, which amused some customers.

Unfortunately, Ethel also saw us and told me I was not setting a good example. I couldn't help but laugh when Erick asked Ethel to dance, and she took off very quickly. I knew she would be calling Bernie to tell her of my outrageous behavior.

Nearly four weeks passed, and I decided to host my first official couples' dinner party. I invited Adam, Megan, Cassie, Mitch, Donna, Anton, Bernie, and Michael. We sat on my patio outside in the cool evening air with a gentle sea breeze playing with our senses. The dinner went off without a hitch. Erick seemed comfortable around everyone as we laughed and reminisced about the old days. He would kiss the nape of my neck, wrap his arm around me affectionately, and gently play with my hair. The way he looked into my eyes made me feel loved and safe, and anyone watching us could tell we were happy. It felt as though we had been together forever.

During our second week of dating, we agreed not to rush into intimacy. This was Erick's suggestion, as he had previously rushed into physical closeness and wanted to avoid making that mistake again. I supported his decision, yet I sensed that tonight was the right moment, and Erick was showing all the signs that he wanted it too.

As the evening came to a close, I stacked the dishes in the sink, thinking we would wash them later, and shortly after, Erick and I waved off our guests from my driveway.

As they drove away, Erick turned me toward him and kissed me. "I had a great time with your friends tonight," he said.

"I had a great time too." I kissed him back.

God, I hoped I was reading his signals right.

I swiftly organized the kitchen, and for the first time, Erick paused to observe the framed photos on my shelves.

"Ah, family photos," he said with a smile. He picked up a frame holding a picture of my family, and I happily pointed out each person. "This is my dad, mom, Adam, and me. It was taken not long before Mom's accident."

Erick held the photo a little longer, then returned it to the shelf.

"Do you want to help me finish this off?" I asked with a playful smile, holding a nearly full bottle of wine, feeling confident that he would say yes and whisk me away to the bedroom.

"Umm, you know what? I think I'll go. I have an early start tomorrow," he said.

"Are you sure?" I was trying to give a seductive smile, thinking he was playing hard to get.

"Yeah, it's late." He seemed in a hurry as he headed for the door.

"Is there something wrong?" I asked.

"No, nothing's wrong. I'm a bit tired," he said, kissing me on the cheek. "Thanks again for a great evening. I'll call you."

And he was gone before I could say another word.

I felt bewildered. Everything had been going smoothly. Was the idea of spending the night with me so frightening that he felt the need to escape? I hurried to the door and opened it to get answers, but he was already gone.

As I sat on the couch, my mind was spinning, still confused about what had happened.

I decided to text him, but stopped. He always messaged when he got home. Maybe I was overreacting, and the night had been a bit much for him.

Don't overthink this, I told myself as I washed the dishes and cleaned up after the party. I was operating on autopilot, my mind racing. Once I finished tidying the kitchen, I went into the backyard, sat on the deck, and cried, feeling crushed with how the night had unfolded.

An hour ticked by, and as I hadn't heard from Erick, I got mad. What was his deal? He had been all over me since we met, and now he had left as if I had a disease.

Keeping my cell phone close, I got ready for bed, hoping he would phone or even text to explain his strange behavior, but I received nothing. Could it be over?

Even though it was late, I decided to text him.

Hi, I hope everything is okay. You left in such a hurry. Call me tomorrow. Good night.

I watched my phone. He typically replied within a minute. After fifteen minutes, I finally received a response.

All okay, speak tomorrow, good night.

Tossing my phone aside, I buried my face in the pillow and screamed.

All night, my mind replayed the evening. He waited until my friends left, then he changed. Was it something I did, or maybe something my friends said? I didn't know what to think.

CHAPTER TWENTY-NINE

Erick
Six Weeks Earlier

Six weeks ago, a man sat in his dark-blue SVU, just in sight of a private school in Oahu, his binoculars trained on his mark. She was a schoolteacher who was now on lunchtime playground duty.

This was a special assignment for the agency, to observe and make sure "the soft target" was safe. He had never been on an assignment like this before, but he didn't question it. He had received special orders two weeks ago, been given a new identity, and ordered to move to the island and stay until instructed otherwise.

He had taken on so many identities that it was hard to recall his original name. For this assignment, he was known as Erick Morgan until he was reassigned.

The man portraying Erick had served as a surveillance officer for the government agency for many years. His role had taken him across the globe, despite not being a high-profile agent. Erick possessed exceptional observational skills and the capacity to multitask without losing focus. His responsibilities included tracking a target's movements, noting who visited them, managing various surveillance devices, and reporting back to his handler to help the agency strategize their next steps.

Throughout his career, he had faced some close calls, but only once did he nearly lose his life. While on assignment in Southeast Asia, Erick let his guard down, allowing his target to shoot him in the abdomen. He vividly recalled the searing pain, the blood, and his inability to move; he was convinced he was going to die. Just as he was about to be taken by enemy forces, another agent emerged from cover, rescued him at the last moment, brought him to a safe house, treated his wounds, and arranged for his flight back home. Although it happened in a blur, he would always remember the person who saved him. He only knew that individual as Wilding, but he promised himself that he would someday repay that debt.

It took months of physical therapy before he was allowed back in the field.

For several weeks, he had quietly observed the soft target from his car and apartment, noting her movements at school, home, and even while shopping. There were no criminal or unusual activities, and the target stayed blissfully unaware of Erick's vigilant gaze.

As he watched the teacher interacting with the children, it was clear that she had a warm and caring nature. He didn't usually feel anything for a target, but this time felt different. What was it about her that made him want to keep a watchful eye and protect her? He wasn't quite sure, and he reminded himself that it wasn't his job to figure it out, yet there was something about her that captured his attention.

He couldn't help but smile when she smiled, and his heart ached for her when she looked sad. The other night, she sat on her back deck with a glass of wine, watching the sunset, her expression heavy with sorrow. He felt an overwhelming urge to ask her what was wrong, to wrap his arms around her, and to gently whisper, "It will be okay." This impulse to connect was stronger than anything he had experienced. What was it about her? Why at this moment?

As he thought of her sadness, it reminded him of the sorrow in his brother's eyes when he first left him. His mind wandered back to when he was growing up and the only other person he ever cared for was his little brother. *One day, I will leave the agency and find him*, he would tell himself.

He understood that Daniel was safe, being raised in a nurturing environment and receiving a good education. One of the requirements for assisting the agency was that his brother be adopted into a caring family, but this decision meant he would never see his sibling again. Daniel's name was changed, and Erick was unaware of what it became or where he was raised.

Perhaps it would be best if he didn't find him. He often had conflicting thoughts and always returned to what was best for his brother: Erick staying away.

As the bell rang to mark the end of lunch break, Erick set down the binoculars, leaned back in the car seat, and sipped his stale coffee. This island was lovely, though it could get hot at times.

His thoughts wandered back to his childhood. While he didn't recall much from before his brother came along, he remembered enjoying school and looking after himself. He also thought fondly of Nora, a wonderfully kind young woman who lived a few flights up in his building. In her early twenties, Nora worked at her brother-in-law's dry cleaners. She was aware that Erick's parents weren't around much, so she would occasionally check in on him. Erick managed to bathe, put himself to bed, do his homework, and get off to school with very little help from his parents. Unfortunately, their main concern seemed to be getting their welfare check and buying drugs.

Erick was about eleven when his younger brother arrived. The nine months of his mother's pregnancy marked the happiest period of Erick's childhood. Although his father left, his mother remained drug-free. She cooked, cleaned their apartment, spent evenings watching TV with Erick, and took him to the park on weekends.

Six months after Daniel was born, his father came back, but sadly, his mother relapsed, and life returned to how it had been before her pregnancy. The only difference was that now Erick had the extra responsibility of caring for his brother as his parents could vanish for days, sometimes even weeks.

Nora continued to live upstairs as a single mother with her baby son. Erick's mother often pressed money into her hands, insisting, "You take him until his brother gets home." Nora welcomed the responsibility of caring for both babies since they enjoyed playing together, and the additional money was a significant help. By keeping his brother and himself under the radar of social services, Erick hoped to avoid being taken into foster care and separated.

After being away for two weeks, their father returned and announced, "Your mother's dead. The city cremated her." Erick didn't ask any questions and felt no need to find out what had happened to her. He wasn't close to them; they had never shown the boys any affection. They merely coexisted to receive welfare benefits.

The only person Erick loved and cared for was Daniel, and his sole concern was to look after him as best he could. He left school at sixteen and found work at the local car repair shop. He could drop Daniel off at kindergarten in the morning and pick him up in the afternoon.

One day, Erick came home to find that their father was gone, with no note and all his belongings missing. Surprisingly, this brought a sense of relief for Erick. Now, he could focus on moving forward in life alongside his brother. With the money from his job and assistance from welfare still coming in, they had just enough to get by. Erick worked hard to keep his brother in school, keep a roof over their heads, and ensure there was food on the table. They lived in public housing, and social services were often too busy to check on their situation. As long as he paid the rent and bills on time and kept Daniel clean, safe, and in class, they were left to their own devices. It was challenging, but he managed to make it work.

Erick was aware that the car repair shop he worked for had a questionable reputation, but he maintained a low profile to avoid any trouble. He focused on fixing cars and often seemed invisible to his boss, who hardly acknowledged his presence.

One day, Erick realized that a black van was tailing him as he walked home from work. Just as he was about to dash into an alley, the van halted, and three men jumped out. Initially, Erick believed he was being robbed. As he attempted to fight back, a surge of electricity coursed through his body, causing him to collapse on the ground. When he eventually regained consciousness, his head throbbed, his vision was blurry, and every part of him ached. He found himself seated at a metal table in a police interrogation room.

"Look, he's awake! Hello, sunshine!"

As Erick attempted to concentrate, he noticed a short man in a business shirt and jeans seated in front of him.

"What happened?"

"We're in charge of the questions here." The man set a soda can in front of Erick, who drank most of it, hoping the sugar rush would sharpen his muddled mind. He heard the man chuckle as the door to the interrogation room swung open, revealing a tall figure in a dark suit.

The first man said, "He's all yours."

The second man introduced himself. "I'm Agent Waters. Do you require medical assistance?" he asked.

Erick's mind started to clear. *They're playing good cop, bad cop.*

"No. I want to know what's going on. I need to get home; I have a little brother to look after, so if you're not charging me with anything, let me go." His assertiveness surprised even him.

"As I said, I'm Agent Waters, and you are not being charged. However, as we're conducting a federal investigation, we can hold you until we get our information."

Erick was confused. "What information? I don't know what you're talking about."

"Let's start with who you work for."

"Who, Manny?"

"Emmanuel Rodriguez. Tell me what you know about him."

"Manny is a good guy. He gave me a job when I needed it. I go in, fix cars, Manny pays me, and I go home. He gives my kid brother a birthday and Christmas present every year. There are no problems." Erick liked Manny, and as he said, he was also good to him.

"So, you've seen no illegal activities while working there?"

"No. A few strange dudes come in and out, but they leave me alone, and I don't say anything. They've never really noticed me. Why, what's this about?"

The two men glared at one another. Agent Waters sat across from Erick at the table and opened a manila folder. He extracted two pages, each featuring two photos, and placed them before Erick.

"Do you recognize these men?"

Erick adjusted his position in the chair and examined the photos. "Yeah, those are the guys. I won't get Manny into trouble, will I?"

"We know what your life is like—how you struggle to keep a roof over your little brother's head, get food on the table, find someone to care for him when you're at work, and keep social services at bay. We know it all. We even know you aren't involved in what's happening with your friend Manny. You seem able to 'blend in,' which is exactly what we require in this situation.

"What are you saying, you want me to spy on my friend?"

The agent sitting opposite Erick looked him straight in the face. "See, it can go either way. You help us, and we will see your brother enters witness security, where he will be taken care of by a wonderful, safe family, or he goes into the foster system because you're in jail, where we can't guarantee your or his safety, especially when it is leaked that you were speaking to us today."

"You can't intimidate me." Erick was shaking with fear.

"Don't you want a safer life for you and your brother? We can make it happen. All you have to do is help us out. We'll leave you for a few minutes to think about it."

They left the room.

Erick fell silent, his mind racing. Was this truly the best way to ensure Daniel could have a good life—a steady, safe life? Erick wrestled with the decision before him, and after an hour, when the agents returned to the room, he knew what he had to do.

"I'll keep an eye on Manny and let you know what he's up to, but I've got a few conditions."

"We're listening," they replied.

"I want my brother out of the way and safe. I want him to be placed in a good home."

"It won't be a problem," Waters said.

Once Erick had signed all the documents, he felt a wave of relief wash over him. Within a week, his brother safely settled into a new home with a new name. To protect Daniel from Manny, Erick decided he didn't want to know where he was or what his new name was. Saying goodbye was incredibly tough, and Erick often found himself remembering his brother's tears and the sorrow on his face.

Manny and his friends were involved in serious illegal activities, including drug and human trafficking and it took nearly a year before they were arrested. After the long, drawn-out court trial and conviction, the agency relocated Erick to another city and offered him a deal. They claimed he would be an excellent asset to the agency and wanted him to keep working for them. Erick promptly declined. Daniel was his family, and he wanted him back.

The agency informed him that Daniel was flourishing in his current environment. Erick had received heartwarming photos and updates about his brother's new family. They had expressed their desire to adopt him. Before making any decision, he would have the opportunity to see his brother at the zoo the next day. This way, he could decide for himself if he wanted to approach him. It left Erick wondering: did he want to take his brother away from his new life?

As he strolled around the zoo, waiting to see his brother, two little boys dashed past him laughing. Their parents followed, calling for them to slow down, but the boys were eager to see the monkeys. Erick realized one of the little boys was Daniel. He was about to shout out to him when Daniel turned and called out to one of the parents.

"Daddy, come see the monkeys." He was ecstatic.

"I'm coming, buddy," said the dad, and as he reached him, he picked him up. Daniel wrapped his little arms around the man's neck and hugged him.

Erick's heart shattered. He knew he could never provide his brother with what he had now. Yes, Erick loved him deeply, but his brother finally had parents who took great care of him. For Daniel to always be safe, Erick knew he had to keep his distance. One day, they would reunite, but not yet.

Daniel gazed past Erick twice without acknowledging his presence. After stealing one last long glance at his younger brother, he knew what he had to do. Erick turned and walked away.

When he arrived at his new home, Erick called the agent and informed him he would take the job, and that the family could adopt Daniel. His safety meant everything to Erick.

After eighteen months of rigorous training, the agency assigned Erick to the field. His role was to observe individuals' movements without engaging and to report his findings. He loved traveling and excelled at his job, with many senior agents eager to collaborate with him. Months turned into years, and suddenly, nearly ten years had gone by.

CHAPTER THIRTY

Night of the Dinner Party

Erick was having a marvelous time with Ally's friends. This is how life was supposed to be, he thought. Someone you cared deeply about next to you with good conversations, good friends, wine, and laughter. It was something he had never experienced before, and he loved it.

He knew this was against the rules, but with every day he spent with Ally, he only wanted to see her more, and if Erick was honest with himself, he didn't care about the rules anymore. He had fallen for her and didn't want it to end.

Ally's friends left, and they waved goodbye to them from the driveway. It felt right. He knew he belonged here, next to Ally. He turned her toward him and kissed her passionately. Ally had been giving him hints all night that tonight would be the night they would sleep together. He couldn't wait.

She started clearing up from dinner when Erick noticed the photos on the shelf in the living room and looked at them for the first time. He picked up frames with pictures of Ally's life and smiled. She was a cute kid.

He spotted the family photo on the shelf. He had never seen a picture of her parents before. But when he picked it up, he had to stop himself from letting it fall.

He stared at one of the people in the photo. The one person he never thought he would see in Ally's family photo.

He heard Ally saying, "This is my dad, my mom, Adam, and me." But Erick didn't hear anything else. He couldn't take his eyes off the picture. Her mother was Wilding, and she had saved his life. A wave of panic washed over him. Ally had told him her mother had died in a car accident a long time ago. But, as far as he knew, Wilding was still alive. At least she had been when she had helped him. It was clear Ally didn't know about her mother, and she could never find out the truth.

He had to get out of there. The past was coming back to haunt him, and he needed to think.

He spotted Ally holding a bottle of wine, inviting him to finish it with her. He understood she wanted him to stay, but he had to leave straight away.

"Umm, you know what, I think I'll go. I have an early start tomorrow," he said. It was a weak excuse, but it was the only one he could think of.

"Are you sure?" she said, smiling seductively.

"Yeah, it's late." He turned toward the door.

"Is there something wrong?" she asked, a hurt look on her face.

"No, nothing's wrong. I'm a bit tired," he said as he turned, walked back, and kissed her cheek. "Thanks for a great evening. I'll call you." Erick walked out the door, closed it behind him, and sprinted toward his car.

He started the car and sped away, feeling regret about how he had treated her. She deserved so much more. As he drove, thoughts of her mother crossed his mind. "Damn it. Damn it," he shouted, hitting the steering wheel repeatedly with his palm.

He reached his place quickly and promptly activated the two camera monitors at Ally's home, positioned front and back. He had covertly set them up to monitor her. He settled on the couch, observing the screens. Ally was on the back deck, in tears. Witnessing her sorrow shattered his heart, particularly since he was the cause of her pain.

He should never have interacted with her. Was it because she was Wilding's daughter that they assigned him to keep an eye on her?

When they had begun dating, he sensed he should take things slowly, unsure of which direction their relationship would go in or if he might be pulled from the assignment. He made up an excuse, and Ally respected his choice. Knowing who her mother was, perhaps it was a good move, but it didn't lessen the pain.

How can I tell her it's got nothing to do with her?

Erick watched Ally go back inside her house on his monitors.

An hour later, his phone pinged. He knew it was her. *How do I answer?* After fifteen minutes, he came up with his second lame answer of the night.

All okay, speak tomorrow, good night.

He despised himself for it, and for the first time in his career, he panicked and didn't know what to do. He wanted to be with Ally, but he had to detach himself before the situation worsened and she got hurt even more.

Erick pondered various scenarios all night. Should I reveal who I am and who I work for? It might put her at risk.

There was no need to tell Ally about her mother, as he didn't know Wilding's whereabouts or whether she was still alive. The agency had no idea what was happening between him and Ally; otherwise he would have heard from them and been removed. He only needed to report if something occurred.

Maybe this assignment had nothing to do with Wilding, and they could carry on as they were, he thought. Perhaps he could convince Ally to run away with him. But did he want that life for the two of them?

Perhaps the best thing to do was to break it off with her. Break both their hearts and go back to watching her, or get someone else to do it. But the thought of someone else watching Ally made him cringe. She was his girl.

He had never questioned an assignment before, but his mind raced all night trying to figure out what to do. He cared for her a lot, but the real question was: What was best for Ally? Then he realized that her safety was the only thing that truly mattered.

He finally fell asleep in the early hours. When he woke up, he knew what he had to do. He needed to muster the courage and strength to end what he had started. It was the only safe course of action. The only question was how he could manage it without hurting her more.

CHAPTER THIRTY-ONE

Ally

Five days later, I had barely heard from Erick. I had asked if something was wrong, and he had sent a few brief text messages saying he was busy.

My heart was broken. How could someone go so cold so fast?

I spoke to my friends who were at the dinner, and they all thought everything had gone well. They were surprised; Erick had acted as though everything was great. We were a "cute" couple.

After class one day, when we were the only two left. I spoke to Bernie.

"I fell for this guy. What a fool I was," I told her. "I'm too old to be playing games. If Erick doesn't want to be with me, then fine, but I want to know one way or another."

"Then tell him. Ring the bastard and tell him to get his act together or get lost," she replied.

"You're right. But I'm going to do it in person." I picked up my phone and dialed his number.

Surprisingly, he answered straight away.

"Hi, we need to talk, but not over the phone. Can you meet me in half an hour at Kapi`olani Park?"

"Sure, I'll see you in thirty minutes," he replied.

I ended the conversation without saying goodbye or even giving him a chance to say anything.

"I'm driving you. I won't leave the car, but you need someone there," Bernie said.

I was pleased she had offered to come with me.

Bernie pulled into one of the parking spaces at the park. As she turned off the engine, I tried to calm my nerves.

"Am I doing the right thing?"

"Yes, you are. No more games," Bernie replied.

"I'm going to be strong, tell him how I feel, and most importantly, I'm not going to cry," I said, hoping my words would give me courage. I touched up my lipstick and powdered my face. "How do I look?"

"Perfect. He'll be a fool if he doesn't get down on his knees and beg for your forgiveness." Bernie hugged me and said, "Be strong and tell him how you feel."

I left the car and saw Erick by "our" bench seat. *At least he showed up*, I thought.

As I approached him, I noticed he was wearing dark denim jeans—the ones that made his butt look great—along with a light-blue polo shirt. His hair appeared messy, and his face was not as cleanly shaven as usual; he looked tired, with dark circles under his eyes.

I stood up straight, put my shoulders back, and walked straight to him. He leant toward me to kiss me on the lips, but I turned my head slightly, and he kissed my cheek instead.

"I wanted to call you—" he started to say.

"Let me talk," I interrupted. "First off, are you okay?"

"Yes, I'm okay." He reached over to hold my hand, and I pulled away.

"Did I do something to upset or embarrass you?" I asked.

"No."

"Did any of my friends upset or embarrass you the other night?"

"No," he said, looking a little ashamed.

My voice started to tremble as I asked the next question. "Is there someone else?"

"You are the *only* one," he said.

I took a few seconds to stay composed, then calmly but firmly asked, "Are you going to tell me why you left abruptly and have ignored me since?"

Erick stared at me, sorrowful eyes gazing back, and when he opened his mouth to speak, no words emerged.

I put my hand on my hip and shook my head.

"Darling," he said, trying to hold my hand again.

But I wouldn't let him. "What? Do you have something to tell me? Please explain to me what's happening."

"I … I can't," he said.

I turned and moved a few steps away.

"Honey, wait!" he called.

I spun around and walked back to face him. "No. You don't get to call me honey, darling, or anything else," I said. I threw my hands up in the air. "God, you know what? I'm too old to play games, and so are you." I was livid. "Either we end it, or you give me a reason why you're acting this way, and we try and mend our relationship. I won't be your casual plaything." I was yelling at this stage.

He was speechless.

"Do you want to end it?" I shocked myself with what I said. It could all be over within seconds.

"No, I don't," he said.

"Then, what? Please tell me," I begged.

He remained silent and crossed his arms.

"You know what, let me know, or maybe I'll let you know because I won't be treated like this."

Still no words from him, only a sad puppy-dog face, but I was mad and would not give in.

"Twenty-four hours. Twenty-four hours to decide. We'll tell each other in person because that's what adults do, Erick. No more games."

My face was red from my rant. I stared at Erick, but he only gazed at the ground, his arms still crossed. *God, he can't even look at me.* My heart was breaking as I knew this could be the last time I would ever see him. Part of me wanted to fall into his arms, but I had to be strong.

I turned and walked away, hoping Erick would run after me, swoop me up into his arms, and tell me he loved me. But he didn't.

I quickly glanced back. He hadn't moved from where I had left him. He still had his arms crossed, his gaze fixed on the ground.

Reaching Bernie's car, she anxiously asked,

"What happened?"

"Drive. He can't see me cry." I held it together until we were out of sight.

CHAPTER THIRTY-TWO

Erick
Thirty Minutes Earlier

Erick had been relieved to hear from Ally. He had missed her so much. But the thought of her being very upset with him tore him up. He didn't know what he would say to her when they met. But he did know he had to find the courage to end the relationship.

As Erick drove to Kapi`olani Regional Park, he remembered all the fun times the two of them had there together. They even had a favorite bench.

He got there before Ally, pacing up and down in front of their bench. After ten minutes, he saw her walking toward him, taking his breath away and what little courage he had. She wore a flowing green floral summer dress that hugged her figure, and her hair had soft curls perfectly framing her face. God, he wanted to run and scoop her up in his arms, tell her everything, and beg for forgiveness, but most of all, tell her how much he loved her.

But the thought of telling her the truth scared him more. Either way, she was going to be hurt. He was unprepared to talk to her. His heart told him one thing, but logic took hold of his mind.

Erick listened to Ally talk but couldn't answer her. Everything she was saying was right. He crossed his arms in front of his chest to protect his heart. But it didn't help. His chest ached, and he looked at the ground as he couldn't watch her leave.

Ally was furious, and she had a right to be. All he wanted to do was hold her and tell her he was sorry, but he couldn't. She had given him the way out he needed, a way to end their relationship before anything more happened.

But instead of being relieved, he felt miserable. He hadn't experienced such sadness since he left his brother all those years ago. Remembering it made his chest ache even more.

He slowly walked to his car and sat behind the steering wheel. He had no energy to drive. *Would she go straight home?* he wondered. He didn't know if he could stand seeing her on his monitors. But it was his job to watch her without her knowing.

When Erick arrived at his place, he turned on the monitors and watched Ally go into her house. He imagined her lying on the couch, probably crying.

Erick lay on his couch, too. *Tomorrow,* he thought, *I'll go to her house and tell her face to face it's over. We have to break up. There's no need to draw this out any longer than necessary.*

CHAPTER THIRTY-THREE

Ally
Twenty-Four Hours Later

Somehow, I managed to get through the day without crying, but I was glad when I got home and thankful it was Friday. I hadn't heard a word from Erick all day. I was hoping he would contact me and tell me it was all okay, but he hadn't, so I tried to resign myself to the fact I would never hear or see him again.

The day was still sunny and warm, and I thought a swim in the ocean would clear my head before I called Erick to tell him it was over. I changed into my swimsuit, grabbed one of the many beach towels off my small clothesline, and walked down to the water.

Standing at the shoreline, waves lapping over my feet, I looked at the horizon and slowly walked into the surf, diving under a small wave. The water was cold and made my body tingle, and it felt good to stretch out as I swam.

I had been there for about fifteen minutes, swimming and diving under the low waves, when I stood up and wiped my hair off my face. I looked back at the shore and saw Erick on the sand. He waved at me, and I waved back.

CHAPTER THIRTY-FOUR

Erick

Erick had followed Ally home from work and was listening to John Legend's "All of Me" playing on the radio as he sat in his car trying to gather enough strength to speak with her.

He had left his car intending to end it with Ally, but when he went around the back of her place and saw her in the ocean, he couldn't take his eyes off her. The water glistened on her skin as she dove under the waves, came up, and swept her hair off her face. She once again took his breath away.

Erick realized he couldn't break up with her. He had never experienced such feelings before and didn't want to lose someone he loved again. He was in a trance as he walked toward the shoreline and stood on the sand.

As Ally turned around and saw Erick on the beach, he couldn't stop smiling. He raised his hand and waved to her, and she waved back.

His emotions took over, and he knew he had to be with her. He took off his clothes to his boxer briefs, and as he started to walk into the water, their eyes locked.

Ally stood still and waited for him to come to her. When he reached her, he put his hands under her arms, lifted her into the air, slowly lowered her to where their lips met, and kissed her passionately. She wrapped her arms around his neck and kissed him back.

After a few seconds, Ally gently pushed him away, and he put her down.

"I'm sorry," he said. "I have been such a fool. Please forgive me."

She looked into his eyes, took hold of his hand, and walked out of the surf to the beach.

At her clothesline, she grabbed another towel and handed it to Erick. "I don't know what to say."

"Good, because I want to do the talking," he said.

They wrapped themselves in their beach towels and sat at the table and chairs on her back deck.

Erick started. "I'm sorry, I'm so, so sorry. I got scared. Plain and simple. I have *never* cared this much for anyone before in my life."

Ally seemed taken aback by his honesty. He continued.

"The other night with your friends was the first time I felt I was somewhere I wanted to belong. Then I looked at your family photos, and it hit me."

He let out a sigh and decided he couldn't bring himself to tell her the truth. Instead, he said, "I could get transferred, and this would all be over. I've done this most of my life, moving from place to place. I've never allowed myself to get too involved with anyone because I could leave at any time, but I don't want to leave you and all this behind.

"So I panicked and thought if I ended it now, no one would be hurt. I didn't realize how much I had fallen for you. Staying away was the hardest and most painful thing I had to do."

Ally shivered as she looked at Erick.

"I know you must have questions," he said. "But why don't you have a warm shower, and think about what you want to ask me? Then we can talk more."

Ally nodded and got up to walk into the house. "Will you be here when I get back?" she asked.

"I promise, I'm not going anywhere," Erick said, crossing his heart with his finger.

"You can use the guest bathroom if you want to shower," she said.

Erick thanked her. It would give him time to think also.

Most of what he was telling her was the truth—everything but who he was working for. He knew he should have followed his plan, but after seeing her in the water with the sun glistening on and around her, he also knew he couldn't leave her.

In two years, his contract would be up, and he would be free to love and stay where he wanted. He hoped it would be with Ally. He only had to work out how to deal with it in the meantime.

CHAPTER THIRTY-FIVE

Ally

When I came out of my bathroom, part of me expected Erick not to be there. I thought of many questions in the shower, but seeing Erick, barefoot, in my kitchen freshly washed, I thought my heart would burst. I wanted to run into his arms, but I had to stop myself. First, I wanted answers and to feel certain he wouldn't flee again.

As I entered the kitchen, he turned and handed me a glass of wine.

"I hope you don't mind. I helped myself to a beer," he said.

"That's fine."

"You want to talk outside?" he asked.

I was a bit standoffish. "Okay."

We sat in the outdoor chairs with the sun setting in the background. I asked him, "So you're saying work could transfer you at any time, and that's why you broke it off without any discussion?"

"Yes. I know it's not a good reason, but it's true. I panicked. I'm not proud of how I acted. I know I should've talked to you about it."

"When do you think you could be transferred?" I asked.

"I'm not sure when or where. My contract ends in about two years, then I can live wherever I want." He took my hand in his. "This is a new situation for me, and I'm not sure how to manage it. Please forgive me. Can we put the past behind us and move on? I want to be with you," he pleaded.

"I don't know. What if you want to run again and shut me out? I don't think I can forgive that a second time."

"I won't. I promise. We'll talk things over, and I won't run again."

My heart melted, unable to resist his beautiful face any longer. "Yes, let's try and move on," I said, putting my arms around his neck and kissing him.

He stood, pulled me up in his arms, and spun me around.

"Wait," I said. "Before you get too excited, we have to discuss this and have a plan if and when you do get transferred."

"Okay, whatever you want," he replied.

"From what I can figure out, if you get transferred, there are three options," I said.

"Three? How do you work that out?"

"Plan A: I go with you," I said.

"But you would have to rent out your place and give up work."

"Okay, Plan B: we do a long-distance relationship. We visit each other when we can," I said.

"It would only be until the end of my contract," he mused. "Then I could return here. Do you think you could handle a long-distance relationship?"

"I could if you could," I said.

"Alright then, what's Plan C?" he asked.

"Plan C," I said. "We have the best time of our lives until you get transferred, then we break up."

"Is it what you want? Because I can tell you right now it's not going to work for me," he replied.

"No, it's not what I want. It's an option."

"Then we go with Plan B," he said. "I might not get a transfer for months or longer. The longer I stay here, the less time I'll have left on my contract and the less time I'll be away from you."

"So, if you get transferred, it will be Plan B, and we'll promise each other to stay true. Agreed?"

"Agreed. I will stay true to you until the end of time," he said, gazing into my eyes.

I felt the weight of despair lift off my shoulders.

We pulled out the blow-up mattress and put it on the lawn, covering it with blankets and lay there holding hands, watching the sunset.

"My dad used to tell me if you listen carefully, you'll be able to hear the sun hit the ocean."

Erick leaned over, put his arm under my neck, pulled me close, and kissed me. When I stared at his face, he seemed tired. I think our short separation had taken a toll on him.

I whispered to him, "Close your eyes."

"Why?"

"Close your eyes and listen to the sound of the waves."

"I'd rather look at you," he said.

"Just do it."

He followed my instructions. It only took a few minutes, and he was sound asleep. He appeared peaceful, and I knew I was deeply in love with him. I closed my eyes as well. Within seconds, I was also in a peaceful slumber.

* * *

Waking up the following morning, I saw the sunlight glistening on the water and Erick sitting next to me. He kissed me as I sat up then handed me a mug of tea.

"I have breakfast for us." Next to him was an assortment of fruit and bagels.

"Wow, this is nice. I could get used to this," I said.

Erick gazed out over the ocean. "The water looks incredible with the sun on it."

"It never disappoints," I said, resting my head on his shoulder. "Let's laze around today, doing whatever we want."

"Mmm, I like that idea."

Then, a voice came from the beach. It was Adam on his morning run. "You two sleep there?"

"Yes," I replied.

Adam stopped, put his hands on his hips, and approached us. "You two okay now?"

"We're great," Erick replied.

Adam nodded. "Well … excellent news." He gave us a thumbs up. "Hey, why don't we all have dinner tonight?"

"Sounds good," Erick replied before I could answer.

"I'll text you after my run," Adam said as he disappeared down the beach.

I knew we had gotten my little brother's approval.

We sat outside for another hour when Erick said he would go home to get a change of clothes and be back in about an hour or so. He kissed me goodbye, and a wave of panic came over me. Was he coming back? The doubt only lasted for a few seconds, then I dismissed it.

When he returned, we decided to go out for lunch and wander the markets. We were like young lovers holding hands and stealing kisses.

It was late when we got back from Adam's place. Erick grabbed me as soon as we got through the door and kissed me hard, and I responded. I knew what I wanted, and as if Erick had read my mind, he swooped me into his arms and carried me to the bedroom.

He was a very gentle and passionate lover, and we slept peacefully in each other's arms as if we had been together for years.

When we finally woke up the next morning, Erick said he needed to return to his place for another change of clothes. I sat up to say goodbye to him, and it hit me.

"Get all your clothes," I said.

"What?"

"Get all your clothes and things and move in with me."

He stared at me. "You're serious?" he finally said.

Maybe I had pushed too much. Perhaps it was too soon.

"I'm sorry. I should ask rather than tell you, and we should talk about it. I didn't mean to order you—"

But I didn't get a chance to finish my apology. "Yes, yes, I will move in with you."

"Are you sure?" I asked.

"Darling, if you're sure, I'm sure," he said with his winning smile.

CHAPTER THIRTY-SIX

Eight Months Later

Ilooked at the ocean and listened to the waves lapping on the shore. Soft music came from the radio in the background, and I softly sang along as I watched the sun setting from my kitchen window. I stood barefoot on the cool wooden floor, looking at my perfect view, a view I could never get tired of.

I took a moment from chopping vegetables for dinner and sighed. Life, at last, was good. I was happy, really happy. My parents' deaths had left a massive hole in my soul, and I had accepted this hole would never close. That was until Erick came into my life. I think Dad would have liked him.

Behind me, the front door opened and closed, and I heard his "Hi." A smile automatically came over my face. I always got a tingle when he arrived home.

"What's for dinner?" he asked as he came up behind me, slipping his strong, gentle arms around my waist and resting his chin on my right shoulder.

"We have chicken and vegetables," I replied. "How was your day?"

"All the better for being home." He softly kissed my neck and sighed. "Come dance with me."

With a smile I had not been able to remove for the last eight months, I said, "If you've not noticed, I am trying to make dinner."

"I don't care. Come dance with me."

I could never resist his request to dance.

He took the knife out of my hand and turned me around. I stood on my tiptoes, putting my arms around his neck. He put his arms back around my waist and buried his face in my neck. We slowly danced to the song on the radio, and I put my head on his chest and heard his heart beating in time with mine. All this felt right. How could it be after only eight months? Could I be so lucky?

Oh God, his aroma was intoxicating. It was a combination of his shampoo, aftershave, and sweat. I don't know why I loved it. He made me feel safe and whole.

Old legends say we all have soulmates, but until Erick came into my life, I never thought I would find mine. My dad always said Mom was his and he would never have another. He said the only good thing about dying was that he would be back in the arms of his beloved. Oh, Dad, I do hope that happened.

Erick's cell rang in his pocket, and he groaned. "Sorry, I have to answer this."

Erick's body suddenly became tense. I could tell this was an unwanted call. He looked at me over his shoulder and gave a half-smile as he left the room. I returned to making dinner, curious about who was on the phone and had made him stressed.

Ten minutes later, he returned to the kitchen, getting a beer out of the fridge. "Want one?" he asked.

"Sure."

He opened two beer bottles and passed one to me as he leaned over the kitchen bench, checking out the dinner preparations.

"Who was that?" I asked.

"Work. A pain-in-the-neck executive is coming, and now I have to go out of town in the morning."

"It's Saturday tomorrow. For how long?"

"Hopefully only for the day. At times, I hate my job."

"This company executive is really bad?"

"The worst," he said as he took a swig of his beer. "Need help with dinner?" he asked, changing the subject.

"No, honey, you go and sit."

"Thanks." He kissed me on the cheek.

There was a tone in his voice I hadn't heard before, and I could tell he was bothered by the phone call. He took his beer, sat on the couch, slipped off his shoes, put his feet on the coffee table, and turned the TV on. I kept sneaking a look at him as I finished making dinner. He seemed worried.

I served the meal and took the plates over to the couch. We didn't usually eat in front of the TV, but I could tell he was comfortable where he was, and I didn't want to disturb him. He accepted his plate without question; I think he was grateful he didn't have to move. We sat eating dinner, watching TV, and making small talk. Erick was unusually quiet. He cleaned up the kitchen, then came back to the couch, and we curled up together and watched a cooking show.

Sitting together, he suddenly pulled me toward him and smelled my hair. Then he softly said, "Let's run away."

"What?"

"Let's run away, disappear."

"Okay," I laughed, "where?"

"I don't care. Somewhere where no one would find or know us. It could be us and Blossom."

"Where would this place be, and how would we live?"

"Wherever we want. It doesn't matter as long as we're together."

He gazed into my eyes, and I took his face in my hands.

"You're serious about this, aren't you? Has work said anything about a transfer?" I said, getting concerned.

He studied me for a few moments, then he put his head on my lap. "No, it was a silly thought."

I stroked his thick, dark hair and asked, "Is this because of your job?"

He didn't answer.

"If you hate it that much, break the contract. I'm serious. We'll get by. Don't let it worry you."

"I'm not able to break the contract. I've looked into it," he explained.

Jokingly, I said, "I was hoping you could be a kept man. I would bring in the paycheck, and you could be here when I get home, waiting for me at the door with a cocktail. I would sit at the table waiting for my dinner because you'd spent all day shopping, preparing dinner, like a fifties housewife."

He laughed as he buried his face into my lap.

"You could wear a frilly apron," I added.

He looked up at me, laughing. "Well, it's a good plan. I'll be your kept man with a frilly apron. I'd have no problems with it as long as I did it with you." His face turned serious. He paused momentarily, got up from the couch, and kissed me on my lips. "You go to bed. I have some work to do. I won't be long." He gently touched my right cheek. "It's going to be okay." He grabbed his briefcase, sat at the dining room table, and sighed.

I got up and kissed his head. "Don't be too long. You're tired," I said, then headed to the bedroom and got ready for bed. I crawled under the soft cotton sheets and snuggled next to Blossom, listening to the waves hitting the shore as I fell asleep.

I don't know what time it was when Erick came to bed, but before he laid his head on his pillow, he kissed my forehead. I half-opened my eyes, and he said, "Shh, go back to sleep."

We were both lying on our sides, facing each other. I gently put my hand on his cheek and whispered, "If you want to run away, I will go with you. Just say the word."

He kissed my forehead again and held my hand, and I drifted back to sleep.

When I woke up the following morning, Erick had already left for the day. I called him on his cell phone.

"Morning, sunshine," I said, "You left early."

"Hi, honey. Yeah, I had an early start."

"You okay?" I asked.

"Sure," he said, "everything will be great. But I do like the idea of being a kept man." We both laughed. "I'm not sure when I'll be back tonight, but it won't be late."

"I love you," I said.

"I love you, too."

My body also tingles when he says he loves me.

CHAPTER THIRTY-SEVEN

After I hung up from Erick, I took my time to shower, put on my red-and-navy summer dress, fed Blossom, grabbed a few rice cakes for breakfast, and sat on my back deck enjoying the warm morning sun. I didn't have a dance class this morning, so I reviewed my to-do list for the arrival of our special visitors. Auntie Ell and Frank had finally decided to get married, and they wanted to have the ceremony on the island.

Then Adam phoned me.

"Hi, little brother, what's up?"

"I need you to come to my house now!" He sounded panicked.

"Are you alright?"

"Yes, just get here and come in the back way."

Megan was away on business, and I was concerned something had happened. Hanging up the phone, I grabbed my keys, locked the back door, and kicked off my sandals as I ran down the beach. When I got there, I saw Adam pacing outside his back door.

As I approached him, I saw his I-have-to-stay-calm-so-Ally-doesn't-freak-out look.

"I have to tell you something," he said.

"Adam, you're scaring …" I didn't finish my sentence. I was speechless as a tall, slender woman appeared in his doorway.

It was someone I hadn't seen for nearly twenty years. A woman I thought had died. My mother.

"Hello, honey," she said softly, coming over to hug me.

At first, my arms wouldn't work, but then I hugged her back and held her tight. We stood facing each other. Yes, this was my mother. A little older, with gray hair within her beautiful curls, but it was her. My mother was back from the dead.

"Okay, we need to move this inside," Adam said, ushering us in the house.

"I don't understand. How? Are you okay?" Those were the only words I managed to say. I turned to Adam. "Did you know?"

"No, she arrived at my door this morning. I'm as shocked as you."

"No one knew, honey. I'll explain, but it's complicated," she answered.

I looked at her and said, "You're dead. We buried you. We *mourned* you." My mind was spinning. I was happy my mother wasn't dead, but confused about why she had been gone for all these years.

Adam stood next to me with his hands on his hips.

"Where have you been?" I asked. "Why did you leave us? Did you know it broke Dad's heart?"

"It broke my heart having to leave my family, but if I didn't, you all would have been in extreme danger."

"How does a teacher put her family in such *extreme* danger that she has to fake her death? That's right, isn't it? You faked the accident?"

She stared at me. "I was in a complicated, dangerous situation."

Confused, I said, "Please don't tell me it's complicated. I can see it's 'complicated,' but we deserve answers."

"Darlings, come and sit down and I'll explain," she said, clearly trying to stay calm. She walked me over to the couch, sat next to me, and patted the cushion for Adam to sit on the other side of her. "First, I loved your father very much, and I was devastated when I heard he had died. Your father, you two, and Eloise mean the world to me, and I was heartbroken to leave you all." She sighed as if to build the courage to continue. "Before I married your father, I worked for a government agency."

"What does that mean?" Adam asked.

"I was a government operative, a spy."

Wham. I felt as if someone had punched me in the stomach. I leant back on the couch, and all I could manage to say over and over was, "A spy. My mother was a spy."

"I don't understand. Please explain how a schoolteacher was a—" "Wait," I interrupted Adam, "was it for *our* government?"

My mother seemed offended by my question. "Of course it was for our government." She took a breath in and let it out slowly. "About six months before meeting your father, I left the agency. I was finished with my spy life and anything to do with it. From the first time I saw Charlie, I fell in love with him. We were inseparable," she recalled.

"I had a wonderful life with your dad and you kids. I was very proud of my family. Then one day, out of nowhere, the agency contacted me. A long time ago, a man I had sent to prison for life had escaped, and they said they had intel he was coming after me and anyone I loved. I was frightened he would find us.

"It wasn't only you kids and Charlie—it was Eloise as well. This man would have done anything to find me, so I did what I had to do to keep all my family safe."

"How long did you know before you … disappeared?" I asked.

"I was informed six days before that it was a possibility, and the agency had put an exit plan together. I prayed it wouldn't happen, that he would be caught, but when they confirmed the threat was real, the plan was executed. I fought to stay until you arrived to take care of Adam."

I thought back to that night and how Adam and I drove off without looking back.

"Did Dad and Ell know?" Adam asked.

"No," she said.

I stood up and paced in a small circle, trying to clear my mind. "I need a drink," I said.

"I think it's a bit early," my mother replied.

"What, you're going to be a mother now?" I snapped back at her.

"Ally, give Mom a chance."

Adam had always been a mama's boy whereas Mom and I had butted heads. Dad used to say it was because Mom and I were alike, but I never agreed with his theory.

"I thought my daughter would be a little pleased I was alive."

I looked at her and felt guilty for my words. "I am happy," I said. "But I have questions, things I need to know, to tell you, I can't … think."

Adam spoke up. "Mom, you must realize this is a shock for us. Are you safe now? Do we have to worry that this person is still out there?"

She took both our hands in hers and said, "Cole can't hurt us—he's dead, and I'm home to stay. I want to be with my family."

I was in shock and couldn't stop the sarcasm pouring out of my mouth. "Okay then, let's wipe out the past two decades and start again. It's 'complicated', but we can be one big family again. No questions asked."

I could see she was offended by my outburst. "I'm sorry," I said, "I didn't mean it that way. I'm trying to put it all together, and it's not sinking into my brain."

Adam asked, "The agency let you go, just like that?"

"Yes. I'm free," Mom said with a sigh.

I needed more information. "Where have you been for all this time?"

"I moved around a lot and finally settled in East Asia. It's easy to hide there."

"Doing what? Do you have another family?" I asked.

"No, I don't have another family," she huffed, seeming to resent another of my questions. "I taught English to local villagers for years, then a few months ago I received word the threat had been neutralized and I was free from my contract again."

"Again. Your contract *again*?"

She hesitated. "Yes."

"But you just told us you were free from your contract before leaving us." Adam's face was turning red. "So, you returned to the spy business after leaving us?"

We seemed to wait for a long time for her to answer.

"Yes, but only to keep you all safe."

"You left us to go back to spying is what you're trying very hard not to say," I said, getting frustrated.

"Yes, I returned to the agency when I left."

"Did you leave us to go back to the agency? Or did you return to the agency when this Cole became a threat?" My voice demanded an answer.

After another long pause, Eva spoke, "You're confusing the situation."

Both Adam and I stood up.

"My God," said Adam.

"Wow." I started to raise my voice. "So, while your family was falling apart from your 'death,' you went back to spying."

She seemed annoyed. "The two of you are making it sound like I had a choice."

"Well, *Eva*, that's what it sounds like." Adam was getting angrier.

"Well, it's not, and stop calling me Eva, I'm your mother."

It was Adam's turn to raise his voice. "Seriously? That's what concerns you, a name. My sister gave up her life—her dreams—to care for me when you left to continue spying."

My brother's words touched me.

Eva looked at me. "I'm sorry. I would have given anything for it not to have happened."

"You're sorry?" I was furious. "I don't know what's true or whether you're trying to manipulate us."

She snapped back, "You've always been quick to judge."

"Well, I am my mother's daughter."

By this time, the three of us were in separate corners of the room. Could this be happening? Our mother, who we thought was dead, was alive and wanted to go back to her old life.

After a few minutes of silence, Eva said, "I want to see my sister."

I looked at Adam. "Auntie Ell. How are we going to tell her? She's arriving in two days."

"Eloise is coming here?" Eva asked.

"She's getting married here in a week, then they're cruising back to the mainland," Adam explained.

"We'll wait until she gets here. No need to tell her beforehand," I said.

"My sister's getting married?" Eva asked. "Who's she marrying?"

"Frank. He's wonderful and good to her," I said.

Eva stood there, shocked.

Adam and I turned to each other.

"Erick and I will pick them up at the airport as planned, and when we're back at my place, meet us there, and I guess we'll tell her then."

"I want to be there too," Eva said.

"It's a late flight; give us time to tell her first," Adam said.

"Who's Erick?" she asked.

I stared at her. "Erick is my boyfriend; he lives with me."

"Are you happy?"

"Yes, we're very happy."

We finally convinced Eva to let us tell Auntie Ell before they saw each other. By late afternoon, we had gone over Mom's story many times, trying to comprehend it, but nothing of what she was saying matched the woman I remembered.

I needed to go home and be with Erick.

* * *

Opening my back door, I frantically called out for Erick, but there was only silence, and my heart sank.

Going to refrigerator and grabbed a bottle of white wine and started drinking from the bottle, sliding down the kitchen wall and sitting on the floor, feeling numb.

What's wrong with me? I thought. I was ecstatic my mother was alive—thrilled—but I was also angry. Angry that Dad died before he found out the love of his life was still alive, angry she had been away, living another life. If she had been here, she would have picked up on his heart condition before his fatal heart attack. And I wouldn't have given up on my dream of being a professional dancer.

I felt overwhelmed with conflicting emotions; I needed Erick.

Fifteen minutes had passed, and I had drunk almost the whole bottle of wine when Erick arrived home. I was distracted and didn't hear him open the door.

He put his briefcase down and sat on the kitchen floor beside me. "Darling, why are you sitting on the floor drinking straight from a bottle?"

"We need more," I said.

Erick took the bottle from my hand. "Tell me what's wrong, then I'll get you more wine."

I turned and buried my face into his shoulder.

"Darling, what's wrong? Whatever it is, I'm here for you, and together we'll fix it."

CHAPTER THIRTY-EIGHT

Thankfully, I was busy with wedding arrangements for the next two days. Eva hung around, wanting to help me, though she spent a lot of the time questioning me about Frank, his family, and his law firm. She was eager to meet Erick, but I wanted to put it off as long as possible. I told her we had arranged a BBQ for the night after Auntie Ell's and Frank's arrival, and she could meet him then. Eva was not pleased about waiting but accepted it. I don't think she wanted to push things at the moment.

The evening came for Erick and me to pick Ell and Frank up from the airport. We had arranged to meet them at the baggage claim, and we flew into each other's arms when we saw each other.

"Oh, my darling girl." She hugged me tightly.

"I missed you," I told her.

She stopped, held me at arm's length, and stared into my eyes as if she could see into my mind. "There's something wrong. I can tell."

"Everything's great," I assured her. I turned and smiled at Frank. "It's great to see you again."

Auntie Ell peered over my shoulder and saw Erick, and before she could move or say anything, Erick had his arms stretched out toward her. "Auntie Ell, I've heard a lot about you." He embraced her.

"Well, I can say the same about you." She pushed him back to get a look at him. "I can see why my niece talks about you all the time."

Her comment made Erick blush. "Back at you, Auntie."

She smiled and turned to me. "I'm going to like your Erick."

Now it was my turn to blush.

Auntie Ell and I took off toward the car with our arms interlocked and left the men to deal with the trolley full of luggage.

My aunt and I settled in the back seat, and as we started driving, she leaned in and whispered to me, "Darling, you seem different; something must have happened, or you're in love."

Not wanting to tell her about Mom yet, I laughed and changed the subject.

When we finally reached my house, and the visitors were settling into their room, I texted Adam so he could come up and we could give her the news about her sister. I prepared Auntie Ell's favorite drink, brandy and water, a scotch for Frank, wine for me, and beers for the boys.

Adam arrived through the back door, and I was relieved Mom had not come along with him.

"Where's Eva?" I whispered to him.

"At my place, but I don't know how long I can keep her there."

"Why are you two whispering?" Auntie Ell had emerged from the bedroom. "Come here, my beautiful boy, and give your old aunt a hug and kiss," she said with outstretched arms.

Adam walked over, and they gave each other a huge hug. Then Adam greeted Frank.

She looked at Adam and narrowed her eyes. "Okay, you two. I know something is going on. I can tell by your faces."

Adam started. "Auntie Ell, come and sit down."

Erick and Frank were in the kitchen with their drinks, and I handed Ell her brandy.

"What's up? What's wrong?" she said.

"Well, I won't say it's something wrong. It's a good thing." Adam started to stumble over his words.

"Adam darling, tell me."

"Auntie Ell, we found out the other day … well, Mom never died in the car accident. She's alive. She was in hiding because she worked as a spy."

Ell gasped and took a long sip of her drink.

"You okay?" I asked her.

She stared at us, but I don't think she saw us. She was silent for what would have only been a few seconds but seemed longer.

"Is she well?" she finally asked.

"Yes. Eva's at Adam's house and she wants to see you. She just turned up on Adam's doorstep." I explained.

She took a bigger gulp of her brandy. "Did your father know?" Then, she responded to her own question. "No. He wouldn't have, and I can see from your expressions that you two weren't aware either. Why didn't she tell me?" She sounded resentful. "Are you kids alright?"

"Yes. Shocked, confused, but okay," Adam said.

Eloise stood up and embraced both of us.

Frank poured more brandy into her glass.

"You know," she said, "I always felt guilty that, when Eva died, I didn't feel the same as I had when my father passed away. I don't know how to explain it, but a part of me couldn't accept she was gone. But I thought it was my way of dealing with her death. Now it all makes sense."

Frank put his arm around her. "Are you okay, darling?" he asked.

"Yes. It's strange, but things I didn't understand in the past are now falling into place." She took another sip of brandy and settled back onto the couch.

I didn't know what to say to her. I was still in shock after two days. Frank was the first to speak. "Honey, it's okay to postpone the wedding."

Auntie Ell kissed Frank and rested her head on his shoulder.

"Please don't postpone," I said. "This week is about you, not Mom. You both have been looking forward to it and deserve your wedding." It was true. My auntie had been alone for a long time. Now she had Frank, they needed to celebrate their love.

Adam piped up, "She's right. You two are going ahead with your wedding. Postponing it would be the last thing Eva would want."

Eloise rose, contemplating her next steps. "First, Frank and I will discuss the wedding, then I'll see my sister, but it's too late tonight, and I'm worn out. One more night won't make a difference. Adam, please tell Eva I'll see her in the morning. I need some time to get my mind around all this information."

Adam wrapped his arms around his aunt. "I think that's fair. You rest, and I will bring her up in the morning."

"Thank you, darling," she said.

Adam said goodbye and disappeared down the beach.

"Can I get either of you anything? Something to eat or another drink?" I asked my aunt.

"No, darling, it's been a very long day. We need to turn in," she said.

I watched the couple walk hand in hand to their bedroom.

Erick came up behind me and wrapped his arms around me. "You okay? I thought you handled it well."

"I'm not letting her cancel her wedding," I said.

Erick rubbed the back of my neck. "Come on, let's go to bed." He took my hand and led me to our room.

My legs felt heavy, and my mind was racing. After we both changed and snuggled into bed, we decided to watch a little TV, hoping to take my mind off things. We had been there for about half an hour when we heard a soft knock on our bedroom door. It was Auntie Ell.

"I hope I'm not disturbing you. I heard the TV on and thought ..."

Erick was quick. "It's okay. Why don't you girls talk, and I'll catch up on some football." He grabbed his robe and, as he left the room, kissed Eloise on the cheek.

Eloise watched him leave, and as she climbed into my bed where Erick was lying, I turned off the TV.

"I like him a lot," she said.

"I like him a lot, too," I said, grinning.

"I can tell he makes you happy."

"He does. He makes me happier than I ever thought possible, similar to you and Frank, so please, no more talk about postponing the wedding."

"Frank and I have discussed it, and the wedding is going ahead as planned."

I was very relieved. "Are you okay with Eva being here?" I asked.

"I noticed you and Adam called her Eva instead of Mom," she said.

"It's a long story that I'd rather not go into right now. I want to know how you're dealing with it."

"It's a strange feeling. I'm very thrilled my sister is alive and well, but annoyed she left it this long to reach out to us."

"I know exactly what you mean. Then you end up feeling guilty."

She nodded and smiled. "Your mother did tend to make others do that," she said.

"I remember," I added. "Do you know what you'll say to her tomorrow?"

"No, I think I'll wing it."

"Well, I have your back," I replied.

Auntie Ell smiled. She knew she could always count on me. "What does your mother think of Erick?" she asked.

"They haven't met yet."

She gave me a look.

"I'm a little cautious about the two of them meeting," I explained. "Besides, Erick has to go to work early in the morning, so they can meet when we have the BBQ tomorrow night."

It wasn't long until we heard Erick and Frank yelling at the referee on the TV.

We both looked at each other and giggled.

"Well, the boys are happy," she said. "You know, I can see some of your father in Erick."

We lay down facing each other.

"I remember lying in bed just like this, talking with your mother the night she told us she was pregnant with you. Your father did the same thing and left us to talk," she recalled. "We talked most of the night. She told me she was excited and scared at the same time. I always thought Eva couldn't be scared of anything. Even at our father's funeral, she was the brave one. I get the feeling she may be a little scared now. When you think of it, it's brave to come back after all this time and face everyone."

I enjoyed hearing my aunt reminisce about her and Mom's past and how she thought Dad and Erick were alike.

"Now, fill me in on all the wedding preparations," she said.

We talked for about an hour while the boys continued yelling at the television. It wasn't long before we had both fallen asleep, my aunt's hand on top of mine.

CHAPTER THIRTY-NINE

Eva

My children had insisted I stay here while they told my sister about my return from the dead. I was frustrated with the decision, but I went along with it. As I anxiously paced the floor, I looked around the house that was once mine and didn't recognize it. It didn't feel like my home anymore. I wondered how long it took them to make the changes after I left.

I was feeling irritated and lost in my thoughts when Adam arrived back. He looked tired.

"Well, how did it go?" I was anxious about my sister's reaction.

"She wants to see you," Adam assured me.

"Great. I'll go up there now …"

"It's late. They've had a long day. Give her time to rest. I said we'd go up first thing in the morning."

I wasn't happy about waiting to see Eloise, but things were fragile now, and I didn't want to make any waves.

"Alright, first thing in the morning. But was she okay?" I asked.

"She was stunned initially, but she wants to see you. She was talking about canceling her wedding, but I hope we talked her out of it. Anyway, let's go to bed. We have a big day tomorrow and a BBQ tomorrow night," Adam explained.

"You're right, honey. I think I'll turn in." I hugged my son and gave him a kiss goodnight. "You and your sister know I love you both very much, don't you?"

"We know." He gave me another hug. "We love you, too. We always have."

I walked into my room and closed the door, but I didn't get into bed. I lay on the covers and decided I wasn't waiting to see my sister.

CHAPTER FORTY

Slipping out of my old house under cover of darkness, I carefully crept up the beach to Ally's place. There wasn't a soul around, and her house was in darkness.

Reaching her home and slowly creeping up the backstairs, I entered, making a mental note to talk to my daughter about locking her back door.

As I stealthily entered her house, I noticed a man sleeping on the couch, facing away from the door. *What use is he?* I wondered. I crouched down and listened carefully. The house was silent. An open door rested down the hall, and I approached it cautiously. The only sound was the gentle breathing of the sleeping.

Peering around the door, I noticed my daughter and sister asleep on the bed. My sister had aged since the last time I saw her, but so had I.

The pain of jealousy filled me with anger and resentment at the sight of them sleeping together. Ell's hand was on top of Ally's, like Eloise and I had slept when we were little. They'd had a close bond since Ally was born, and obviously they still did. I had never really experienced jealousy before, and this hit me hard. I was getting angrier, but at which one? Is my sister caring for my daughter as if she were her mother? Or is my daughter replacing me?

None of my feelings made sense, of course. After all, my actions were what had made them closer. But I couldn't quiet the envy or anger. Why couldn't I be happy for them?

I knew it was time to go, and I crept my way back down the beach to Adams. No one was the wiser.

CHAPTER FORTY-ONE

Ally

The sun was shining through the windows when I woke up. Auntie Ell was not beside me, and I could hear noises in the other room. Putting my robe on, I walked into the kitchen to see Erick and Frank making breakfast.

"Morning, gentlemen."

Erick handed me a cup of tea and kissed me.

"Where's Ell?" I asked.

Frank answered, "In the shower. I'm taking her some coffee."

Erick grabbed his phone. "I'm going. You have a *wonderful* day today," he said, his voice dripping with sarcasm.

"Coward. You could stay and support me." I felt like I was pleading.

"I love you, darling, but something tells me I should go. Besides, you'll be running around finalizing wedding stuff."

With the thought of the sisters seeing each other for the first time in years, I had momentarily forgotten we also had to deal with wedding preparations today and the BBQ tonight.

He kissed me again. "I promise I'll get home early and pick up the drinks on my way. You had better get into the shower before Eva arrives."

He was right. I needed to be ready.

It didn't take me long to get showered and dressed, slipping on my navy, sleeveless dress with a V-neck and pockets. When I returned to the kitchen, Frank was eating breakfast and offered me some bacon. I declined.

"Where's Ell? Is she okay?" I asked.

"She's fine. A little nervous, but she can handle anything."

I was putting peanut butter on my rice cracker when I heard the back door open. It was Eva and Adam. Eva said an extremely nervous hello and gave me an awkward hug.

Adam decided to do the introductions. "This is Frank, Ell's fiancé, and this is Eva."

They didn't move toward each other.

"Where's Eloise?" Eva asked.

From across the room, my aunt appeared in a pink floral skirt and a white blouse. "Hello, Eva."

She turned, and the twins faced each other.

Neither of them moved. I think everyone was holding their breath. Then they collapsed into each other's arms.

"I never thought I would have this moment again," Ell said.

"Me neither."

They pulled apart slightly, still in each other's grasp, and looked at each other.

"You got old."

"So did you," Eva answered.

They both laughed.

Holding onto her sister's arm, Ell gently led her to the couch. "Come sit. I have so many questions."

"I know. The kids have probably told you a lot, but there are other things we need to discuss."

Auntie Ell sat up straight. "Christmas at Uncle Mike's place after he died? You knew what you were going to do then. Right?"

"Yes. I wanted to tell you, but I had signed an agreement that meant that if I told you … well, let's say it wouldn't have ended well."

Auntie Ell sighed. "I understand, but it's hard for me to hear you kept such an important secret from me."

"I get it. I do. It was tough for me as well. But there is something else," Eva started to explain. "I was initially recommended to the agency by someone we both knew."

Eloise looked at her sister's face, puzzled by what she was saying.

"Uncle Mike was an operative as well. He recommended me to the agency," Eva said finally.

We all seemed to gasp at the same time.

Eloise remained silent for a long time before asking, "How long have you known about this?"

"I found out the day I joined the agency. Uncle Mike was an analyst and operated from the university."

I couldn't hold my tongue. "You never told your sister this? How many other secrets aren't you telling us?"

Eloise got up from the couch and came over to Adam and me. "Out. Come on, out. Wait on the back porch and let me talk to my sister alone."

Her words surprised me, and her actions shocked me even more as Adam and I were ushered out the back, the door closing in our faces.

"I got kicked out of my own house," I said, staring at the closed door. "*My* house. Pushed out as if I were a child."

Adam was still unable to speak.

"Should I go back in and say something?" I asked.

"Not unless you want to be kicked out again," he said.

He sat on the top step, and I joined him, trying to process what had happened.

"Did you know about Uncle Mike?" he eventually asked.

"No, did you?"

"No," he grumbled.

I turned to my brother. "You're not a spy as well, are you? Now's the time to tell me."

"No." Adam turned to me, irritated. "Are you?"

"Seriously?"

We gazed at the beach, unable to hear what was happening inside and afraid to go in. After twenty minutes, the door opened and Frank came out. We stood, thinking we could go back in, but he closed the door behind him.

"Is Auntie Ell okay?"

"She's fine, they're both fine, but Eloise wants us to go and finish the wedding plans while she talks to Eva." He handed me my handbag and keys.

"But we need her to approve everything," I tried to point out.

"I'm coming with you to give the final approval. This is what she wants." He noticed the worried expression on my face. "It'll be okay. Let's give them some time."

"I don't have to go," Adam said.

"Yes, you do. The three of us are going," Frank said.

Once again, we were escorted off like children.

It was going to be a simple outdoor wedding at a beach resort with around fifty people, with most guests visiting from the mainland and staying at the resort. Eloise and Frank's honeymoon was a cruise back to the mainland, leaving the night of the ceremony.

It took most of the day to do all our errands, and when we got back, the sisters were nowhere to be seen. They had left a message that they were walking along the beach.

Thirty minutes later, Erick got home and as promised, was preparing the grill. Adam went to fetch the meat from his place and collect Megan, and I quickly changed into my lilac floral dress and made salads. Bernie and Michael were away, and Donna and Anton arrived with Cassie and Mitch in tow. The men headed straight to the BBQ area, and the girls helped me in the kitchen. I could always count on them.

Eva and Auntie Ell finally returned from their walk, arm in arm. It was obvious they were happy to be together again.

I could finally introduce Erick to Eva.

"Eva, wonderful to finally meet you." She was a bit cold toward him, putting her hand out first to shake before Erick had a chance to hug her.

"My daughter said you only moved here recently. Where were you previously?"

Before I let Erick answer, I grabbed his arm. "You'll have plenty of time to interrogate him later, Eva. I need his help. Go talk to Frank." I said, dragging Erick away.

Erick whispered into my ear, "I'm going to have to talk to your mother sooner or later."

"I know, but I don't want her badgering you with questions, not tonight."

The night air was warm, and the smell of food cooking mixed with the salt ocean air was delightful. There was a lot of chatter, laughter, and background music, with everyone enjoying themselves. I was running around barefoot, attending to the guests, making sure everyone had drinks. At one point, I saw Eva and Erick talking alone, away from the others. Erick forced a smile when he noticed me watching them. Eva moved to speak to Eloise, and Erick came over to me.

"Come dance with me," he said, grabbing me in his arms.

"What did my mother say to you?" I asked, annoyed she had singled him out.

"Oh, she's a mama bear protecting her cub. Listen, this is our song," he said, trying to change the subject. "Kiss Me" by Ed Sheeran was playing. "Dance with me," he urged. He wrapped his arms around my waist and pulled me onto the lawn. As usual, I put my arms around his neck, but I couldn't let his conversation with Eva go.

"Tell me what she said," I insisted.

"Shh, dance."

He was humming along, and I melted into his arms. He held me gently but firmly, and in between his humming, he kissed the nape of my neck. I couldn't love anyone more than I did right then.

In the corner of my eye, I could see others watching, but I didn't care. My mother wasn't smiling until Auntie Ell whispered something, then she seemed to relax.

At the end of the song, Erick dipped me backward, and before he pulled me up, he said, "I love you more than anything." Then he kissed me firmly on the lips. It was the type of kiss that made my whole body weak.

* * *

The party went long into the night, and after everyone had left, my aunt approached me to help with the dishes.

"Where are the boys?"

"They may have overindulged a bit and gone to bed." She grabbed a tea towel.

"Did Eva say anything to you about Erick?" I asked.

She smiled at me. "No, but I told her I had never seen you happier. Leave these. The men can help tomorrow. Let's go to bed."

Tiptoeing into my bedroom, I saw Erick was already asleep. Thinking of our dance and his kiss, I thought of how much I loved this man. My chest felt as if it was going to burst open. Approaching his side of the bed, I gently stroked his face. He woke up and looked up at me, and I kissed him passionately as he gently unzipped my dress.

<h1 style="text-align:center">CHAPTER FORTY-TWO</h1>

Before we knew it, it was the wedding day.

All the men got ready at Adam's, with supervision from Megan. The bride, Eva, and I went to the resort. Auntie Ell wanted her sister to be involved, so the day before we bought Eva a dusty-rose chiffon A-line scoop-neck dress with three-quarter sleeves with lace from the neck to just past her waist. She didn't complain once about wearing a dress.

While Eva was getting ready, I took Auntie Ell a glass of champagne. She was calm while being fussed over. I took my champagne to the balcony to watch the guests arrive. I could see Mitch and Erick laughing at something. Even from this distance, I could see how handsome they were. Frank was standing at the side of the altar, having a very intense conversation with his brother. At one point, Sean tried to walk away, but Frank placed his hand on Sean's shoulder, stopping him from leaving. Sean gave in to Frank's hold and looked down at his feet as Frank seemed to continue to lecture him.

"Frank and Sean seem to be having an issue," I yelled to Auntie Ell.

"What, darling?"

I turned to repeat myself but became distracted. My auntie had come out of her room dressed in her beautiful off-white wedding gown. She was stunning. Her princess-line gown was made of chiffon and lace. It had three-quarter length sleeves, the hem falling just above her pearl-colored shoes. Her hair was slightly above her shoulders with soft curls and a pearl clip to one side, and her pearl necklace hung around her neck.

"Wow, you look …" I started crying.

"No crying. You'll ruin our makeup," she said, holding back tears.

Eva walked out looking amazing.

"Wow, Mom, you look beautiful." My words took both of us by surprise.

Eva took her twin's hands. "My darling sister, you are breathtaking. Dad would be proud."

Then Eva lightly touched the pearls Eloise was wearing and quietly said. "They still look beautiful on you."

I remembered I was wearing Mom's pearls and took them off, placing them gently around her neck. "You should be wearing these."

"Are you sure, darling?" she asked.

"I'm completely sure."

Adam whistled from the doorway. "Well, don't you all look wonderful."

Then I had an idea.

"Adam, I know you were going to walk the bride down the aisle, but I think Mom should do it. It's the right thing to do."

There was a brief silence.

"You're right. Mom should do it. Okay with you two?" Adam asked the twins.

"Adam, you're sure?" Auntie Ell asked, not wanting to disappoint him.

"Definitely. I'll escort this one," he said as he put his arm around my shoulders.

"Mom, are you okay with that?"

She didn't hesitate. "Yes. It would be a great honor."

"Okay, let's get this party started, or poor Frank will think you've run off with someone else," Adam joked.

Adam and I were the first to head down the aisle, followed by Mom and Auntie Ell. People whispered when they saw my mother, which made the twins hold their heads higher.

As I stood listening to their vows, I looked around at all the people I cared for. I saw my mother near her twin, and the love she had in her eyes for her sister made me emotional.

The reception seemed to go by fast. Frank and Ell did their first dance to the song "At Last." I teared up as we watched the newly married couple dance tenderly wrapped in each other's arms. Erick gave me goosebumps as he very softly sang along in my ear.

When the sun started to go down over the ocean in a beautiful golden sunset, it was time for the happy couple to leave on their cruise. We all stood outside the resort to wave goodbye as they drove off in a white limousine.

The day was perfect, and my family was nearly whole again. Maybe things were changing.

I never handled change well, but I finally felt close to my mother again. I wanted to make things work with her.

CHAPTER FORTY-THREE

I was busy with work the following week, and Erick worked late most days. When he arrived home, he was quiet. He looked stressed lately, and when I asked him about it, he would say, "It's okay."

Things were starting to feel familiar with Mom around, and we even met for dinner a couple of times. She said she would like to visit Ell and Frank after their honeymoon and asked if I would go with her. I surprised myself with my quick response of "yes".

Two weeks after the wedding, Erick and I were getting ready for work when he suggested we go on a date.

"The two of us haven't been out alone for a long time, and I want to take my best girl on a date tonight," he said.

I couldn't argue. Erick wanted to return to the restaurant where we had our first date, and I was keen for a much-needed romantic evening. Throughout the day, I looked at the clock frequently, waiting for it to end. He texted me at lunchtime to say he couldn't wait for tonight.

When the school day finally ended, I rushed home to prepare and decided to wear the same green dress I had on our first date. As I was finishing my makeup, Erick texted me to say he was a bit held up and that I should get a cab to the restaurant, where he would meet me in the bar area. I felt a bit disappointed but understood.

I called a taxi and quickly reached the restaurant. Expecting Erick to be there, I was surprised to find he hadn't arrived yet. I took a seat at a small table by the door, ordered a glass of wine, and began to wait. While I sipped my drink and daydreamed, my cell phone pinged with a message from Erick.

I'm sorry, darling, I'm caught in traffic.

It's okay. Do you want to make it another night? I don't mind.

I'm nearly there.

I ordered another glass of wine while I watched people coming and going, but not one of them was Erick. I panicked a bit but reassured myself he was just running late.

An hour had passed since his text when I called him. The call didn't go through, so I dialed again. This time, an automated message informed me that his number had been disconnected.

A chill ran through my body; I knew something was wrong. I vaguely remember leaving money on the table for my drinks as I dashed out. There were no taxis around, so I walked until one finally showed up.

When I got home, all the lights were off, and Erick's car wasn't in the driveway. I dashed into the house, calling out his name, hoping for a response, but all I heard was silence.

I was worried that something had happened.

Grabbing my cell, I rang Adam. When I explained what had happened, he told me to stay calm and that everything would be alright, but I had a bad feeling in the pit of my stomach.

Adam was at my place in no time. I wanted to contact the police, but Adam convinced me to wait for another hour to see what happened. He also tried to contact Erick and got the same message.

I watched every minute tick by. When an hour had passed, I grabbed my car keys and said I was going to the police station. Adam took the keys from me and said he would drive.

He called Mitch on the way, who met us at the station. The police took Erick's description and said they would check accident reports and assign detectives for further investigation if he hadn't appeared within twenty-four hours. Mitch said he would contact the hospital when we got home. I wanted to drive around the streets all night looking for him, but I didn't know where to start. I didn't even know where he had been last. Although I remained silent during the car ride home, my brain raced at a million miles an hour.

When we arrived home, Erick's car was still absent from the driveway, causing my heart to sink even further. I scoured the house, hoping he might have returned, but he hadn't. Panic set in completely; no amount of reassurance from others could halt my pacing. I repeatedly checked his cell phone and called my friends to see if they had any news about him.

By that time, Eva had arrived. She had been at the movies when Adam called her. I could hear Mitch on the phone asking questions about anyone being brought into the ER, but there wasn't anyone matching Erick's description.

Then the questions I didn't want to hear started from Adam and Mitch.

"Are you sure you two didn't argue?"

"No, we didn't argue." My frustration grew.

"Is there an office?"

"There's no office on the island. He travels to see clients, then comes home to work on his laptop. And before you ask, he didn't tell me what his schedule was today."

The last twenty-four hours kept playing over in my head. Had I missed something?

Then Mitch asked the question no one else had dared ask.

"Have you checked his closet?"

I was confused. "Why would I check his closet?"

"Let me go check for you," he insisted.

Looking at Mitch with my mouth open, I noticed Adam and Eva hadn't asked why. They seemed to realize what Mitch meant. I ran to our bedroom and opened the closet door. Only empty hangers remained.

My brain didn't want to comprehend what it meant, so I ran into the spare bathroom he used. His things were gone from there too—his toothbrush, shampoo, shaving cream, everything had gone.

"I don't understand. Where are his things?" I asked as I re-entered the living room.

Adam finally said the unthinkable. "Sis, check your bank accounts and the deed to the house, please."

I lashed out. "You think he was only interested in my money? I don't have any money for him to take, and the house deed is safely in the lockbox under the bed. Anyway, he's not like that and you know it."

"I know, but the police suggested we check."

My laptop was on the dining table, and I logged into my bank accounts. "There, look. No money has been taken, and Erick wouldn't get far with what's in there anyway."

I got the lockbox from the bedroom and showed them the house deed was still there. "And before you say anything, all my jewelry is still here too. Now, can we please concentrate on what could have happened? He didn't leave me, okay? He wouldn't."

"How do you explain his missing clothes?" Mitch asked.

It wasn't possible. Erick wouldn't leave me. I had to believe it with all my heart and soul.

"If you aren't going to help me, go," I yelled.

They all stood there.

Eva walked over and took hold of my hand. "Nobody is going anywhere. We want to help find him. But as your brother said, sometimes tough questions need to be asked to rule things out. Come and sit down. You're shaking."

Eva led me to the couch, where she put a blanket around my shoulders.

"I'm sorry," Mitch said. "I didn't want to upset you. We all want to help."

"So, what do we do now? Can we try the police again?" I asked.

Adam spoke up. "What about his friends? Do you know any of them?"

Erick didn't have any friends here and never really spoke about friends on the mainland.

A wave of nausea struck me, and I quickly ran to the bathroom and threw up. Eva came in behind me and gently rubbed my back, then placed a wet facecloth on the back of my neck.

When I stopped vomiting, I leaned over the sink and rinsed my mouth. Standing up, I saw the look of concern in my mother's eyes.

"You all think he ran off and left me, but he wouldn't. Twice today, he told me he loved me. Why would he do that if he was going to leave?"

"Shh, come and lie down" was all she could say as she led me back to the couch, placing a pillow on her lap. "Lie down," she said again, patting the cushion.

I put my head on the pillow and wept as Eva gently stroked my forehead, as she did when I was little.

"Something's happened to him," I whispered.

Mitch put a cup of tea in front of me, but I couldn't stomach drinking anything.

"I've spoken to Megan, and she said she'll use her contacts at the courthouse to see if she can find any information. We'll get to the bottom of this, sis."

As the night passed, there were still no calls from anyone. It was as if Erick had disappeared off the face of the earth.

Adam and Mitch seemed to take turns dozing off, but I didn't close my eyes for a moment. I couldn't take them off the door, hoping he would arrive back at any moment.

It hadn't been twenty-four hours, but it felt like a hell of a lot longer. The sun started to peek through my kitchen windows, so Adam and Mitch decided to go home to shower and change. Eva was in the kitchen making breakfast, trying to get me to eat, but I couldn't.

"Darling, when was the last time you ate?"

"I don't remember."

"At least drink some water, you must stay hydrated."

She handed me a glass of water, but I could only manage a few sips.

My mother's hovering was starting to get on my nerves, and I needed time to myself, so I decided to take a shower. Looking in the bathroom mirror, I saw a woman with a pale face and red eyes—I was emotionally drained.

Returning to the living room, Adam said Eva had gone home to change. I lay back down on the couch and stared at the door all day. I turned on the TV to try to pass the time, but the day dragged on. I tried Erick's number every fifteen minutes and got the same disconnection message.

Out of sheer exhaustion, I finally closed my eyes, sleeping for about an hour until my cell phone woke me. It was the police. They wanted to know if we had heard anything. When I said no, they informed me that detectives would come and take my statement.

At last, some action. Finding Erick wouldn't be far away.

Detectives Thomas and O'Brien arrived within forty minutes with a crime-scene tech. The detectives sat on the couch and asked me the same questions everyone had been asking me.

Did we fight?

Could he be on a business trip?

Was anything missing?

I was getting impatient.

Adam stepped in and told them Erick's clothes were missing, and the detectives looked at each other and raised their eyebrows. Detective O'Brien asked if she and the tech could see the bedroom and closet.

Detective Thomas continued to ask questions. "Have you checked your bank account?"

I was about to lose it when Adam stepped in again. He told her we had checked everything, and all was normal.

"So, it's only *his* items that have gone? Ms. Kane, is there any possibility he has … left on his own?"

How could I make people understand?

"No, he hasn't. I can't explain it, but I know something has happened. Please, can you help me find him?" I was pleading.

Detective Thomas seemed more compassionate than her partner and told me they would take my statement, check to see if anything had been reported, and also check the airport manifests. They asked for a picture of him and a description of his car.

The tech walked around the house, shining a special torch, making me very nervous. What if something had happened here, and I didn't know?

Half an hour later, the tech announced everything seemed clean. Detective O'Brien handed me her card and said, "Ms. Kane, as there is no evidence of a crime here, we'll go back to the station and send out his photo and car description to patrol cars to keep a lookout. In the meantime, if you hear anything, please let us know." With that, they were gone and, once again, I was in limbo.

There were too many people hovering around me, and I was getting agitated, so I suggested they all go home. It was early evening, and everyone was tired; besides, there was nothing more anyone could do.

Reluctantly, they left after I promised to ring if I needed anything.

The house was eerily quiet as I stood in the living room, not knowing what to do. Lying back on the couch, I turned on the TV again, flicking through the channels with one hand and dialing Erick's number with the other, barely sleeping.

It was eleven o'clock in the morning when my phone rang, causing me to jump. It was Detective O'Brien telling me they had found Erick's car at the airport. She explained that the tech's report showed there wasn't any evidence of foul play in the car or house. The detective apologized and said her captain had closed the file as it was apparent to the police department that Erick had left of his own free will.

I couldn't speak. My chest had a relentless tightness and searing pain. I tried calling Adam to see if Megan had found out anything, but he wasn't answering his phone.

I knew he would be at his office at the airfield, and decided to go there, calling a cab as I couldn't find my car keys. On the ride over, my anxiety grew, unable to accept the possibility that he had left me without a word.

CHAPTER FORTY-FOUR

My heart was beating fast, and I was panting as I reached the top of the stairs. I didn't notice the people around me. I was only focused on getting to Adam's office to find out if there was any information from Megan. She was my last hope.

As I approached the doorway of Adam's office, I saw Eva and Mitch standing inside. I could tell something was wrong by their facial expressions, but they hadn't noticed me yet. "You have to tell her, Eva, and you have to tell her now," Adam said sternly.

"Tell who what? Is it about Erick? Did you find him?" I asked, finding it hard to breathe.

They all turned and noticed me for the first time, exchanging glances.

"Please, tell me. Erick's hurt, isn't he?" I said, thinking the worst.

Eva took me by the hand and led me to the two chairs. We sat facing each other.

"Oh God, please tell me," I said.

"He's not hurt." She paused, steadying her voice. "Remember when I told you I had to leave because things became dangerous again?" she said.

"Yes, but just tell me about Erick." I didn't want to hear about my mother's past again.

"I'm trying, darling," Eva said. "Someone I sent to prison threatened to hurt anyone dear to me when he got out, which is why I left home. This man, Cole, was a sadist who enjoyed watching young women being tortured."

"What does this have to do with Erick?" I sneered at her, getting impatient.

She looked up at Adam for help, desperate, but he shook his head.

"You have to tell her everything," he said.

Eva took a slow breath in. "About eleven months ago, there was intel that Cole may have had *your* photo and location, so I assigned Erick to watch over and protect you. I wasn't going to take a chance with your life and let that monster do to you what he did to me," she blurted out.

Her words didn't make sense. "What?"

"Erick was assigned to keep you under surveillance. He wasn't supposed to contact you, but he did."

"How can you *assign* him?" I asked, confused.

"He works for the same agency as I did."

I quickly pulled my hands away from her and stood up. Slowly, her words started to sink in.

"He's a spy too, and you were his boss? No, it doesn't make any sense." I said in disbelief.

"He was only supposed to watch you from a distance, to keep you safe. He was under orders not to get involved with your life."

"Orders. From you. He was under orders. No. It was real. What we had in our lives was real. You're wrong," I said firmly. "We love each other." I didn't want to believe her. She had been lying to us for twenty years. Why was she still lying now?

"It may have been real, but he got too close."

I looked into her eyes and knew she was telling the truth. I couldn't find any words. My mind spun, and the pain in my chest grew.

"It was all a lie, and my mother set it up! You both lied to me." I turned quickly to Adam. "Did you know about this?" I yelled at him, "Did you know?"

"I swear I only just found out." I could always tell when Adam was lying, and he was telling me the truth.

Still, I threatened him. "If I *ever* find out you knew—"

Mitch stepped in. "It's true. Adam and I didn't know until today."

I put my hands on my pounding head and started to pace. "How? Why would you do this to me?"

"I was scared for *your* life," Eva explained.

"Not good enough!" I yelled. "It was all too good to be true. Oh, my God. I'm so stupid for not seeing it was all a big lie." I couldn't believe it.

Eva tried to hug me.

"No, you don't get to hug me. How could you do this?"

She stood there.

"Where's Erick now? I want to talk to him. I want to talk to him now," I yelled.

"You can't," Eva said, "he's gone. Erick's been compromised."

"What do you mean 'compromised'? Where is he?" I was mad. I hated her and wanted to hit her.

"I don't know where he is," Eva said. "He broke protocol, Ally. He chose a relationship over his assignment, which made him a liability, and the agency had no choice but to remove him from the situation."

I moved to Adam's desk and picked up his phone. "You get on the phone *now*, call your spy friends, and find him. Tell them to bring him back to me *now*," I demanded.

"I can't. I've been locked out of any involvement concerning Erick. All anyone will tell me is that he's been reassigned."

I started to sob uncontrollably. "Please, Mom, please call. Bring him back to me. I'll do anything you want. Please, Mommy, do this for me." I put my palms together and begged her.

Eva was crying as well. "Oh, darling, I can't."

My chest and head were pounding harder and faster, and the room had no air. "I have to go," I said.

"No, don't go. Let's talk," Eva tried to insist.

"*Talk*? I don't even want to look at you," I yelled as I backed out of the room. As soon as I was clear of the doorway, I turned and ran, feeling very alone and betrayed.

As I ran down the stairs, my breathing quickened. All I could think of was going home. I had a vision in my head that when I got back, Erick would be there, put his arms around me, and tell me it was all a mistake.

As I stepped outside, I tried to take a breath, but nothing would go in. I could hear someone calling me from behind, but I didn't care.

"Ally, wait." It was Mitch. He caught up to me and grabbed my arm to stop me from running further.

My world was spinning out of control.

"I can't …," I tried to say.

Mitch put his arms around me. "It's okay, I've got you."

And I passed out.

CHAPTER FORTY-FIVE

earing sounds in the distance and the hospital smells, I slowly opened my eyes and, for a brief second, forgot the drama earlier at Adam's office. Then it all came rushing back, and I felt a heaviness in my chest.

"Hey." Adam was sitting by my bed. "You're okay," he assured me.

"What happened?" I asked.

"You passed out."

"I'm going home," I said as a male doctor in dark-blue scrubs entered.

"Hi there, I'm Dr. Dane. Do you remember your name?" he said.

"Of course I do. Let me go home." My head was still throbbing, and I could barely lift it, but I still tried to sit up.

Dr. Dane gently touched my shoulder to stop me. "You can go soon. But your blood pressure is extremely high, and you're also dehydrated. You have an IV to get you rehydrated and medication to reduce your blood pressure. Once that's all stable, you can go," he said. I could hear the care in his voice.

Settling back down, I was a little relieved as I didn't think I could have stood up. I didn't have any fight left.

"The medication for your blood pressure, along with a mild sedative, might make you a bit drowsy, so try and relax. I'll be back to check on you again," He smiled and left the room.

Mitch came in as the doctor left.

"You're looking a little better. You had me worried."

I gave him a smile of thanks and turned to Adam. "Is it all true what Eva told me?"

"I believe her," he said. "It would explain why he suddenly left. I'm sorry this has happened to you."

I wanted a black hole to open and swallow me.

Adam shifted his weight in the chair. "I know this might be the wrong time, but Eva's in the waiting room and wants to come in."

"No," I said. Feeling the medication taking effect, I closed my eyes.

"I'll go to the waiting room and update her on how you are, then I'll be right back, okay?" Adam left the room, leaving Mitch holding my hand.

"Just close your eyes. I won't let anything happen to you," he softly said.

His words were reassuring, and I fell into a deep sleep.

CHAPTER FORTY-SIX

I woke up with a start, forgetting for a second where I was. "You're okay, don't try and get up." Mitch was still sitting by my hospital bed. He touched my shoulder to ease me back onto the pillow.

"How long have I been out?" I asked.

"All night," he said.

"All night?"

"Yeah. Here, drink some water." He handed me a plastic cup. "The doctor's removed the IV and said you must stay hydrated."

My mouth was dry, and I savored the cool water soothing my throat. "Have you been here all night?"

"Adam and I took turns. He's in the corridor with the doctor," he explained.

Adam walked into the room with the same doctor I saw yesterday. This time, I paid a bit more attention to him. He was tall, attractive, and had dark curly hair.

"Good morning. How do you feel?" he asked.

I tried to sit up. "A bit groggy, but okay."

"The IV has rehydrated you, but more importantly, your blood pressure is stable. Your brother mentioned that you received some upsetting news yesterday."

Feeling embarrassed, I couldn't answer and hoped Adam hadn't told him.

"Here is a week's supply of medication. Take it twice daily and consult your GP for blood pressure checks." He handed me the bottle. "If you have any questions or concerns, feel free to call."

I nodded and thanked him.

"I'll send the nurse with the discharge papers. Take care." Then he left the room.

"I want you to come and stay with us," Adam said.

"No, please take me home." I was feeling anxious again.

"I don't want you to be by yourself, Ally."

"I'll ring Cassie or Donna. One of them will come over. Besides, Eva's staying at your place, and I don't want to see her."

"She's worried and wants to talk to you."

"I don't care. I want to go home." I started to get out of bed and was a little wobbly on my feet. Adam grabbed my arm, but I steadied myself and said, "I'm okay."

"Are you sure?"

I knew he was concerned about me, but I wanted to be alone. I felt humiliated.

"I have to go to the bathroom, and I can do it alone, thank you." I grabbed the back of my hospital gown—no need for them to have a peep show.

Adam raised his hands and said, "Sure, but if—"

I cut him off. "I'm fine."

As I gazed into the bathroom mirror, I noticed how red and puffy my eyes appeared, making me look as though I hadn't slept in years.

"God," I said to my reflection, "what the hell happened? Seventy-two hours ago, I was happy." I started to think of Erick, and tears welled in my eyes. No, I won't cry. Not yet. I had to keep it together until I got home.

I splashed my face with cold water, and ran my damp hands through my hair. My dress was hanging on the back of the bathroom door, and I changed into it, taking one last look in the mirror before pushing my shoulders back and walking out of the bathroom to where the boys were waiting by the bed.

"Can we go now?" I asked, grabbing my sandals from Adam.

"You have to sign discharge papers at the desk …"

Before he could finish his sentence, I was heading to the nurses' station. A nurse went over the paperwork with me, and I signed it without reading, then walked toward the elevators.

As we reached the front entrance, a warm breeze hit my face.

"Just stand there with Mitch, and I'll bring the car around," Adam ordered.

"I can walk."

But he was already sprinting toward the car.

"Just let him do it. It makes him feel like he's helping," Mitch said. He put his arm around my shoulders.

"Thanks," I said.

"For what?"

"For being there. You didn't have to be," I put my head on his shoulder.

"That's what family does," he said, and he was right.

"I really appreciate what you and Adam have done for me. I'm lucky to have my two brothers."

The drive home was mostly in silence—none of us knew what to say.

As I entered my house, it felt empty.

"Did someone tidy up?"

"Megan came over," Adam replied.

"Thank her for me."

Mitch whispered, "Family, remember?"

"Can we get you anything? Something to eat?" Adam started to fuss.

I could see the signs of exhaustion and concern on their faces. "I really need to rest. Cassie or Donna can come over if I need help, so you two should go. I promise I'm fine." I smiled to reassure them. "You've both been swamped with work and haven't had much sleep in the last seventy-two hours either. I promise I'll let you know if I need anything at all."

"Are you sure?" Adam checked.

"Yes, go." I hugged them both.

Once they had gone, I crumpled onto the floor and sobbed. I felt embarrassed, humiliated, and annoyed with myself for being so naïve. I got off the floor and headed to the bedroom. Blossom came up to see what was wrong as I curled up on my bed.

I dialed Cassie. When she answered, I couldn't speak.

"Hello, Ally?"

She heard me crying.

"I'm coming."

I hung up the phone, closed my eyes, and fell asleep.

CHAPTER FORTY-SEVEN

I heard female voices and the TV softly playing in the living room before I opened my eyes. I knew straight away Cassie was there with Donna.

Slowly getting out of bed, I came up behind them as they sat on the couch. They got up and hugged me, then I noticed the girls had brought the remedies for heartbreak. "You okay? You want something. Food, water?" Donna asked.

"Wine?" asked Cassie.

"Yes, to water and wine, and those chips," I replied.

"Adam told us some of what happened. You want to tell us the rest?"

I downed Cassie's half-full glass of wine in one go. I needed the courage to share my humiliating story with them.

"Okay, let me get you your own glass," she said, quickly returning from the kitchen with a bottle of wine and another glass. She filled it and handed it to me before topping up hers.

As I settled on the couch, the two girls positioned themselves next to me, prepared to support me.

"When you're ready to talk, we're here."

"Thanks." I took another big gulp of wine.

At that moment, my back door swung open, and Bernie walked in.

"Hi, I thought we might need more supplies." She was juggling several grocery bags.

I smiled at her, and Donna said, "Great, I hope there's more wine in one of those bags."

"There is," Bernie replied.

Before we realized it, Eva had appeared behind Bernie, yet all Bernie noticed was the shocked expression on our faces.

"What are you all looking at? I did bring wine," said Bernie. Then she turned around and saw Eva. "Can I help you?" she asked, having never met my mother.

"I'm Ally's mother, and I want to speak to my daughter alone," Eva sharply replied.

Looking unimpressed, Eva gazed at Cassie and Donna.

"Hello, Mrs. Kane," they both spoke in unison.

Bernie turned into Principal Bernie. "Unfortunately, ma'am, your daughter doesn't wish to speak with you, so I believe it's best you leave now."

Eva's face flushed red, and she began to rant. "Listen here, lady. I don't know who you are, but I strongly advise you get out of my way because you don't want to mess with me right now."

At this point, Bernie stood between Eva and me, while Cassie and Donna were also on their feet. Eva had to navigate past all three of them to reach me. Bernie showed no fear—her expression was serious, and she was prepared to confront Eva.

But before Bernie could reply, I stood up and shouted, "Stop, just stop." I walked past my friends. "It's okay. I've got this."

Bernie placed her hand on my shoulder as I passed her before moving next to Donna and Cassie.

I took Eva's arm and turned her around to face the back door. "First, do not *ever* speak to my friends like that again. They have been there for me more times than you."

My words caught Eva by surprise. "I'm sorry, but I need to talk to you."

I leaned closer to her and said, "I think you should go."

"Honey, please give me a moment. Let me explain."

My voice was steady, "I don't want to hear what you have to say."

Eva gently placed her hand on my face, but I pulled away. Startled by this, she moved toward the door.

"Wait, I need to ask you a question," I said.

She turned and looked at me. "Anything."

I bit my bottom lip to stop myself from trembling. "Did Erick leave because you told him to, or did he leave because he wanted to?"

"Would it make a difference?" she asked.

I shrugged my shoulders and held my breath, bracing myself for the answer.

"Erick left because it was the best thing for you," she said, her voice quiet.

Her words didn't change the turmoil I was feeling. "You're right. It doesn't make a difference."

Eva stepped closer, her face still flushed. By not allowing her in and sending her away, I was pushing her buttons and making her more frustrated with me, and part of me found satisfaction in it. I wanted to hurt her for what she had done with Erick and how she had left us all those years ago. I wanted her to experience the pain of the rejection they both had caused.

"You know, ever since I came back," she said, "I sensed you weren't pleased I was alive and, frankly, it hurt. You always thought life would be one big fairy tale with happy endings, and I blame your father for putting ideas in your head. Well, my darling girl, life is not a fairy tale, nobody's life is, and I didn't raise you to think that. I did, however, raise you to be respectful."

Maybe she thought I would fall crying into her arms after her little speech. She was mistaken.

"You're right," I replied, "the mother who raised me taught me to respect, love, and care for people. She never promised me a fairy-tale life, and that was okay because I knew my mother loved me and would always be there for her family. My mother was kindhearted, warm, loving, and not the cold-hearted bitch standing before me now."

My words took Eva by surprise, and without a moment's hesitation, she raised her hand and slapped me across the face. The slap stung, but I didn't flinch.

I leaned closer to her. "My point exactly."

I could see that Eva was astonished, both by what she had done and by my reaction. Left speechless, she turned, walked to the back door, opened it, and left, slamming it behind her.

"Wow," said Cassie, "she was intimidating before she died, now she's scary *and* intimidating."

I turned to face my friends, and we broke into laughter, then I burst into tears again. The three of them came to me, and we formed a group hug.

"We need wine," Bernie said.

CHAPTER FORTY-EIGHT

The girls stayed for a few hours. We drank and cried as I explained everything. I could always tell them more than I could my own family.

After a while, I was emotionally exhausted and had trouble keeping my eyes open. They insisted I go to bed.

"I'll stay," Donna said. "Anton is visiting his sister in Cuba."

I thanked her but assured them it wasn't necessary. I needed to be alone. Besides, they had their own lives. I promised to tell them if I changed my mind or wanted to chat during the night.

Reluctantly, they left, having cleaned up and fed Blossom, and I was alone again. In the bathroom, I washed my face and took one of the doctor's tablets.

Blossom had already occupied her usual position on the bed, so I crawled beside her. I was too exhausted to cry anymore. My head was pounding, and with Blossom purring beside me, I fell into a deep sleep.

* * *

I lay facing Erick's side of the bed when I slowly opened my eyes.

Erick was lying next to me.

I didn't move. Was this real?

I looked into his eyes and asked, "You said you loved me and wanted to be with me forever. Was it all a lie?"

"I'm sorry," he softly replied.

"You broke my heart."

"I'm sorry," he said again.

My hand reached out to touch his face, but before I could, my phone rang. Startled, I turned to look at the phone then quickly turned back to Erick. He wasn't there. It had been a dream.

I let it ring for a few seconds more before I answered it. It was Adam.

"How are you?" he asked. "I talked to Cassie, and she told me Eva came to see you yesterday."

"It's okay," I replied.

"Do you want me to come over?"

"No, I think I might go back to sleep. I have a headache."

"Okay, but please eat something and drink plenty of water."

"I will." I hung up and turned to stare at where Erick had been lying a few seconds earlier. My hand felt his pillow—it was cold. I took a few deep breaths and asked myself how long this pain in my chest, along with the feeling of emptiness, would last.

I got up, fed Blossom, had a glass of water, and took another tablet. I wanted to drift back to sleep, hoping Erick would return in my dreams. I didn't know who had hurt me more, him or Eva.

It is a fact that some people have died from a broken heart. This occurs when extreme emotional distress causes the heart muscles to weaken due to the rush of blood. It's a rare condition known as broken heart syndrome. I knew I wasn't about to die, but it felt as if I was.

CHAPTER FORTY-NINE

Nearly a week had passed since Erick left. I had taken a week's sick leave from work and hadn't left the house or really got out of bed. People came and went and brought me food, but I still wouldn't talk to Eva. Adam told me she was going to the mainland to visit a friend, but I wasn't listening. Anyone could have told me anything, and I wouldn't have been able to repeat it. I was numb.

The girls came over again to cheer me up. They talked about how I had to move on, and I understood what they were saying and appreciated their care, but I needed some time to myself. After they left with the promise that I would at least get out of the house the next day, I climbed back into bed. As I lay staring at Erick's side of the bed, feeling numb, I closed my eyes and let the sounds of the waves crashing against the beach do their job and lull me to sleep.

It was the early hours of the morning when I felt a familiar hand stroking the side of my face. It was soothing, and I thought it was a dream. I didn't want to open my eyes.

"Honey, wake up." It was my mother.

I opened my eyes and saw my mom lying on the bed facing me, her hand on my face. I opened my mouth to say, "What do you want?" but before I could get a word out, she gently put her finger to my lips and whispered, "Shh, please listen. I'm leaving in a few hours." She held up a small photo. "This is you and me, the week after you were born. This is the only photo I have kept with me all these years."

I had never seen the photo before.

"I'm very sorry I hurt you. I have tried all your life to keep you safe. Remember when you were young and you were trying hard to do a silly dance on the surfboard with Cassie? One day, I was watching you and you slipped." She placed her hand back on my cheek. "You were a few feet away from me, and I couldn't stop you from falling. It happened quickly, but you were under the water when I reached you. I was frightened when I dived in and pulled you up. You were breathing, but unconscious, and I think my heart stopped as I ran with you in my arms and drove like a mad person to the hospital, pleading with God to let you be okay. I hated feeling that, even though I was there, I couldn't stop you from getting hurt."

Eva sighed. "You eventually came to, with a bump on your head. I knew then I would protect you no matter what happened so you would never get hurt again." She gently stroked my forehead as she used to do when I was young. "You're my baby girl. We did a lot of firsts together, you and I."

She stopped stroking my forehead and took my hand in hers. "I was doing the right thing when I left my family years ago. I did the only thing I knew I could do to save you from being hurt. This year, when I found out you might be targeted, that feeling of being powerless to protect you terrified me, especially now that your father's gone. I called in favors to get an operative to watch you. Erick wasn't supposed to get close. I'm sorry. I was busy keeping the physical hurt out. I didn't think of the emotional hurt."

By now, both our eyes had filled with tears.

"Soon, you're going to have to forgive Erick and me. Not for us, but for you, my darling baby girl. You will never move on with your life if you hold all this sadness and anger inside you. You deserve to be happy." She leant over, hugged me, and said, "I love you very much. But I must go. Your brother's waiting to take me to the airport."

I finally found my voice. "When will you be back?"

"I'll be gone for a few weeks. My friend needs help, then I'll be back. I promise." She looked at me with a warm smile and lovingly ran her fingers through my hair. "Can we chat more when I get back?"

I couldn't speak, so I nodded.

Eva rose from my bed. When she reached the door, she paused, turned back to me and smiled, then left.

The front door closed, and I heard a car driving away.

When I woke up later that morning and checked the clock, it was nearly ten-thirty. I didn't want to get out of bed, but Blossom had other ideas. She wanted her breakfast and had waited long enough.

I fed Blossom, donned a T-shirt, shorts, and sunglasses, and, as promised, I left the house and headed to Adam's. It felt great to have the sun on my skin and the warm sand beneath my feet as I strolled along the beach.

I reached his back door and took my sunglasses off once I got inside.

"You look as good as I feel," he said.

"Same back at you, bro."

"You want some coffee or tea?"

"Tea, please. Is Megan here?"

"No, she had to work."

"Eva told me you two talked before she left."

"Yeah, it was pretty intense."

Adam handed me a mug of tea. "Want to tell me about it?"

"No. I'm tired of talking and very tired of being sad. Do you think Eva will be back?"

He paused, sipping his coffee. "I hope so. I still have questions I want answers to."

"I'm not sure she will be back," I confessed.

Adam seemed a bit taken aback by my comment. "I guess we will see."

"Well, bro, this has been a hell of a month."

"Boy, that's an understatement. You know what Dad would say," he said, "we need to laugh again."

"What do you suggest?"

"A beach picnic with friends, beer, wine, and burgers. What more could we need?"

He was right.

CHAPTER FIFTY

After two weeks, the only message we got from Eva was a text.

I'm fine. Everything is okay. I love you both.

For the next three weeks, we tried reaching her on the cell number she had texted us from, but it was disconnected. Adam found out later it was a burner phone.

Another two weeks passed, and Adam made some inquiries with one of his buddies in Air Force intelligence. A week later, he was informed Eva had gone off the grid.

Had Eva returned to her old life?

Adam later mentioned he had also inquired about Erick, but there was no information. It felt as though they had both vanished completely.

When we finally shared the news with Auntie Ell after her honeymoon, we couldn't help but ask if she had heard from Eva. Sadly, she replied that the last time they spoke was at her wedding. You could hear the pain in her voice at the thought of her sister disappearing once more.

We continued as though the past year was a fading memory. At times, it felt like it had all been a dream.

I did more dancing and taught a few ballet classes to younger students. Cassie purchased her parents' house, which they had rented out when they moved to Maui. It was hers now, and we were neighbors again. It wasn't surprising to any of us when Cassie and Mitch announced they were moving in together. Finally!

Realizing that life was too unpredictable, Adam finally asked Megan to marry him. He told me he was proposing but was worried I might be upset after losing Erick; however, I couldn't have been happier for him. I already loved Megan like a sister, and she was perfect for him. When they announced their engagement, Megan asked if I could help her plan the wedding and be her maid of honor. They got married four months later on the beach outside their house. It was simple and beautiful, with only close family and friends, which included Auntie Ell and Frank.

On the day of Adam's wedding, Eva called to wish him all the best. He was surprised that she knew about it, just as I was. After their chat, he handed the phone to me.

"How are you, sweetheart?" she asked.

Still furious with her, I said, "I miss my mother."

"Oh, darling, I miss you too."

"You don't get it. I miss my mother. The mother who raised me and wouldn't skip her son's wedding for anything. But she passed away years ago."

Silence fell as she hung up.

I shared with my auntie what I had said to Eva, but I chose not to mention it to Adam. I recognized that it was a hurtful thing to say, yet I didn't feel sorry. I missed the mom I had twenty years ago.

Besides Eva's call, Adam's big day was a success, and I was happy for them.

Frank had urgent business and flew back home after the wedding, but I was delighted that Auntie Ell could stay with me for the week. One morning, before going to my four-to-five-year-old dance class, she asked if she could come and watch.

I always enjoyed teaching the little ones. They were cute, trying hard to point their feet, but after an hour of pointing, dancing, and standing straight, I was ready for them to go. It doesn't look like hard work, but keeping ten little girls focused and doing the same thing can be mentally exhausting.

After the girls said their goodbyes, I sat next to my aunt.

"You're a wonderful teacher. I'm proud of you," she told me.

"Thank you."

She approached the piano in the corner and inquired whether she could play it.

"Please, I love hearing you play," I said.

"All right, but you dance too."

There's nothing more fulfilling than dancing while my aunt plays the piano. It's a very special moment for us, and it always will be.

CHAPTER FIFTY-ONE

Eva

The day my son got married, I was there on the beach watching. No one noticed. I stayed far enough away not to be noticed but close enough to see the beautiful bride walk down the sandy aisle. Adam looked very handsome, like his father, bringing back memories of my wedding day. I was proud of Adam and wished Charlie had been here with me. Maybe things would be different if he was.

I had to summon all my strength to resist the urge to run up and hug my kids, to tell them I was sorry and that I wanted to come home. But I just didn't feel confident I would be welcome; I had made a mess of my life and theirs.

When I rang Adam to wish him every happiness, I hoped he would give me a sign he might want me there. I was ready to take the chance … until I spoke to my daughter. When she said she "missed the mother who died years ago", I was lost for words and couldn't reply. The hardest part was that she was right.

As I stood watching my son and his bride take their vows, my daughter beside them, I couldn't help but wonder if things would be different if I hadn't broken my promise to Eloise not to search for our mother. Maybe I wouldn't feel so torn and conflicted with the fear of being rejected again. I remember that day as if it were yesterday. I had finished training and was about to be sent overseas, unsure of when I would return home, so I used the agency's resources to find our mother, Emily.

* * *

It was a chilly autumn morning when I finally got the courage to knock on Emily's door.

When she opened it, I held my breath. She was beautiful, just as I had always imagined, with her slightly graying auburn curly hair and Eloise's green eyes.

"Emily?" I was excited.

"Can I help you?" she asked softly, a kind smile playing on her lips.

"I'm your daughter." I waited for her to throw her arms around me and smother me with kisses.

"Sorry, I don't have any daughters," she said, closing the door.

"Wait," I yelled, as my hand stopped the door from closing. "You said, 'daughters.' I never told you I had a sister."

Her smile instantly morphed into fury. "I told Ben never to look for me! I foolishly trusted him. I never wanted kids," she proclaimed, her eyes filled with hatred.

Her words left me speechless, and I took a step back.

"Leave now. I have nothing to give you. Hell, I didn't even want to give birth to you, and if I had my way, you and your sister would've been aborted," Emily said, almost snarling.

I was too shocked to even cry.

As she started to close the door again, she paused. "Wait, here is some advice I'll give you. The truth about life." She leaned closer to me and in a low voice, "Never get attached to anyone. It doesn't matter who, as people will suck the life out of you, and it will never be your own. You will end up hating them, and they'll hate you. Those closest to you will always betray you."

I couldn't believe what I was hearing.

Emily continued. "Never forget what I said, as it will be the only thing you'll get from me. Now get off my porch or I'll call the police." She closed the door in my face, rejecting me. She never even asked my name, let alone anything about me, Eloise, or Dad.

My world shattered, and with my mother's words echoing in my mind, I retreated into my work.

I never saw her again, and I never told Eloise. My sister was right, and I felt ashamed for breaking my promise to her.

My mother's damaging words repeated in my head during my time with the agency, but when I met Charlie, the words disappeared.

After my children were born, Emily's voice began again and grew louder over time. I managed to ignore it and enjoy life with my family. Now, I could no longer block her words out.

Is this the reason Ally and I frequently clashed? Adam was an easygoing child, while Ally had always been a daddy's girl. I loved my daughter deeply, but there were moments when she truly tested my patience. Charlie said we were alike. Maybe he was right.

I was horrified to think that my words and actions may have affected Ally just as Emily's had affected me. My mother's words still torment me after all these years. Would my life have been different if I'd had the courage to talk to my sister when it happened instead of running away? It was a long time ago, and much has happened since then.

Watching my family gather to congratulate the newlyweds made me feel quite depressed and alone. I hung around for a few days, watching and wanting to approach them, but I was afraid to do so. I had done too much damage, and that pain in my chest that I'd had for years grew. Once again, I ran.

CHAPTER FIFTY-TWO

Ally

Ten months had passed since the day Erick left, and we were now heading into spring.

After a month, I took his pillow and hurled it against the wall. For the next week, I would stomp on it every time I left or entered the room until I finally threw it in the trash.

Three weeks later, I got a new bed and decided to sleep in the middle.

I was going through the stages of grief, and the anger was taking a little longer to pass, so I focused my energy on work and dancing. I even did a Teaching Children with Learning Difficulties course over the summer in Virginia and took some time to do a bit of sightseeing.

My friends offered to set up blind dates for me. It was too soon. I couldn't get rid of the foolish notion that I would be unfaithful to Erick. I became angry with myself and decided if I were alone, I couldn't be harmed.

I made a concerted effort not to think about Eva or Erick. The time I had spent with them felt like a film about the life of another person.

Mitch arrived at my doorstep one night. Flushed with excitement, he said before he entered the house, "I'm going to do it. I'm going to ask Cassie to marry me."

I threw my arms around his neck before ushering him inside. "Does Cassie suspect anything?" I asked, dying to know the details.

"No, not yet, but I need your help," Mitch said.

"Whatever you need."

"It must be perfect. Can you come with me and look at the ring I've chosen? I'm not sure if it's one she'll love, and I don't know her size. Anyway, keep it a secret."

"It would be an honored." Cassie was my oldest friend, and I wanted everything to go flawlessly for her.

"Can you come tomorrow morning?" he asked. "I've arranged a dinner on a sailboat for the two of us the day after tomorrow, and I want to have the ring to give her."

"Gosh, you're not wasting any time."

"I woke up this morning and knew this is what I wanted to do, so I went out today and looked at rings. I don't want to wait any longer. Besides, I can't keep it a secret for more than two days."

"Me neither." I laughed. "I'll have to avoid Cassie until you ask her."

He stopped and looked at me. "You're okay with this?"

"More than okay. I thought it would happen ages ago." I tried hugging him again, but he wouldn't stand still. "Stop pacing. I'll get you a beer—sit and tell me all about it. Have you told Adam yet?"

"No, not yet. I love Adam, he's my bro, but the guy can't keep a secret."

"I know."

We arranged for Mitch to pick me up around eleven the following morning.

* * *

Mitch arrived at my front door the next morning, scooping me up in his arms and smiling from ear to ear.

208

Thirty minutes later, we were at the jewelers. Mitch had already picked out a ring and wanted my approval. Cassie and I were the same ring size and when I tried it on it was perfect. It was a beautiful pear-shaped diamond in a rose-gold setting, simple but elegant. I knew straight away this was the ring for her.

Mitch insisted on taking me to lunch—he wanted to go through all the proposal details. I was impressed by how much planning he had done, although he had been in love with Cassie since they first met.

After lunch, Mitch dropped me home, and I asked him to let me know what else I could do to help, promising not to tell anyone.

Later that afternoon, I looked out my kitchen window and could see people on the beach, young and old, playing in the water and on the sand, laughing. I was overjoyed by Cassie and Mitch and my brother getting married but sometimes wondered if I was doing the right thing by not taking another chance with love. Losing Erick left my heart in unbearable pain.

I sighed and went and sat on my back steps to watch the happy people on the beach. Dark rain clouds started to cover the sun. As tiny raindrops fell, people hurried out of the ocean and off the beach, and I ran over to my clothesline and grabbed my washing. By the time I got inside, the rain was pouring down, and my sunny kitchen had turned dim.

I was sitting on the couch folding my laundry when the doorbell startled me.

When I opened it, Erick was in front of me, dripping wet.

CHAPTER FIFTY-THREE

I gasped and put my hand over my mouth as I stepped back in shock.

"Ally, please," he stepped into my house and closed the door.

I was too stunned to do or say anything.

"I need to talk to you, it will only take a minute, I promise," he said.

I still couldn't speak.

"I know I don't have any right to be here, but please, he doesn't love you as I do. He's a great guy, but please don't marry him."

His words slowly sank in. I managed to utter "What?"

"Mitch. I saw you two together today. I saw you trying on engagement rings. But he's not the one for you."

"You saw us?"

He stopped, his mouth hanging open, realizing what I had said.

Anger rose within me. I stepped closer to him, and this time *he* stepped back.

"You followed me. You spied on me *again*. Are you serious?" I didn't give him time to answer. "How long have you been spying on me? And what gives you the right to come charging in here telling me what I can and can't do?"

"I … I got back yesterday, and I was coming to see you this morning when I saw you get into his car. Look, I get you didn't want to wait for me. It was a big ask, but Mitch, please. He isn't the one for you."

I was outraged by what he had said. "I didn't want to wait for you? Unbelievable. You take off and leave me, no goodbye, no message, and you say I didn't want to wait for you." I was irate.

Erick's face turned red, and he raised his voice. "I did leave a message." He slowly let out a sigh. "Look, let's calm down. All I'm saying is I think you should wait before marrying Mitch."

His words hit me. Quietly, I asked, "What message?"

He stopped and looked at me, confused as well.

"What message?" I demanded.

"I told her to tell you Plan B," he said.

"Who? Who did you tell?"

"Eva. The night we were supposed to meet for dinner, I got a message from you saying you were at home. But when I got here, Eva and two other operatives were waiting with my stuff already packed. They told me I had compromised my assignment by getting involved with you. They took my cell phone and ushered me into a waiting van. That's when I told Eva to tell you Plan B, as we discussed." He saw my confused look and realized what had happened. "She never gave you the message."

"No." I could barely speak.

"Where is she? I'll get her to tell you the truth."

"She left not long after you. We received a few messages after she left, but haven't heard from her since Adam's wedding."

"Do you know where she is?"

"No. The last we heard, she was off the grid."

We stared at each other for what seemed like minutes.

A puddle of water had formed at his feet.

He moved toward me to take my hand, but I stepped back.

"I'll get you some towels." I was numb.

Erick was still in the same spot, wearing a blank look when I walked back in. I handed him one of the towels, which he rubbed over his hair and face, and I placed the other on the floor where the puddle was.

When he had stopped drying himself, he said, "You thought I'd abandoned you. Eva promised me she would give you the message."

"You should have told me yourself," I yelled at him.

"I wanted to. I argued with your mother over it, but I was given two options before they pushed me into the van. If I stayed or tried to contact you, there would be disciplinary actions—I could have gone to jail for years. The other option was to leave quietly and finish my contract at a desk job in a remote part of Alaska. I wouldn't be able to contact you, but I would eventually be able to come back to you."

I could feel him trying to catch my eye, but all I could do was stare at the towel on the floor.

"I honestly believed Eva would explain this to you, and you'd know I'd be coming back. It was the only thing that got me through being in Alaska."

I still couldn't look at him.

"So, is that why you're marrying Mitch?" he asked.

Oh my God, he refused to let it go. I wanted to lie and say yes, make him suffer, but after looking into his eyes, I couldn't bring myself to do it.

"Mitch is marrying Cassie. I went with him today to help him with the engagement ring."

"So it's Cassie and Mitch, not you and Mitch?"

"Yes. It's a secret. No one knows yet, including Cassie."

He put his arms around my trembling body.

"No, no, I can't do this," I muttered, retreating as my anxiety about getting hurt again increased. "You need to leave. Go." My voice rose.

"But—"

I wouldn't let him finish his sentence. "But what? Did you come back thinking we could pick up from where we left off? After all the lies and no communication, did you think I would fall back into your arms and trust you? How can I trust you? Please go." I walked to the door and opened it. I didn't care that it was still raining outside.

Erick was lost for words. He handed me the towel and slowly moved toward the door. He stopped before he got outside and asked, "Can we please meet for coffee or lunch tomorrow, anything?" he begged.

"No … I don't know. I have to think, and you need to go." I closed the door, leaning against it as my heart urged me to run after him. My brain kept my feet firmly planted on the ground.

Things may have turned out differently if Eva had just been honest with me from the start. I was scared to let him in again now that the trust had been lost.

Before I knew it, I was running on the beach to Adam's place in the rain. I barged through his back door, dripping wet, with sand stuck to my feet and legs.

Adam was relaxing on the couch when I burst through the door, startling him.

"Ally, you scared me to death. What the hell?" His hand was on his chest as he spoke.

I dropped to the kitchen floor, my lungs burning from a lack of oxygen.

He took a blanket from the back of the couch and wrapped it around me.

"What's wrong?"

I finally told him about Erick and Eva, being careful not to mention Mitch and Cassie. I was crying so hard that I didn't notice moving to the couch. He did not speak. He allowed me to say everything until I couldn't speak or cry any longer.

"How could she? She saw what I was going through and never mentioned a word."

Adam rubbed my back as I used to do to him when he was young. Finally, he asked, "What are you going to do?"

"I don't know. How do I trust him not to take off on me again?"

"Did he say he knew where Eva was?"

"No. He thought she was still here."

We sat and talked for a while before I decided I wanted to go home.

Erick texted and phoned me several times the next day. Initially, I didn't take his calls as I didn't know what to say. When I finally answered, I was conflicted and emotional. Part of me wanted to be with Erick, which scared me as I didn't know if I could trust him.

Adam visited and said Erick had reached out to him. They had talked over a few beers about how Erick needed a job. Adam then told me that he had given him one in the office at his helicopter business. I felt a bit betrayed.

I realized the only way to work things out in my head was to not see Erick for a while. When I told him this, he stayed quiet. My heart broke to treat him this way, but I was confused about what to do. I had Cassie's and Mitch's engagement party to plan, and I could only handle one thing at a time. Now, Erick would have to wait for me.

CHAPTER FIFTY-FOUR

There was much laughter on the night of the engagement party as we sat around the restaurant table. I was delighted for Cassie and Mitch, but I still couldn't get Erick out of my head. Every time I thought about him, my mind went into turmoil. My heart wanted to trust him again, but my head sent warning signals.

Cassie's parents had come over from Maui for the party, overjoyed by their daughter's upcoming wedding.

As I sat discussing wedding ideas with Cassie and her mother, a large spotlight hit the center of the dance floor. People slowly looked up, and Cassie grabbed my arm and pointed. Erick was in the middle of the circle of light.

He smiled at me, and before I realized it, Adam stood up, took my hand, and led me over to Erick. I was in such a state of shock that I didn't put up any resistance.

Adam whispered to me, "You deserve to be happy, sis. I know he loves you, and you love him too, so give him a chance. I trust him, and you should too. Don't let this be another thing Eva takes away from you." He placed my hand into Erick's and moved off the dance floor, leaving the two of us standing there.

Erick slowly put his arm around my waist and gently drew me to him. He whispered into my ear, "They're playing our song."

My arms went limp by my side, feeling so heavy that I couldn't move them. I didn't dare look up to see everyone gawking at us, waiting to see what would happen. Part of me wanted to leave, but his arms around my waist felt good.

As the band played "Kiss Me," we started slowly dancing. I was staring at the buttons on Erick's light-blue shirt, not strong enough to look into his eyes. I could feel my heart beating so hard I was sure you could see it through my dress.

I slowly placed my right hand on his chest and felt his heart. It was pounding as hard as mine, and once again, our heartbeats were in sync. It was something I loved about us. *Is this the sign I'm looking for? The sign we should be together?*

I did love him. That was never the issue.

By this time, others had joined us on the dance floor, and I slowly put my arms around his neck and laid my cheek on his chest. Between his wonderful smell and his heartbeat, I melted into his arms.

He pulled me closer, putting his head on my shoulder as if we had never been apart, then whispered, "I will say sorry to you every day. I love you and want to be with you forever."

His words snapped me out of my trance. I looked up at him, and my old fears came flooding back. Pulling out of his arms, I went to the table to grab my purse.

Erick was still on the dance floor with his head lowered. I knew what I had to do. I quickly went to him and took hold of his hand.

"We need to talk," I said.

This time, it was Erick who was stunned as I led him off the dance floor and out the door.

The restaurant backed onto the beach, and as we reached the sand, I let go of his hand and took off my shoes.

"Let's walk along the beach," I said to him.

Still a little stunned, he replied, "Whatever you want."

"This is not about what I want. You're saying whatever you think I need to hear. I want honesty every time. Even if it will upset me. There have been too many secrets, and I don't know who or what to trust anymore."

I turned and began walking again, and he followed. We walked for about ten minutes along the sand before Erick took hold of my arm and turned me toward him.

"Okay, my turn to talk. I get what you're saying, and I promise to always be honest. But you have to know I *was* honest when I told you I loved you and am sorry for what happened. You are the most important person in my life. You are the *only* one I want to be with, and I will beg for your forgiveness every day if need be." His eyes were welling up with tears. "Please, can't we start again?"

I stood there for a moment with my heart and my head fighting. Could I trust him again?

"How do I know that one day, when I come home, you won't be there? I can't go through it again." There I had said it, my greatest fear.

He looked into my eyes. "I can tell you every hour I'm not going to leave, but the truth is, you're going to have to trust me and believe me when I say I'm not going anywhere."

He was right. But could I put my heart on the line once more? I didn't think I was strong enough to be hurt again. It would break me for good, and there would be no coming back from it.

"I don't know. It scares me." I started to shake.

Erick pulled me into his arms and held me tight. I belonged there.

"I know, darling, but only you can decide if we're worth the risk."

God, he was right again.

I gently pulled out of his embrace and looked up at him, and he kissed me.

Finally, I said, "We can't just pick up where we left off."

He looked shocked, but I wasn't finished.

"Maybe we could start over again. A new first date where we tell each other the truth about everything, don't leave anything out, then go from there. One step at a time."

A grin spread across his face. "I'm okay with that. I can tell you about my life before the agency, but even after leaving, I'm still not allowed to divulge certain facts."

"Start by telling me whether Erick is your real name."

"Well, I was born Scott Jackman, but I legally changed my name to Erick Morgan recently."

I looked at him, curious. "Why?"

"Honestly, I realized I didn't come alive or know who I was or what I wanted out of life until I came here and met you. You know me as Erick Morgan. I was loved as Erick Morgan. I liked who I was when I was him, so I decided to stay with that name."

His answer took me aback, but I understood.

We walked further along the beach and talked more. When we finally made our way back, we sat on the sand outside the restaurant. Erick told me about his life growing up and his brother Daniel, and how he had struggled with the idea of finding him. He had realized over this past year that he would only harm his brother by searching for him. It could change Daniel's life for the worse if he knew the truth, and it was best to leave him happy.

Adam checked on us, and I told him Erick would drive me home.

Soon after, we had our first date again, and it didn't take long before we were back in each other's arms.

CHAPTER FIFTY-FIVE

It was a perfect night in every way, the weather, the food, the company. All my family and friends had gathered for a BBQ in my backyard. Auntie Ell and Frank were over to meet their new great-nephews, Charles Alexander and Mitchell Adam Kane, Adam and Megan's twin boys. Mitch and Cassie had settled into married life and were still in their honeymoon bubble. Donna was beaming as she and Anton were expecting a child, Bernie and Michael were about to leave on a world trip, and I had the love of my life next to me.

Erick was working with Adam and Mitch in their helicopter business, and he was studying to get his pilot's license. He was excited about it, and so was I. He had moved in about eleven months ago, and although we weren't married, it felt as if we were. We hadn't talked about marriage, and I was okay with it. I was no longer scared when he was late home, although it took time and a few arguments. In the end, he had my complete trust.

We hadn't heard from my mother again, and I had made peace with the fact we might never.

The men were gathered around the BBQ, as men do, watching Erick cook and throwing in their expert advice. I was sitting with the women fussing over the babies when my cell phone rang.

I excused myself and grabbed it. "Hello," I said.

"Is this Alexandria Kane?" a male asked.

"Yes, it is."

I realized it was the voice that, until two weeks ago, I had not heard for nearly two years. The voice of the man who had trained me not long after my mother and Erick had disappeared.

I turned my back on my guests and walked toward the beach.

"Security code?" he asked.

"Dancer," I replied.

"Were you successful in your assigned task?"

"Yes," I answered.

"Is the target secured?"

I turned and looked at each person in my backyard. I smiled at them, and some of them smiled back.

"The target is secured," I said.

"Further instructions will follow." Then the line went dead.

Pure exhilaration ran through my body, and I couldn't help but smile.

The target was none the wiser.

PART THREE

Dancer

CHAPTER FIFTY-SIX

Two Weeks Earlier

My long day had finally ended, and I was relieved to be leaving work. Lately, I had been questioning my career choice. I wasn't enjoying teaching anymore, but didn't know whether I should change my career or take a break.

My cell phone rang as I got in my car. I sighed, thinking it was Erick saying he would be late home again, but to my delight, it was my beautiful auntie. And she had news. She and Frank were moving to the island for several months for Frank's work.

She explained that Frank's law firm, Ronan and Ronan & Associates, was involved in a merger with a Chinese shipping company on the island, and they needed to be there. She didn't sound very impressed about moving, and she wouldn't say why, so I suggested they stay with me and Erick while they organized a fully furnished rental. She could spend some time with Adam's twin boys, who she couldn't wait to hold.

I asked her what she thought and if she wanted to talk to Frank about it first.

"No," she replied. "If I have to move into an oversized house, we can stay with family first."

Her one request was a dinner party with family and friends once she arrived.

I was ecstatic about having my aunt on the island. I missed her. It was also an excuse to take some time away from teaching and get painters to paint the spare bedroom. Erick had promised to do it, but he had been busy getting his pilot's license and working for Adam.

I booked painters to come four days before my guests arrive. We covered all the furniture in the bedroom, and Erick hadn't long left for work when a white painter's van arrived. I thought only one or two painters were coming to do the job, and was surprised when four men in white overalls showed up. Two men asked me about the painting I needed, and a third man seemed to be guarding my closed front door. It was creepy. When the fourth man approached me, I didn't recognize him immediately.

"Ms. Kane, do you remember who I am?" he asked.

It was Agent Donaldson. He had been the special agent in charge of my training in Virginia nearly two years prior.

I nodded. Could this be happening? When I hadn't heard anything from the agency, I convinced myself I hadn't been accepted and dismissed it from my mind.

"Ms. Kane, I need your security code."

I remained silent.

"Ms. Kane, I insist you answer before we proceed," he said.

The adrenaline rushed through my body. Feelings I hadn't felt for a long time kicked in, and I was excited. "Dancer," I answered. "What's happening?"

"Are you expecting anyone, or are you expected anywhere?" he asked.

"No. I'm not expecting anyone home until this evening." I could hear them setting up the ladders and painting equipment in the spare bedroom.

"Please sit down. This may take a while," Donaldson instructed.

"Okay," I said as we moved to the dining room table.

Agent Donaldson took out a pen and a manila folder filled with documents. "First, I need to remind you of the confidential agreement and conditions you originally signed."

"Wait, what about my painting?" I almost laughed at my question. I was about to be briefed by a government agent, and I was concerned about painting.

A half-smile came over his face. "The men will complete the work. Now, I need to clarify a few things before we proceed. Have you discussed your recruitment with anyone? Think very carefully before you answer."

Who would I have told? No one would have understood. I hadn't considered telling Erick when he returned, as I didn't know the agency was still part of my life.

"No, I have neither told nor discussed this with anyone," I replied.

Donaldson studied my face and wrote something in the file. "Do you remember the privacy clause in the contract declaring you would not speak to anyone regarding the agency?" He handed me the documentation with my signature on it.

I considered how Erick and I had been forced apart due to his involvement with the agency. He had vanished because he was unable to tell me the truth. It took some time for trust to recover in our relationship. What would happen to us now that the tables were turned?

Donaldson was growing impatient. "Ms. Kane, I need an answer."

"Yes, this is the contract I signed, but things have changed since then."

"We know you are involved with an ex-operative known as Erick Morgan. Mr. Morgan can be informed of the situation once he agrees to our terms and conditions, but the agency will decide what information he will receive," he said, his voice firm.

I hesitated again.

"Ms. Kane, as discussed during your training, we would only use you if needed. We can leave, but the situation has become critical and time sensitive. We only have a few months to stop this illegal activity," he explained. "If we're wasting our time, let us know now, but we may not get the same results if we bring in another operative."

I was starting to panic. "Does it have something to do with my mother?"

"We can't provide further information until you agree to all terms and conditions."

I paused, then said, "On the condition that this is the only time I work for the agency, and I can tell Erick."

"Fine. However, as I said, the agency will decide what information Mr. Morgan is to know."

I decided there was one other condition I needed to make, and I wanted it in writing. It had to do with my mother. When I told Donaldson, he shook his head.

"You're making this difficult, and I can't guarantee it."

"Try, then we'll proceed," I said.

Irritated, his cheeks flushed slightly, and he stood up, walked into the kitchen, and placed a phone call. I sat at the dining room table, trying to figure out what to do if the agency denied my requests.

For fifteen minutes, the discussion continued. "Agreed," he said as he walked back to the table. "However, if you withdraw from the operation for any reason, your demands will no longer be valid."

I accepted those conditions.

He wrote in the file and said, "Read this agreement, initial, and sign, and we'll proceed."

"I want a copy of it." I knew I was pushing it.

Donaldson was annoyed with my demands. "You'll have a copy by tomorrow. I will also leave the agreement for Mr. Morgan to sign." He handed me the documents.

I read it, initialed it, and signed it without hesitation.

* * *

Our meeting continued for hours. Agent Donaldson explained that an organization known as Gemini had appeared on their radar approximately two years ago. It began with a few anomalies, such as money laundering and gang connections, but now it had grown, and the agency feared the company could be very destructive and dangerous once it started operating internationally. Their intel also showed it could be involved in terrorism and illegal firearms.

They hadn't officially confirmed who the Gemini organization was or who its leader was. However, their information did point to one company and its owner.

"All the information we have to identify the Gemini leader points to Frank Ronan." Donaldson paused and waited for my reaction.

I couldn't speak.

He continued. "Ronan and his firm were red-flagged not long after his marriage to your aunt. Unfortunately, at the time, we didn't have enough information to proceed. This is why we approached you two years ago, to prepare you if and when the situation developed."

I couldn't believe what I was hearing. Frank. The love of my aunt's life.

"Is my aunt in danger? Does she know?" I was frantic.

"Our sources believe your aunt is unaware of what is happening. Therefore, under no circumstances will she be informed of the situation. It would put both your aunt and the operation in danger. However," he continued, "you have my word that if there is any danger, we'll get her out immediately."

I sat slumped in my chair. My head was spinning. "If someone is watching them, why do you need me?" I asked.

"We hoped to have another operative for this mission. However, we now feel you are the only one who can get close enough without suspicion. Ms. Kane, this is what you trained for."

"Who was the other operative?" I asked.

"That person is now a liability," he said abruptly. He quickly continued. "We know Ronan and your aunt will be arriving on the island soon and staying with you for a short time. Have they indicated why?" he asked.

"My aunt said Frank is doing business here, and his law firm is renting a house, but my aunt insisted she wanted them to stay with family for a few days before moving into the rental property."

"Thanks to your aunt insisting on staying with you, we now have a small window of opportunity," he explained. "Our intel indicates the Gemini organization will merge with a foreign company while they are on the island. *It is critical this doesn't happen.* Our information also tells us Ronan has already hired a high-tech security team for the rental property to set up security before his arrival. They will search for anyone entering the premises; therefore, placing monitoring devices prior to them moving into the rental house is out of the question. The devices will need to be placed once they have moved in, which will be the second phase of the operation."

"Second phase? What's the first phase?" I asked.

"Here's where our small window of opportunity comes into play. While Ronan stays with you, you must insert this into his laptop." He handed me a small USB thumb drive. "We've installed spyware on it, and you must plug it into his computer while it's on. The spyware will help us gather most of the data we need."

I wanted reassurance about their plan. "How sure is the agency that Frank is the leader of this Gemini?" I asked.

"Our information is incomplete as the organization is very secure, and we have limited time to act. We need to get into Ronan's network before he enters the rental house. Until then, we can neither confirm nor deny his position. However, illegal activities are occurring within his company, and our information regarding Gemini is pointing to him."

Agent Donaldson explained the thumb drive would only take five minutes to upload the malware. I kept telling myself I would only need to access his computer for a short time.

Donaldson said he would give me a few days while Frank was staying with me to complete the task, then he would contact me to confirm if I was successful.

I felt conflicted about not telling Auntie Ell. She had already had her sister lie to her throughout most of their lives, and possibly Frank, and now me. But I knew I had to do this. I made Donaldson give his word again that if there were even a hint of trouble that he would get my aunt out, no matter what.

"In the second phase of the operation, you will have to be invited to stay with them. Would that be a problem?" he asked.

I hesitated for a moment. Then I said, "No, I don't think so."

Donaldson continued laying out the operation. "Once you have secured an invitation to stay, you'll meet with an operative who will slip you a pen at a pre-arranged drop-off location before you enter the house. We have a replica of Frank's pens. The top section of the pen is hollow and will screw off to place a listening device in the space. Our information also reveals that the wine cellar is secure and a possible meeting place. Therefore, you will also be issued a second listening device to plant in the cellar. The device will have a stronger signal to penetrate the rock foundation."

My head was spinning with all the information, but Donaldson kept talking.

"The devices will be color-coded. Silver for the pen to go into his office, and brown for the cellar. The brown device will include special tape to attach it under a table or wine rack," he said.

"We cannot risk you entering the property with the devices, and our research indicates that using the exclusive bay at the back of the residence is the most secure alternative. As a result, once you've been invited to stay, we'll schedule a time and location for you to collect the dead drops from the water."

When I told Donaldson that when I paddleboarded, I always had a ChapStick wedged between the strap and my ankle, he thought they would use a fake ChapStick to relay the listening devices.

On my first morning at the rental house, I needed to paddle out a set distance, stop, and rest with my legs dangling in the water while a diver surfaced beneath me to swap my ChapStick for the fake one. Then, I had to hide it until I could place both items inconspicuously in Frank's office and the cellar.

"Ms. Kane, this is what we trained you for."

I reflected on my basic training. It included hand-to-hand combat, weapons training, lock-picking, and executing a dead drop. There was nothing in my training that prepared me for manipulating computers, placing listening devices, and spying on my aunt and her husband.

Donaldson informed me the agency had rented the house next to Frank's, which was reassuring.

We finished reviewing everything in the late afternoon, and I was mentally exhausted. And I still had to face Erick, which scared me.

When they all left, I pulled out a frozen lasagna for dinner. There was no way I was cooking. I made sure there were cold beers in the fridge for Erick, as I knew we would be having a difficult conversation tonight. Then I rang him and asked what time he would be home.

"In about an hour. Is the painting finished?" he asked.

I assured him it was.

I sat and watched the clock, drinking a glass of wine and staring out at the ocean through the back screen door. I was lost in my thoughts when Erick arrived.

"Hey, why are you sitting in the dark?"

Erick turned on the light, and I squinted at the sudden brightness. "I didn't realize," I said.

"What's wrong? Did the painters mess up?"

Since he had been working with Adam and Mitch, Erick always came home happy. Sometimes it was a little annoying.

I felt I was losing my courage fast and gulped the remainder of my wine.

"You're starting to scare me, Ally. What's wrong?" Erick asked as he pulled the other chair over and sat opposite me.

Without saying a word, I stood up and walked to the fridge, poured myself more wine, got Erick a beer, returned to him, and kissed him. "You're going to need this," I said as I handed him the beer and settled back in my chair.

"Darling, we need to talk, but first, I want you to know I love you more than anything, so please don't leave me." I let out a long sigh. Then I told him my secret.

CHAPTER FIFTY-SEVEN

Erick

Erick sat listening to Ally, unable to move. He thought it was a bad joke, but from the intensity on her face, he knew it wasn't.

Was Ally getting involved with the agency because of what he and her mother put her through?

Anger ran through his body, followed by a sick feeling in the pit of his stomach. *The agency would always have its claws in us,* he thought. Would they ever break free from its grasp?

When Ally finished explaining, Erick begged her to call it off. But she kept saying how important it was and how the agency had given her permission to tell him only the basics. Still, she felt she had to inform him of everything, and he needed to sign the agreement and not tell anyone else, not even Adam.

"I know the rules, Ally. I lived with them for most of my life."

Heated discussions, more beers, and wine continued for hours. Then, finally, they stopped going around in circles. Erick wanted to wipe his hands of it all. He had left the agency behind and never wanted to get involved with them again. He had already lost his brother to them, and he had nearly lost Ally more recently.

But when he looked at Ally, he could see the stress on her beautiful face, and the same old feeling hit him. She was the love of his life, and he would do anything for her, even sign the agency's agreement.

They both fell silent.

Finally, Ally spoke. "I need you to understand how this all happened."

She saw him roll his eyes.

"Please don't. Let me explain." She sighed. "I'm not blaming anyone, and it's not an excuse, but please listen to me." Ally was pleading.

"Okay, explain." He was frustrated.

Ally took another sip of her wine and tried to steady her trembling voice. "When you and Eva disappeared, I didn't know what to do. I was heartbroken, lost, and very alone," she said. "I kept thinking, what did I do that was so terrible it would drive my mother and the man I loved away? I wondered what the agency had that was more powerful and addictive than being with someone you love. Why did you both choose the agency over me?

"So when the agency came to me, and *they* came to me, I thought it was my chance to find out what the addiction was, what felt so great to be a part of it. I went along with it to try to understand. I did the basic training, and never heard from them again, leaving me feeling even more rejected. I didn't get the same feeling you two must have had, so I put it all behind me. I realize now the agency was preparing me for this."

Erick leant forward in his chair. "What I'm finding hard to comprehend is why this agency keeps coming after your family. I know how I got involved, but why your mother and now you?" he asked.

"Eva came highly recommended by her uncle, and, well, I am my mother's daughter, and I can get close to Frank. If he hadn't married Ell, I wouldn't be involved," she said.

"I find it hard to believe Frank is the head of this organization. Are they certain that Ell's not in danger?"

"She could be. Which is why I have to do this." Ally added.

Erick felt conflicted. He understood what Ally was saying, but he was still angry.

"I will do this with or without your approval, Erick," Ally said. "But I would like your support."

He looked at the beautiful face in front of him, the face he had fallen in love with at first sight. He adored everything about her, even how she drooled in her sleep.

"I'm as mad as hell, Ally, but I will never leave you. You have my support, but I won't condone what you are about to do. God, this has to be the only time."

Ally let out a sigh of relief. "It will be," she assured him.

Erick stood up. "I need a shower."

"What about us?" Ally called after him.

"We'll get through this, but I need time to process it," he said without turning around.

CHAPTER FIFTY-EIGHT

Ally

Even though Erick said he would support me, his mood changed daily. He grunted at me at times and asked me the same questions again and again. We kept having the same discussion, where he wanted to plant the malware on Frank's computer for me, but I kept refusing. I didn't want him to get involved. It took Erick a long time to get away from the agency, and there was no way I would let him get back in its grasp.

When Ell and Frank arrived, Erick did a great act, thank goodness. To them, everything was normal.

I don't know if I was looking for something or whether there was a little tension between my aunt and Frank. They seemed happy, although when Auntie Ell wasn't looking, I watched her and saw sorrow in her eyes. Frank had stopped calling her "darling." He was more formal, calling her Eloise. His demeanor had also changed. There was a coldness about him now, and I felt he was looking down his nose at us. When I asked her if Frank seemed different, she said he had a large project he was working on with many people depending on him.

When they arrived, I couldn't take my eyes off Frank's computer, waiting for the right moment to get my hands on it. It was making me anxious. Erick noticed this, which only made him moodier toward me.

When the opportunity finally arrived, it was the day of the dinner party. Erick was at work, and I was setting up. Megan had left the twins with us to watch as she did some shopping. Auntie Ell was in her element, playing with the boys in the shaded area of my back deck in their playpen.

Frank and I were in the kitchen. I was preparing the food while Frank worked at the end of the kitchen bench. Auntie Ell called out to him to bring her some water. Without saying a word, he got a bottle of water from the fridge and headed out to the deck, leaving his computer open.

At first, I froze. I had been carrying the thumb drive around for days, waiting for Frank to leave his computer unattended.

I looked outside and saw him giving her the water, then he sat next to her. She picked up one of the twins and put him on Frank's lap. I quickly grabbed the drive out of my pocket and inserted it into his computer's USB port, then casually placed a tea towel on the table to cover it. I needed a clear five minutes. I thought if I took photos of the two of them with the boys, it would give me the time needed to delay Frank from returning to the kitchen. I grabbed my cell phone and went into the yard.

"How about some photos of you two with the twins?"

"No, I don't think so," Frank grumbled.

"Please, darling," Ell pleaded. "They're our great-nephews, and I want them to have photos of us with them. They grow up fast."

Frank surrendered to the idea, and I slowly took the photos. It took a little while as I spent as much time as I could trying to "get the perfect shot."

Then one of the twins spat up on Frank.

"Enough," he declared, passing the baby back to Ell.

"Stay there, I'll get some water," I said. Before he could answer, I was heading for the kitchen.

My heart was racing a thousand times a minute as I reached the computer and moved the towel.

The download was complete.

I quickly took out the thumb drive, placed it in my pocket, and got another water from the fridge to give to Frank.

As I got to the back door, he was already there.

"Here you go," I said, handing him his drink and a towel to sponge the spit-up off his shirt. I turned back to the counter. Without looking at him, I asked, "If you want to change your shirt, I can wash it for you." I was sure he was staring at me, and I wasn't game to check.

He walked up to his computer, looked at it briefly, closed the lid, picked it up, and moved toward the bedroom. He said, "My shirts are dry cleaned. I'll have someone take care of it."

As he disappeared into the bedroom, I slowly let out the breath I had been holding. I was proud of myself for completing my first task. Phase one was complete. Now all I had to do was wait.

CHAPTER FIFTY-NINE

Our dinner party was a big hit. It had been hours since the phone call with Agent Donaldson, and I was still feeling energized. After watching our guests drive away, I looked for Erick and found him sitting on the back step in the cool evening breeze, drinking another beer. I sat next to him and put my head on his shoulder and looked up at the clear sky overflowing with stars. The only sounds came from the waves softly washing onto the shore.

"That was the agency before, wasn't it?" Erick asked.

"Shh, keep your voice down," I abruptly said as Auntie Ell came out the back door behind us.

"It was a wonderful evening catching up with everyone, but Frank and I are exhausted, so we're off to bed."

"Good night," we replied, and I watched over my shoulder as she walked back into the house.

Erick grabbed another beer from the ice cooler and opened it.

"Another beer?" I asked, getting irritated.

Erick turned and glared at me. He had been unhappy with me for days but had concealed it from others around us. "Are you going to answer my question?" he asked.

I pulled my arm out from his and whispered, "Yes, it was."

"Geez, Ally," Erick said as he grabbed yet another beer from the ice cooler, got up off the step, and walked toward the water's edge.

I followed him. "What do you want me to say? We've discussed this more than once." I was getting impatient with him. "You know what I have to do. There's no other option," I said.

"There *are* options. You could have said no and let someone else handle it," Erick yelled.

"And as I have told you before, no one can get as close as I can," I pointed out again.

"When you agreed to this, did you stop and think about how this could affect our family? No, you didn't."

Trying to get my point across again, I said, "And if I don't do this, it *will* affect our family. You know I would do anything to protect them."

"Let me do it. I know what I'm doing," Erick begged.

"We have discussed this, and there is no way you're getting involved with the agency again," I said, finding it difficult to stay calm.

"Look, it's different for me. It's only this one case, and I'm out, but the agency would keep you in for who knows how long. Besides, I can get closer."

He drained the bottle of beer he was drinking, tossed it on the sand, opened the other, and started drinking again.

I was tired of going over the same argument with him, and I was losing my patience. "It will be okay. I'm going in, doing what I need to, then leaving."

He gave a short, condescending laugh.

"Look, darling, I know you're scared for me," I said. "But it will be fine. I'm not worried."

He looked out over the water, not saying anything for a few seconds, then he turned back to me. "I admit this operation scares me, but you know what scares me the most. You can't wipe away the excitement and the happiness from your face. You've been smiling since you got the call, and that, my sweet darling Ally, scares the hell out of me." Erick didn't wait for my reply. He bent down, picked up the empty bottle he had tossed on the sand, then went back to the house, disappearing inside.

Watching him walk away, I was a little shocked by what he had said, but then I realized he was right. My body was tingling with excitement, and I hadn't tried to hide the smile on my face this whole time. Part of me wished I hadn't told Erick. I thought I was doing the right thing, but now I regretted it.

I stood with the cold water washing over my feet for a while, gazing up at the beautiful night sky and inhaling the ocean air, then I slowly walked back to the house.

Inside the house was silent, and Erick was already in bed, lying on his side, asleep.

I got into bed next to him and lay on my back. He didn't stir. "Very softly, I asked, "Are you asleep?"

There was no answer.

"Are you pretending to be asleep?"

Still no answer.

I sighed, whispered, "I love you," and closed my eyes.

After a few seconds, Erick reached back and held my hand in his.

CHAPTER SIXTY

The next morning, Auntie Ell awkwardly explained how Frank was eager to get into the rental house and would be leaving that morning instead of when planned. I was a little suspicious, so I waited a few days before I phoned her and asked if she wanted a visitor. She was glad to hear from me and immediately invited me over. She said she was lonely and needed the company, and I was only too happy to oblige.

When I reached their driveway, a security guard with a list of names stopped me at the front gate. He asked me to step out of my car and scanned me with an electronic wand while another security guard used an electronic device to look under and in my vehicle. Once given the all-clear, I drove to the mansion's front entrance, where a valet took my car keys to park my car.

Standing in the middle of the enormous wooden front doors was a woman in her late forties who came to greet me.

"Ms. Kane, I'm Ming, the house manager. Mrs. Ronan is on the patio. Please, follow me," she said.

As I followed Ming through the large foyer, I was amazed at the beautiful, big open rooms. There were extensive living and dining areas, which featured open floor-to-ceiling sliding-glass doors to enjoy the view. It was very elegant, and I felt I was visiting royalty.

Auntie Ell met me before I got to the patio. Her arms were open wide, and she hugged me as if we hadn't seen each other for years. I noticed her eyes were puffy as if she had been crying.

"I'm glad you're here."

"Is everything okay?" I asked her.

"Everything is fine."

We walked toward the patio. It had a large dining table in an undercover area.

"This place is amazing," I said as we sat down. I couldn't take my eyes off the rectangular infinity swimming pool. When I looked over it, I could see the calm blue water of the bay.

My aunt looked sad. "I guess. It's too big for me. I'm having trouble getting used to it."

I leant over and put my hand on hers. "Have you told Frank this?"

"I mentioned it. He said I could get an assistant or companion to help with things, but I'm uncomfortable with a stranger. There are already too many changes."

I heard a familiar voice behind me, and Frank appeared, dressed in a three-piece suit. "Ally, your aunt has been looking forward to you visiting."

"It's always great to see her. How are you settling in?" I asked him. "I'm sure the scenery is a little different from what you're used to."

"Yes, it is. Unfortunately, I'm too busy to enjoy it, which leaves my darling wife alone." He paused for a moment. "I've told Eloise to hire an assistant or companion. What about you? You could be Eloise's companion. It would make her happy to have you around. You could move in and stay until she's more comfortable here."

Before I could reply, Frank's brother, Sean, approached us. He stood hunched over as if carrying the world's weight on his shoulders. When Frank saw him, he rolled his eyes.

"Hello," Sean said. "Nice to see you, Ally. How have you been?"

Before I could answer him, Frank spoke up. "Ally is going to be Eloise's companion," he said without looking at his brother.

"Frank, Ally has her own life and job," my aunt snapped. "She's a teacher. She has responsibilities."

"Of course. I would pay you, but it's up to you two. But I think it's the perfect solution. Inform me of your decision before leaving." He kissed his wife's cheek and walked off with Sean trailing behind.

Ell looked embarrassed. "Frank shouldn't have asked you. He can't expect you to leave Erick and your job because it'll make me happy."

She looked vulnerable. It was a side of her I had not seen before.

"Auntie Ell, what's going on? You don't seem yourself."

"It's a big adjustment, and we don't know how long this merger will take. I guess I'm a bit overwhelmed." She looked as if she was about to break down.

"Has Frank been ..." I tried to pick my words carefully. "Difficult?"

"I've seen a different side of him. I feel as if everything he says to me is a command," she confessed. "And how he speaks to Sean reminds me of how the Colonel spoke to Uncle Mike, making me miss my sis ..." She stopped talking.

"Your sister?" I asked.

"At times, I miss her very much."

"I miss her at times too." It was the first time I had confessed that to anyone, even myself. "Well," I said, "I've been thinking about taking time off from teaching, and it's coming up to school break anyway, plus some space from Erick wouldn't hurt."

"Darling, I hope you two aren't having problems."

"No. Erick's great. He's enjoying his job and flying, and I'm pleased he found a job he's passionate about, but I don't see much of him."

As she watched me, I felt I needed to explain more.

"I'm happy for him, but I want that same feeling in something I do," I explained.

My aunt kept staring.

"I know what you're going to say. I was the one who decided to give up dancing and go into teaching, but I didn't realize I would be a teacher for so long. And, yes, I can hear Dad saying, 'Well, Alexandria, it was your decision."

"Are you still teaching ballet on a Saturday?" she asked.

"No. Donna sold the studio. She did ask me if I wanted to buy it, but I don't have my certification. Lately, I've been thinking I want to teach dance to underprivileged children. Maybe this is my opportunity to take a break from work and consider getting my qualification. So, I have options, but until I decide, I'm all yours."

"What are you saying?" she asked, clearly trying to contain her excitement.

"I'm saying I will come and be your companion for a little while. Besides, it will be great hanging out with you."

My aunt gasped. "Are you sure? Do you need to talk to Erick first?"

"I'm sure. Besides, Erick will be okay when he hears it's for you. He'd do anything for you."

She squealed with delight, got up, and threw her arms around me. "Darling, you being here will make things much happier. Let's have lunch first, then I'll show you around before we tell Frank."

And without trying, I was in Frank's inner circle.

* * *

The property was stunning. Set amidst a tropical garden on one-and-a-half acres of land was a two-story main home and a one-story guest home. Auntie Ell, Frank, and his brother Sean resided in the main house. Frank's office was off the large foyer downstairs, with a view of the bay. Adjacent to the dining room was a gourmet kitchen featuring off-white marble countertops, top-of-the-line appliances, and beautiful light-colored oak cabinetry. A baby grand piano stood at the base of the sweeping staircase in the foyer. I smiled and thought of Auntie Ell playing it. Each of the five bedrooms upstairs had its own ensuite with lovely outdoor views of the courtyard and bay. The primary bedrooms included his-and-hers sinks, a jacuzzi, and even a flat-screen television.

The Hawaiian chef, Anna, and the house manager both came in every day, and Frank's security staff stayed in the guest house.

A few doors from the primary suite, Auntie Ell opened the door to another bedroom. "I think this is the prettiest room," she said.

It had silvery gray walls and a king-size bed covered in a pastel floral design. The bedroom led out to a lanai looking over the bay that was big enough for a small table and two chairs. The bathroom was soft gray and pale pink, with fluffy towels in abundance. It was bigger than my bedroom at home.

"Do you like it? This will be your room," she said.

I hugged her. "I love it."

"We're going to have a lot of fun!" My auntie was practically bursting with excitement.

She led me back downstairs, continuing the tour. She pointed to the closed wooden door to Frank's office. Opposite was another wooden door that led to the wine cellar. The cellar wasn't locked, and when she opened the door and flicked the lights, I could see the rock walls and spiral brownstone stairs leading down. It was spacious, but dark and cold with a musty smell. A small redwood table, which would be a perfect spot to place the listening device under, was in the middle of the room, surrounded by racks and racks of every wine and champagne you could imagine. Although it was impressive, I felt rather confined.

We went to see Frank upstairs again. He was sitting behind a big oak desk in his office, and Sean was seated at a smaller desk close by. Like kids in the principal's office, we stood in front of Frank, hoping he would notice us.

Finally, she said, "Darling," and we waited for him to acknowledge our presence.

He looked up from his computer.

"Ally has decided to come and stay with us," she informed him.

"Good. It's nice to have family that is willing to help." He glared at his brother, and Sean lowered his head.

The atmosphere in the room was very uncomfortable.

I spoke up. "I'll go home to do a few things, pack a bag, then come back in the morning."

"I'll send a car for you," Frank said. It was a statement rather than an offer.

"It's okay. I'll have my car here, and I can bring my paddleboard," I said.

"It's unnecessary, we have paddleboards. Paka takes care of the sporting equipment. Tell him what you need."

I was about to insist when Frank looked up and gave us a chilling stare. "Let me make it very clear so there is no miscommunication. Your car is not required; you and Eloise will use a driver while we're here. It's not negotiable."

Frank's words stunned me, and I had trouble finding the correct response.

"Okay, I'll let Auntie Ell know tonight what time, and you can arrange a driver."

"Good," he said, and he returned to his work. We were both dismissed.

"Are you sure you want to do this? I understand if you've changed your mind," she said after we had left the office.

I placed my arm around her. "It'll be fun. Wait and see."

A sense of remorse flooded over me as I considered my major reason for being there. But when I glanced at my aunt, I noticed I had never seen her appear so frail, and I knew she would need me here regardless.

As I drove away from the house, my anxiety grew as I realized I had to tell Erick.

CHAPTER SIXTY-ONE

I had arranged with Agent Donaldson to stop at the grocery store near home when I left the mansion. It was the same store where Erick and I had met. As I strolled up and down the aisles selecting food for Erick and Blossom to eat while I was away, a man I had never seen before came up to me and said, "Excuse me, I'm shopping for my aunt. Is this a good fabric softener?"

That was the code. My reply would give Donaldson the information he needed.

If I had succeeded, I would say "yes" to the fabric softener, the agent would know to drop the special pen in my bag, and I would proceed as planned. If I were negative, they would know I wasn't in yet.

So, when asked about fabric softener, I said, "Yes, it's a great product." The agent thanked me and placed it in his basket, slipping the pen into my handbag before he continued shopping.

When I got home and unpacked the groceries, I changed our bed sheets, as I knew Erick wouldn't do it while I was away, and I put on a load of laundry. I wanted to make everything easy for Erick while I was gone; I thought maybe it would help him take the news better.

I was folding clothes and packing a bag in our bedroom when Erick showed up.

"Ally," he called out.

"In the bedroom," I shouted back.

Erick stood at the doorway. "Going somewhere?"

"Auntie Ell wants me to stay with her for a while. She's finding the move and the house overwhelming. She and Frank asked if I could be her companion for a bit. I didn't think you would mind. You've been busy with work lately. Besides, it's not far away, and you could come over anytime." I was rambling.

Erick sat on the bed and looked at me with a raised eyebrow.

I felt the need to keep explaining. "As I said, she feels overwhelmed, and I think she needs someone with her."

"I know. Frank rang and told me."

I stopped folding. "What?"

"Yeah, he said he was very grateful to me for '*letting*' you come and stay with Eloise."

"'*Letting* me' as if I have to get your permission?" I was astounded.

"Yeah. I thought it was a little weird."

"What did you say to him?" I asked.

"I told him the truth. You don't need my permission to do anything, and we both would do anything for Ell." He put his hand on mine. "To be honest, I was surprised how fast you got in."

"I know. And it was Frank's idea." I stopped and thought for a moment. "Do you think he knows?"

"*Now* you're asking for my opinion?" Erick said sarcastically.

His comment annoyed me, and I pulled my hand away. "Forget it."

Erick got to his feet. As I watched him leave the room, he said, "I'm going for a run before dinner."

We decided to eat dinner on the back deck. Spaghetti bolognese and salad, one of Erick's favorite meals. The warm sun slowly disappeared, and a cool sea breeze surrounded us.

We were eating in awkward silence when Erick said, "No, I don't."

"You don't what?" I asked.

"I don't think Frank knows."

"Thank you, that's good to hear."

"Ally, I will keep asking you this until it's all over, so don't get mad, and don't do the eyebrow-raising thing you do every time I ask. Are you sure about this?"

Reaching over, I took his hand in mine. "Yes, I'm sure."

"I want us to have a safe word. If you need me and can't say it, text or call me and say the word, and I'll come running." He looked and sounded concerned.

"Sure, if it makes you feel more at ease."

"It will." His face relaxed a little. "It should be an everyday word that wouldn't raise suspicion."

"What about pizza?"

"Pizza is good," he replied.

Then a wave of panic suddenly hit me. "Auntie Ell's going to hate me if she finds out, isn't she?"

Erick sighed as he stood up and cleared the empty plates. "Think of it this way, my darling. How well did you take it when you learnt about your mother and me?" He kissed me and walked into the kitchen.

I sat there, unable to move. She would end up hating me, and I couldn't do anything about it.

* * *

Later in the evening, as Erick and I sat close together on the back deck looking at the stars, I phoned my auntie to organize the car to pick me up in the morning. I was terrified, but I would never tell Erick.

"Part of me hoped you would change your mind," he said, heading into the house.

Following him inside, I took a slow look around my small home. My father bought the house for me with my mother's insurance money when Adam entered the Air Force. I missed my dad, and I was surprised to realize how much I missed my mother.

I told my brother that I would be staying with Auntie Ell for a few weeks. I had already informed Bernie that I was taking leave from work, but I needed to contact Cassie and Donna, which I planned to do tomorrow. Tonight, though, I craved Erick holding me.

I went into the bedroom, and he was already in bed watching TV with Blossom curled up beside him. I changed and snuggled in next to them. I waited for a few minutes before saying anything. The last thing I needed tonight was another fight or the cold-shoulder treatment.

"I'm a bit nervous," I finally admitted aloud.

Erick put his arm around me and pulled me close. "You're the love of my life, Ally, don't ever forget it."

We stayed in each other's arms all night. It felt safe, and I wondered when I would feel this safe again.

* * *

Morning came quickly, and Erick surprised me with breakfast in bed. He had decided to stay with me until the car arrived. We sat on the couch, his arm around me as if we were waiting for bad news.

A knock on the front door startled us. When I opened it, a man with a gentle smile stood there, dressed in a black suit, white shirt, and black tie. He was around fifty, with dark hair graying at the temples.

"Ms. Kane, I'm Andrew, Mrs. Ronan's driver. I'm here to pick you up. Can I take your bags?"

Erick was by my side and handed the bags to Andrew, who loaded them into the car.

Erick hugged me tight and whispered, "It's not too late. You could stay."

Part of me wanted to stay right there in his arms, but the thought of Auntie Ell in the house alone with Frank made me cringe.

"It will be fine. *I* will be fine and be home before you know it." I think I was trying to convince myself more than him. I reached up and gave Erick a long, passionate kiss. "Something to hold you over till I see you next."

Walking toward the black BMW, Andrew already had the back door open. As the car drove off, I noticed Erick trying his best to force a smile. He wasn't successful.

CHAPTER SIXTY-TWO

The drive took twenty minutes. Twenty minutes of silence. My mind raced the whole time, going over what I had to do without getting caught and without my aunt hating me in the end.

When I finally arrived at the house, Auntie Ell was waiting for me at the front door. She ran up and hugged me tightly; I didn't think she would let me go.

"Darling, I'm thrilled you're here." She finally stopped hugging me. "Let me take you to your room." She hooked her arm in mine and led me up the grand staircase.

"My bags," I said, turning to get them.

"Andrew will bring them up," Ming said. She had seemingly appeared out of nowhere.

As she led me upstairs, I noticed Kyle, one of the security guards, checking my bags with an electric wand. My heart skipped a beat even though I knew they wouldn't find anything in there.

Auntie Ell had put fresh flowers in my room.

"It's perfect. You know this room is bigger than my house," I joked.

"Wonderful. Now come downstairs and see Frank, and I'll introduce you to the staff." Once again, she took my arm. It was as if she didn't want me to escape.

Frank was on the telephone when we entered his office, and he waved us off.

Chef Anna inquired about the type of food I preferred, then she informed us she had prepared a chicken salad for lunch and would serve it outside. We walked out to the patio overlooking the beautiful bay.

"Will Frank and Sean be joining us for lunch?" I asked.

"I'm not sure. Frank's been very busy," she replied.

Behind us, I heard Frank's voice, "Now, Eloise, I wouldn't miss Ally's first lunch working for me."

His comment made the hair on my arms stand on end. I managed a smile and said, "Anything for Auntie Ell."

He kissed her on the cheek, and she cringed slightly, surprising me. Frank pulled out Ell's chair at the table and sat next to her, pointing for me to sit opposite him. Sean appeared and was instructed to sit next to me.

As Sean sat down, Frank asked, "Did you finish what I asked you to do?"

"It's all taken care of," Sean replied.

There was an uncomfortable silence.

"So, Frank, do you have any instructions for me while I'm here?" I joked, trying to break the silence.

"Take care of Eloise and keep her out of trouble." He was harsh when he said it, and again, I was lost for words. Then he laughed. "You're so serious, Ally. Be supportive and help Eloise get settled, then we'll see."

"Easy," I replied. Then I turned to Sean. "How are you liking it here?"

Sean looked up. "It's very nice. I've always wanted to visit the islands with my family but never got around to it." He caught Frank's eye and fell silent.

I tried to keep the conversation going, but it was challenging. Auntie Ell asked me how Erick and Adam were and commented on how the twins had grown. I asked her if there was anything she wanted to do while I was staying with them. Before she could reply, Frank immediately informed us we had to get his approval before leaving the premises for security reasons and reminded us we were not to go anywhere without her driver, Andrew.

The table fell silent again. I was about to say something when Frank spoke up.

"Both of you, must take a walk along the beach." It was another order. He got up from the table, kissed her, and walked off with Sean in tow.

Auntie Ell said, "Yes, let's go for a walk."

Before I knew it, she was up from the table and heading to the sand.

"Is Frank serious about checking with him before we go anywhere?" I asked.

"He didn't mean to make it sound so strict. He wants to make sure the driver is available for us. We can go anywhere," she said, dismissing it as if it were nothing.

We strolled along the beach chatting, the warm sand shifting between our toes. I wanted to ask her so many questions but didn't want to upset things on my first day.

"Do you think we can catch up with the girls?" she asked me.

"Of course. Donna and Anton are away, but the other two would want to see you. Do you want me to ask them over or—"

Before I could finish my question, Auntie Ell jumped in. "No, let's go out somewhere fun. Yes, let's get away from here."

I reached out and took her hand. "I'll phone them when we get back to the house and set it up."

My aunt seemed happy.

CHAPTER SIXTY-THREE

It was a beautiful morning. I woke at six o'clock as the warm sun started hitting the water. The night before I had told Frank I was going paddleboarding in the morning. I planned to sneak out early as I had to be on the water waiting for the delivery by seven.

When I got to the area with the sporting equipment, Paka was already waiting for me. He startled me at first.

"Morning, miss."

"Good morning. You didn't have to get the board out for me. I would have done that." I said, removing my shorts and T-shirt, which were covering my black one-piece swimsuit. Fastening the bungee strap, I placed the ChapStick between it and my ankle.

Paka offered to take the board to the water's edge for me, but I declined. I picked up the board and headed into the water.

The ocean was calm and a little cold. When I reached the correct depth, I stood up and began paddling. Looking over my shoulder, I saw Paka on the beach watching me. Chills ran through my body, and it wasn't because of the temperature. But all I could do was keep paddling until I got to what I hoped was the right spot, then sit down and look like I was resting.

I paddled for around twenty minutes. After determining that I was in the proper position, I sat on the board with my legs hanging in the water. Looking back at the shore, I noticed Paka had moved on. Now all I had to do was wait.

Within minutes, I felt someone under the water at the bungee strap. I flinched at first, and the hand gently held on to my ankle. I could feel the diver taking the ChapStick and replacing it with another. Then I got three taps on my leg, signifying all was okay. I didn't see the diver arrive or leave. If anyone was watching from the shoreline, they wouldn't have known.

I stood back up on the board and started paddling again. I paddled around for about fifteen minutes, decided it was long enough, and headed for the shore.

When I reached the beach, Paka appeared out of nowhere, took the oar from me, and handed me a large beach towel. I bent down to pick up the board, but Paka got to it first.

"Oh, thanks. I'm not used to such service."

He didn't smile or acknowledge that I had spoken.

As I took off the bungee strap, I dropped the ChapStick, and Paka quickly picked it up. My heart skipped a beat.

I put my hand out for it and said, "Thanks. I never go out on the water without it. The saltwater dries my lips out."

He handed it to me without hesitation.

Wrapping myself in the beach towel and with the ChapStick clutched tightly in my hand, I picked up my clothes and headed for the house.

When I walked in, Frank and Auntie Ell were having breakfast on the patio.

"Did everything go well?" Frank inquired.

His words stopped me in my tracks. "Sorry?"

"Your paddle. Did Paka have everything prepared for you?" He wasn't even looking at me, too busy eating his eggs.

"Yes. I felt very spoilt having everything done for me."

"And did you enjoy it?" he asked, still eating his breakfast.

"The water's lovely at this time of the morning. I'll go and shower." I was eager to get to my room.

But I only took a couple of steps before Frank spoke again.

"Your aunt told me the two of you are meeting up with your friends today. Since Eloise is eager to go with you, I decided you ladies should have lunch at La Mer. I've organized a table for twelve-thirty, and the car will be ready to take you at eleven-thirty."

"Frank, that's very kind of you, but my friends and I can't afford La Mer. We were going to catch up at a little café …"

"This is my treat. Besides, I don't want my wife in some outdoor café," Frank said, looking over his coffee cup.

We locked eyes. I think he was waiting for me to challenge him.

Auntie Ell, sensing the tension, said, "It will be a wonderful day whatever we do."

"I'll change and call them with the news." I didn't wait for a response, but all the while, I could feel Frank's eyes on me. The urge to run up the stairs as fast as possible was great, but I had to make my actions look normal.

Reaching the second floor, I suddenly stopped when I saw Ming leaving my room.

Before I could ask her why she was there, she said, "Ms. Kane, I've made up your room and put a white robe on your bed to wear when you go swimming. Mr. Ronan suggested you wear it. I'll be downstairs if you require anything else."

Ming coming out of my room made my heart pound harder. As I entered my tidy room, I quickly locked the door and sat on my bed next to the robe. It took a second or two to calm myself, then I ensured the new ChapStick contained the two devices. Thank goodness it did. I went into the bathroom and put the stick into my makeup bag with my other lipsticks. I was a nervous wreck.

After my shower, I rang Cassie and Bernie, told them where we were going for lunch, and that we would pick them up at Cassie's house. I dried my hair, put on my navy-blue short-sleeved dress, and dabbed on a bit of makeup. Before leaving my room, I double-checked that the ChapStick was secure at the bottom of the makeup bag and headed downstairs.

As I reached the foyer, I saw Frank and Auntie Ell having a conversation on the patio. She was looking down, her head nodding while Frank firmly held his hand on her shoulder. They didn't see me at first, but when they did, Frank turned and headed for his office. My auntie turned away from me momentarily, then faced me with a fake smile.

"Darling, did you tell the girls we'd pick them up?" she asked me before I could ask her what had happened.

"Yes, they're looking forward to it. I told them we'd pick them up from Cassie's house."

"It'll be great to catch up with them," she said. "I know they're your friends, but I greatly enjoy their company."

I was about to ask her if everything was okay when Ming appeared out of nowhere.

"Mrs. Ronan, it's eleven-thirty, and the car is waiting." Ming walked directly to the front door and opened it.

"We can't keep the car waiting," my aunt said sarcastically as she picked up her handbag.

When we reached the door, Andrew was outside with the back door of the BMW open. He was finishing up a phone call. I thanked him as we got in, and he nodded, closed the door, and got into the driver's side.

"Andrew, we're picking up some friends first," I informed him.

"Would that be at Cassie's or Bernie's address?" he asked.

His question took me aback. "Cassie's. I'll give you the address—"

But before I could finish my sentence, Andrew said, "That's alright, Miss. I have both addresses."

"How do you have my friend's address?"

"It's on the information sheet from Mr. Ronan," he replied as he drove off.

I looked at my auntie, waiting for her to explain, but she was looking out the window.

"Why is Frank giving out my friends addresses?" I asked her.

"Everything is fine," she said, still not looking at me.

I was speechless. We drove the rest of the way in awkward silence.

CHAPTER SIXTY-FOUR

When we arrived at Cassie's, she and Bernie got in the car, and the mood changed from awkward to happy. We were like teenagers on a field trip, all talking at once. I noticed that Bernie didn't stop smiling.

When we got to the restaurant, the waiter showed us to a private table on the terrace and brought over a bottle of champagne. "Mr. Ronan ordered this," he said, filling our glasses. "Mr. Ronan has also selected this menu," he added, handing it over.

The ladies said how wonderful it was, but I knew Frank was controlling the lunch. I wanted to say, "We'll pick our own," but I saw how cheerful my aunt was, and I didn't want to embarrass her.

We all chatted as the waiter brought out our food and topped up our drinks, then my aunt asked Bernie if she was looking forward to her upcoming trip.

Bernie smiled again and cleared her throat. "Well, we're not going now."

There was a chorus of "Oh, no" and "Why?"

"I've been dying to tell you all but didn't want to jinx it. Some time ago, Michael and I applied to be foster parents, hoping to adopt. It's been something we've always wanted to do because Michael grew up in the foster system and wanted us to be good parents to kids who needed a family like he did. When we planned our trip, we hadn't heard anything in a while about it, but we found out last week that we've been accepted and we're getting two little girls, sisters Kaloe and Nakeli. Kaloe's the oldest," Bernie said. "It's killed me not being able to tell you all." She began to cry. "I'm happy and scared all at the same time."

We congratulated her, asked her about the girls, and raised our glasses. I knew she would be a great mother.

My aunt wanted to celebrate by shopping and buying something special for the kids. Bernie said it wasn't necessary, but I whispered to let my aunt do it as it would make her happy.

After lunch, Andrew drove us to a fancy children's store, where Auntie Ell bought a dollhouse for the little girls. When we left the shop, we saw Andrew holding the car door open.

"Andrew, we're not ready to go." I couldn't hold my tongue.

"Sorry, miss. Mr. Ronan messaged me to pick you up. I'll take your packages."

Before I could reply, he took our bags and put them in the car's trunk.

Auntie Ell was embarrassed and flustered. "We were having fun, I didn't realize the time," she said climbing into the car like an obedient wife.

In any other circumstances, I would have told Andrew to leave and that I would let him know when we were ready, but I had to be careful. I still had a job ahead of me and didn't want to make waves, so I got in the car. We dropped off Cassie and Bernie, and we drove back to the house in silence.

Two black Land Rovers drove out of the gate when we approached the driveway. I tried to see who was in them, but they had heavily tinted windows. Important guests. Maybe this is why Frank wanted us out of the house today.

Andrew let us out at the bottom of the stairs, and Ming was already waiting for us at the open front door. She took our bags and said she would put them in our rooms.

"I think I could do with a cup of tea," my aunt said.

I wanted to shake her and yell, "What is wrong with you?" but all I could say was, "I think I'll go for a swim."

When I arrived at my room, the first thing I did was check the ChapStick to make sure its contents were still there, and I let out a sigh of relief when I saw they were. I changed into my black swimsuit and robe and headed to the pool. Auntie Ell was sitting on the patio, sipping her tea.

The water always calmed me, and the repetitive strokes of swimming laps helped me think. It also burned off any anger that had been building up. I had to think with my head; otherwise, this could be dangerous for both of us. I needed to adapt to Frank's methods and begin considering how I would deploy the devices and gather the necessary information for the agency. Then, I could focus on my auntie.

I must have been in the pool for half an hour when I looked up and saw Ming on the edge of the pool with a towel and my robe in her hands.

"Mr. Ronan suggested you start getting ready for dinner, which is strictly at seven-thirty," she said.

As I got out of the pool, I snatched the towel from her, dried myself off, and put on the robe without saying a word to Ming, whom I had quickly come to dislike.

In my room, I felt sad and isolated. I needed to hear Erick's voice, so I called him after I got changed. He was home from work.

"Hey, beautiful," he said.

I wanted to cry and tell him to come over and hold me, but I had to be strong. "Hi, yourself. What are you up to?" I asked.

"Heard the great news about Bernie and Michael, so the guys are going out for burgers and beers to celebrate."

"That sounds wonderful," I replied, wishing I was going with him.

"What about you? I heard you had a very fancy lunch today," he said.

"We sure did." That was all I could say.

"You okay, honey? Do you need pizza? Because you know I can bring you some," he asked.

It took all my strength not to reply, "Yes, bring pizza," but I couldn't.

"No, it's fine. I miss you and wanted to hear your voice. Have fun tonight, and hug the boys for me," I said instead.

"Umm, I don't think I'll hug them, but I will tell them you send hugs." He added, "I can hear you smiling."

Whenever he told me that, it always made me smile more. "My hero. You have fun, and don't forget to feed Blossom before you go."

"Already done," he assured me.

I hung on a bit longer, listening to him breathe. But then I looked at my watch. "I must go. Dinner is strictly at seven-thirty, and I have to do something first."

"I'm not going to ask what. Just be careful and keep smiling. Love you," he said before hanging up.

I looked in the mirror again, practiced my fake smile, and walked quickly and quietly downstairs.

CHAPTER SIXTY-FIVE

Earlier, I had made a little hole in the inside hem of the dress I was wearing and slipped in the device. Once I reached the cellar undetected, I decided the table would be a good place. I took out the device and positioned it underneath the tabletop and waited for a minute to ensure it was secure.

"Can I help you?"

Hearing Ming's voice behind me, I jumped. "Do you have to always sneak up on people?" I was annoyed.

"Dinner is about to be served," she announced.

"I thought I'd pick a wine for dinner," I replied, wanting to explain why I was there.

"It's already been taken care of by Mr. Ronan," Ming said. She stood aside with her hand pointing up the stairs. "After you."

I was the first at the table and thought I would get in before Ming and tell Frank I was in the cellar before she could. Frank soon arrived with Auntie Ell on his arm.

"Frank, I went to the cellar to select a wine for dinner, but Ming said you'd already selected one."

"You don't need to concern yourself with wine selection," he said, his voice stern.

Before I could reply, Sean arrived and asked Frank if he could take a conference call after dinner. He excused himself, and they walked away.

"Let's sit," my aunt said, "the boys won't be long."

Dinner was great. Anna was an excellent chef. However, the conversation between the four of us was difficult. Auntie Ell talked about lunch and shopping. Sean, as usual, barely looked at anyone, while Frank pretended to listen.

The serving staff only topped up the wine glasses once. If they tried anything else, Frank would wave them off.

After dessert had been cleared, Auntie Ell tried to hide a yawn.

"You've had a big day, Eloise. You need to turn in early," Frank said. It sounded like another order.

"I will in a minute, darling. Are you going back to the office? You're working too hard."

"Don't you worry your pretty little head about it," he said.

Condescending bastard, I thought. Auntie Ell smiled as he and Sean headed for the office.

I looked at my auntie. "Are you happy?"

It took a moment for her to answer, and when she did, she sounded a little defensive. "Of course. Why would you ask that?"

"I'm concerned. I know this move has been an enormous change for you," I replied.

She sighed. "Yes, I'm happy, but also tired. I think I'll turn in." She got up from the table and kissed my cheek. "Thank you for today."

After she had left, I looked up at the stars and felt the cool evening breeze flow over me. I decided to plant the pen in the office that night once everyone was asleep.

"Do you want anything else, Ms. Kane?" Ming's words startled me again.

I wanted to yell, "Don't creep up on me," but instead politely said, "No, thank you," and went to my room.

I changed into my light-gray sweats and a long-sleeved pink top and sat on my little balcony off my bedroom in the dark for hours, watching the movement around the house and grounds below me. I watched as the house lights were switched off and the security guard patrolling the beach settled in a chair near the patio entrance.

When I heard Sean's and Frank's bedroom doors close, I knew it was time.

CHAPTER SIXTY-SIX

Standing at the top of the stairs, I stopped and listened for a few minutes. No noise. The house was quiet, and everyone had left or gone to bed except the security guard at the front gate and the guard patrolling the beach. I slowly tiptoed down the stairs. It reminded me of when I was little and crept out of my room at Christmas to see if Santa had been. When I reached the bottom of the landing, I quietly looked around the lower level before proceeding to Frank's office.

I checked the office door and, as I suspected, it was locked. Putting my ear to the door, I listened for voices inside but heard nothing.

In training, I found picking locks exciting, and I happened to be very good at it. I had the two small tools I needed in my bra and the pen holding the listening device inside my long-sleeved top. I took out the tools and carefully picked the lock. The door opened without any trouble, and I quickly popped my head in the door to check the room was empty. When I saw it was, I slipped inside and closed the door behind me.

When the door was securely closed, I noticed two security monitors in Frank's office. The monitors were of the beach and at the front entrance. I wondered when he had put those up. They weren't there the last time I was here. I watched the screens for a moment to ensure they didn't pick up anything in the office. They didn't. He was only concerned about those two areas. I would have to find the cameras in the morning and see if I could avoid them.

Once I was certain it was safe to proceed, I removed the pen from my sleeve and sought a spot to put it. Frank's desk was neat, except for a few files. I placed the pen next to the telephone, which seemed a logical position.

I quietly went to the door and looked back at the desk to ensure everything was in the same place as when I entered, and the pen wasn't noticeable. It had taken less than a few minutes, but my heart had raced the whole time.

Pausing, I listened before opening the door. Nothing. I slid carefully out of the room, then swiftly and gently shut it behind me and checked that it was locked.

As I started to move away, I heard Frank's voice.

"What are you doing at my office?" His face was red, and I thought he was going to explode.

"Oh, there you are. I was about to knock to see if you were still working. I'm making some herbal tea and thought you might like a cup." I was surprised at how fast I produced an answer.

He eyed me for what seemed like forever, my heart still pounding.

Frank walked over to his office door to check if the door was still locked. Then he looked me up and down, and said, "I'm going to bed, and you should as well."

"I'll get my tea first. Goodnight."

As I headed to the kitchen, Frank shouted, "Wait."

I froze in my tracks. I slowly turned to face him, ready to deny everything.

"You staying here has made your aunt very happy, and I want to thank you."

His words took me by surprise.

"As I said before, I would do anything for her," I replied.

He gave a strained smile and headed toward the staircase. I watched him walk up to his room, waiting until he had disappeared before I entered the kitchen to make the tea.

When I reached my room, I quickly closed the door. My heart was still pounding, and I could feel my anxiety building. I sat on the bed and stared at the door, waiting for Frank to burst into the room. All I could think about was Erick and how he would calm me down if he were here. I knew it was late, but I needed to speak to him.

His beautiful voice was music to my ears.

"I'm sorry I woke you," I said. Secretly, I wasn't.

"Is everything alright?" He sounded concerned.

"Yes, I wanted to hear your voice. I miss you."

"You must miss me. Two calls in one day. However, I must tell you I have a female next to me in bed."

I could tell he was joking and asked, "Oh, what does she look like?"

"She's got a lot of fur."

I imagined Blossom curled up next to Erick, which made my heart ache.

"Honey, are you sure everything's okay?" he asked again.

"Everything is fine. I miss you. Tell me about your night out with the boys." I climbed into bed as he told me about his evening. I was only half-listening to what he was saying, but his voice soothed me, and I could feel my eyelids getting heavy.

"Goodnight, sweetheart," Erick finally said.

"Goodnight, darling," I answered. I was asleep within seconds of hanging up the phone.

CHAPTER SIXTY-SEVEN

I had a restless night and woke up as the sun broke through the evening sky. I decided to go paddleboarding to look for confirmation that the devices I planted last night were working. Now that I knew there was a security camera on the beach, I would have to be cautious.

I hadn't told any staff I was going out, so Paka wasn't around to prepare the board for me. However, I preferred to do it myself.

Once I entered the cool water, I paddled out far enough to see the flagpole on the property next door. If the Hawaiian flag was at full mast, the devices worked, and the agents were receiving audio. If the flag wasn't up, we had a problem. If it was half-mast, I needed to go out the next day to receive further instructions.

When I saw the flag at full mast, I was so relieved, I fell off my board. I didn't care. The devices were working. I climbed back on the board and lay down, feeling the sun slowly warm my body.

When I finally paddled back to shore, Paka was on the sand waiting for me. He took the board without speaking or making eye contact. Putting on my robe, I walked up to the house. Frank and my aunt were already on the patio eating breakfast.

"You didn't inform us you were going paddleboarding this morning," Frank said.

"I only decided when I woke up this morning. Is that a problem?" I asked.

Frank rose from his chair, and moved toward me. "It's a safety issue. Don't let it happen again," he said, walking off.

Auntie Elle looked down at her plate, avoiding any eye contact.

"I'll remember for next time," I said.

Later that morning, I offered to deliver Frank and Sean's coffee to their office. I wanted to see if the pen was still in the same location. When I entered the office and approached Frank's desk, I was relieved to see the device was where I had left it.

CHAPTER SIXTY-EIGHT

The next morning, from the top of the sweeping staircase, I heard my aunt playing the baby grand piano. I grinned because I hadn't heard her play in a long time.

Unable to take my eyes off her, I descended the stairs and stood by the piano, watching my aunt, not wanting to disturb her. You could tell by the happiness on her face she had become one with the music. I understood that feeling. I used to feel the same way when I danced. In the middle of playing, my aunt glanced up and smiled. Then she motioned with her head for me to sit next to her. She never missed a beat.

I sat beside her. My eyes fixated on her hands gliding quickly and effortlessly over the piano keys. It was beautiful to watch. I gently lowered my head onto her shoulder, closed my eyes, and became immersed in her music. She made me forget why I was there.

Neither of us saw Frank leave his office until we heard him yell.

"Eloise, for God's sake, stop. How do you expect me to conduct business with that goddam noise in the background?" he shouted.

We were left speechless by Frank's cruel words. Frank returned to his office, slamming the door behind him.

My heart broke as I watched my aunt's hands recoil from the piano keys, as if she were a child being scolded for doing something wrong. She softly closed the piano lid.

I was angry and wanted to follow Frank and confront him for what he had said, but as if Auntie Ell had read my mind, she said, "Don't, Ally; leave it."

"I won't let him talk to you that way," I said, starting to stand up.

"Ally, I said leave it." She looked hurt. She must have noticed the look of fury on my face, as she gently placed her hand on my cheek and said, "Come, take a stroll along the beach with me. It's a beautiful day."

When we got to the sand and kicked off our shoes, I was still fuming. "Has Frank spoken to you that way before?"

She put her arm around my shoulders. "When you're angry, you look like your mother. You reminded me of her back there. Eva wouldn't let anyone say anything against my playing either."

I took it as a compliment, but I wasn't going to let it go. "You haven't answered my question. Does Frank—"

She wouldn't let me finish. "Frank is under a lot of pressure. He doesn't mean the things he says or does. This deal he's in the middle of is critical for his firm, and it's all on his shoulders." Then she changed the subject quickly before I could say anything else. "You know what I want? My family here for dinner. All the family together again. Yes, that's what I want," she said.

"And how will Frank feel about all the 'noise' around him?" I asked sarcastically.

"He'll love it. I guarantee it," she said as she powered on with our walk.

The incident was over for her, but it wasn't for me. I would wait for my chance to say something to Frank.

My opportunity arose later in the afternoon. Auntie Ell was in her room, and I was in the kitchen getting a bottle of water when Frank came in to refill his coffee cup. I ignored him at first.

"Eloise tells me the family is coming over for dinner soon. It should be enjoyable," he said, breaking the silence.

I couldn't hold my tongue. "I hope we don't make any 'goddamn noise' that disturbs you."

Frank stopped in his tracks and slowly turned to face me.

"I'm sorry for what I said. I regret my words."

"It's not me you should be apologizing to. Auntie Ell won't tell you, but your words hurt her."

"I know, and I have apologized to her, and I will make it up to her," he said.

I should have left it at that, but I couldn't. "My aunt means the world to me, and I will come after anyone who hurts her."

Frank leant over to me. A darkness surrounded him. Suddenly, I was afraid, but I forced myself not to show it.

"Are you threatening me?" he asked, a little amused.

"Take it however you want. My only concern is my aunt's safety and happiness."

Frank backed off a little, still staring at me with a nasty grin. "As I said, I will make it up to her. Eloise and I are going out to dinner tonight." Then he stepped in so close, I could smell his aftershave. "And I assure you, *niece*, your aunt will always be safe with me." He turned and left the kitchen.

I felt so intimidated that I was shaking. Some agent I was. I had to get out of the house to get some distance from Frank. I walked to the water's edge and ran as far as I could along the shoreline until I reached the stone-wall boundary. I collapsed on the sand, out of breath. I wanted to climb the wall to escape and tell the agents on the other side that I quit and wanted to go home. But all I could think about was my aunt playing the piano and how destroyed she had looked when her "loving" husband crushed her spirit. I couldn't leave her alone with him.

After I pulled myself together, I slowly strolled back to the house. That's when I noticed Sean on the beach. He was sitting on the sand, talking on his phone, looking out over the water. As I quietly approached him, he saw me and hung up.

"Just checking in with the family," he explained.

"You must miss them very much."

"I do," he replied.

"If you don't mind me asking, why didn't they come with you?"

"Frank felt it would be best if they stayed home. I would have fewer distractions. Besides, they have school, friends, and sports … but I do miss them." He sighed.

Sean seemed lonely, and I felt very sad for him being here without his family.

"But, I must say, looking out over the water is calming," he said.

"It is. I've solved a lot of problems looking out over the water. Hey, I have an idea. Frank and Ell are going out to dinner tonight. why don't you and I have a beach picnic dinner?"

"Frank's going out?" He was surprised by this news.

"Last I heard," I said.

Sean let out a sigh of what seemed to be either relief or concern. "Thanks for the offer. Can I let you know?"

"Sure, if not tonight, then another night," I replied.

Sean looked back at the mansion. "I'd better get back to my desk before … well, I'd better get back." He got up, looking a little broken.

"Sean, you know I'm here for you if you want to talk. Just between us, okay," I suggested.

He smiled, placing his hand on my shoulder. "I may take you up on that one day." He strolled up the pathway toward the house.

I was relieved when I didn't hear from Sean about dinner. I was tired and wanted to have a quiet meal alone on my little lanai and watch TV. Auntie Ell had told me before she went out about the family coming over tomorrow afternoon. I couldn't wait to see them, especially Erick.

CHAPTER SIXTY-NINE

Auntie Ell was up early the following day, fussing around. She was eager to see the family, and everything had to be perfect. Unfortunately, Donna and Anton were still away, and Bernie and Michael were meeting with Kaloe and Nakeli's social worker. I looked for Auntie Ell and found her humming while picking flowers in the garden. She looked content. Last night, I heard her and Frank laughing as they returned from their night out. I smiled when I recalled my parents coming home giggling after being out together. Mom would hum the same way.

By early afternoon, everything had been taken care of, and there was nothing for me to do. I decided to swim laps in the pool to try to get rid of my nervous energy.

I was swimming laps, in my own little world, when I looked up and saw Erick smiling down at me. I squealed with glee as I jumped out of the pool into his arms and wrapped my legs around his waist.

"You're getting me wet," Erick said, laughing while holding me tight.

"Don't care," I said, smothering him with kisses, then whispered, "Just hold me."

He held me tighter.

My aunt appeared out of nowhere. "Ally, you need to change. The others will be here soon. I'll keep this handsome man company. Besides, I need his help with the drinks."

I didn't want to let him go; I wanted to take him upstairs and make passionate love to him.

"Hurry, honey. I'll help Ell," he said as I finally let go of him.

"I won't be long," I said before kissing Erick's perfect lips. I grabbed my robe and ran upstairs.

When I returned, Adam and Megan had arrived with the twins, and Auntie Ell was cooing over the sleeping boys. I left them to go into the kitchen to check on Chef Anna.

Anna had prepared the salads and appetizers, but Adam and Erick had insisted they would do the cooking on the grill and asked Sean if he wanted to help. Sean looked a little lost with this crowd, and the boys tried to include him.

My aunt turned to Anna in the kitchen and said, "Why don't you leave early today? You've organized everything, and we're all capable of serving ourselves. Your family would love to have you home early for a change."

"If you're sure, Mrs. Ronan. My daughter is in a play tonight," Anna said.

"Then you must go. I insist. Get your bag and have a good night with your family."

It was good to see my auntie as her old self again.

Cassie and Mitch soon arrived, and Auntie Ell and I were in the kitchen getting the appetizers plated when Frank entered the kitchen. We didn't notice him at first, but after a few seconds, I felt his presence as if the air had been sucked out of the room.

"Where's Chef Anna?"

Auntie Ell immediately froze; she looked too afraid to move. Her mouth opened, but no words came out.

Wanting to protect her, I spoke up. "I gave her the night off. With everyone here and the boys wanting to cook, I thought it would be nice for Anna to spend time with her family."

The room fell silent as Frank glared at me.

Erick appeared at the doorway and sensed the tension. "Is everything okay?"

"Yes, they were about to take the appetizers out," I said with a smile as I handed Frank the tray.

Auntie Ell finally found her voice. "Come, darling, say hello to everyone." She took the platter from Frank, breaking his glare at me, and he followed his wife out of the kitchen.

I let out a sigh. I wanted to collapse in a heap but knew I couldn't.

"What was that about?" Erick asked, concerned.

I didn't want to get him involved, so I assured him all was okay and told him he had better check on Adam and Mitch.

He kissed me. "You're sure everything is okay?"

"Yes, go," I insisted. I wanted to be alone to pull myself together.

As I was taking the salads out of the fridge, I heard Frank behind me. "You're taking your position in my house for granted."

I knew he wouldn't have let it go.

"You're right, Frank. I apologize. I should've checked with you first. It won't happen again," I said, hoping my apology would stop him in his tracks.

He moved toward me. "Watch your step."

His threat scared me, and I couldn't move. I remember my father saying, "Don't poke the bear."

Cassie came into the kitchen, oblivious to what had happened. "Erick told me to bring you a glass of wine, and we also need another knife. My stupid husband dropped it. At least he didn't drop anything else." Then she looked at us. "Sorry, did I interrupt something?"

"No, we're done here," Frank said, leaving the kitchen.

Cassie handed me a glass of wine, and I downed it in one gulp.

"Wow, you needed that. Was Frank always that scary?" she asked.

"He is lately," I said, wanting to change the subject. "I think we've left those boys unsupervised for too long, and I need more wine."

Cassie agreed, and we joined the others. When we did, Frank was sitting at the table next to Auntie Ell, his arm firmly around her shoulders. The last thing I wanted to do was make eye contact with him.

* * *

Dinner was over, and we were all laughing and talking at the same time, which wasn't unusual for this crowd. Sean joined in, and Frank made an effort, which I suspected was for show.

The twins started to fuss.

"There they go, my little Geminis," Megan said.

Her comment took me by surprise. "What did you say?" I asked.

"Their zodiac sign is Gemini, and it fits them," Megan said as she got up to check on them.

"Frank is a Gemini also, aren't you, darling," Auntie Ell said.

Frank took her hand and kissed the back of it.

I froze. Erick touched my leg under the table. I knew he was trying to tell me to stay calm.

I felt as if there was no air around me. I quickly stood up to clear the table.

"Here, honey, I'll help you," Auntie Ell said.

Erick was quick to speak up. "You sit there, Ell. We've got this."

We collected as many dishes as possible and headed for the kitchen. I dumped the plates in the sink and put my hand over my mouth. I wanted to scream. Erick put his strong arms around me.

"I didn't want it to be true," I said, "but his behavior and this bit of information …"

Erick turned me around and hugged me tight. "It could be a coincidence—don't read anything into it," he said.

Mitch appeared in the kitchen with the rest of the dishes. "You guys need a hand, or do you want some cuddle time?"

277

"It's okay. We only need to load the dishwasher," I said pulling away from Erick to organized the dirty plates.

"We've got this. Why don't you go back and entertain everyone with your wit," Erick joked.

"Funny guy," Mitch said as he left the kitchen.

Erick massaged the back of my neck. "Why don't I stay the night?"

I wanted him to stay more than anything, but I didn't want to risk him getting involved. "Thank you, but it'll be fine. As you said, it's probably a coincidence."

Erick whispered, "Just remember our emergency word, and I'll be here in a flash."

I felt a little calmer.

Adam and Megan were getting the twins ready to leave when we got back outside from packing the dishwasher.

"We must get these little guys home. They've been good all night, and I don't want to risk a meltdown," Megan said.

Megan was a natural mother. To my surprise, Adam had turned out to be an excellent dad. Whenever I saw my brother with his boys, I thought how proud Dad would have been of his son. When this was over, I wanted to get closer to my nephews. I wanted to be the best aunt to them.

"We're going too. It's been a great evening," Cassie said, hugging me goodbye.

Everyone asked where Frank was, but he was nowhere to be seen. Only Sean had stayed. Auntie Ell apologized for her husband's absence, saying Frank had an urgent business matter and she would pass on their farewells.

As Auntie Ell, Erick, and I watched the guests drive away, a voice behind us startled me. It was Sean. I had forgotten he was there.

"I wanted to thank you both for a delightful family evening."

"You're welcome," I replied.

Sean turned and started up the stairs, then stopped a quarter-way up, turned around as if he was going to say something, but only smiled, then continued up the staircase.

Erick was still next to me. "I'm going to take my girl for a walk along the beach before I go," he said to Ell as he led me outside.

As we reached the cool sand, we kicked off our shoes and Erick led me to the water's edge.

"I don't want to talk about what's happening," I whispered.

"Neither do I. I miss dancing with you." Erick hummed our song, pulled me into his arms, and we started to dance.

"Be careful. There's a security camera on the beach," I whispered.

"I know—I saw. Let's give them something to watch," he whispered back as he held me closer.

I missed putting my arms around his neck. Feeling safe, I leaned against his warm body with his "Erick scent," as I called it. We danced to him humming in my ear on the sand as the cold water washed over our feet. It was as if we were the only people in the world. After we danced, we walked in the moonlight along the shoreline then sat on the sand outside the main house. We wrapped our arms around each other and didn't talk. I could have stayed there all night, but the guard patrolling the beach stopped to speak to us.

"Sorry, Ms. Kane, but Mr. Ronan wants the beach secured. Can you please take your guest to the patio area?" The guard stood there until we moved.

"I guess that's my cue to go," Erick said as he stood up and pulled me to my feet.

Once we were far enough away from the security camera and the guard, I quietly said to Erick, "This is Frank's way of controlling us. He does it all the time."

He whispered, "Let it go, honey, play his game now. Be patient. As you always say, *'karma's a bitch.'*"

I smiled and buried my face into his chest. I did say that, but I didn't think he was listening when I said it. Erick gently took my hand into his as we headed up the patio stairs. At the top, he pulled me into his arms and kissed me.

Just as he did, I saw a glimpse of Frank watching us from his office window. But as Erick kissed me, I forgot about it.

I led Erick to the front door; we were still wrapped in each other's arms.

"I love you," he sweetly whispered. "My offer to stay still stands."

"Go," I said. "Phone me when you get home."

Auntie Ell appeared at the door, and Erick wrapped his arms around her and thanked her for the evening. He hugged me again and kissed me ever so softly.

As I watched Erick drive off, I desperately wanted to go after him.

Auntie Ell looked exhausted and said she was going to bed. I told her I would clean up the kitchen as I didn't want any mess left for Anna. I also didn't want to give Frank any excuse to be displeased.

Later, as I left the kitchen, I heard loud, muffled voices from Frank's office. I should have listened to what they were saying, but I was tired and didn't want any more confrontations.

As I got to my bedroom door, I saw Frank ahead of me entering his bedroom. I was sure I had heard him in his office. Maybe I should go back downstairs and check it out. I was deciding what to do when my phone rang, and it was Erick.

"I'm home," he said.

When I heard his voice, I forgot about anything else.

"Are you in bed yet?" he asked.

"Nearly. I wanted to be sure the kitchen was perfect first. Want to talk to me until I fall asleep?"

"Sure."

We didn't talk long, and I was asleep when my head hit the pillow.

When I came downstairs the following day, I entered the kitchen and was surprised to see a male chef working.

"Hello, I'm George, the new chef. What can I get you?"

I was stunned. "Where's Anna?"

"I don't know. I was hired last night," he said.

I headed to the patio where Auntie Ell and Frank were finishing breakfast. Frank got up from the table, kissed Ell, and approached me.

"Your action had consequences," he said before going to his office.

I looked at Auntie Ell for her response.

She raised her hand and said, "Please, Ally, don't say anything. It's done, and I'm not going to discuss it." She got up from the table and left the patio.

I was left alone with my mouth open, not knowing what to say.

CHAPTER SEVENTY

We all spent most of the day apart; Frank and Sean were in their office, and my aunt sat in the corner of the living area reading, looking very unapproachable. I decided to go out paddling to check the flagpole. Thankfully, the flag was still at full mast.

Frank informed Auntie Ell that he and Sean were attending a dinner meeting. When my aunt told me, I thought this was my opportunity to talk with her without Frank around, so I suggested we have dinner on the beach like we used to when she visited my brother and me when we were younger. She thought it was a good idea, and thankfully, her mood changed toward me. We asked the new chef to prepare a simple dinner of grilled marinated chicken and salad.

It was starting to get dark as we sat in our beach chairs, and we watched the moonlight glisten on the water while we drank our wine, talking and laughing about old times.

"Why don't you play the piano more?" I asked her.

"Oh, it's a long story," she said as she looked at the water.

It was apparent she didn't want to talk about it, so I asked her to tell me stories about her and Mom growing up. I had heard them before but wanted to listen to them again. It was the most relaxed I had seen my aunt since she arrived on the island.

We were halfway through our second bottle of wine when my aunt suddenly said, "It hasn't been easy staying in this house, but you being here, supporting me, well, you don't know how much I appreciate it. I love you more than life. You know I don't have favorites, but you're the daughter I never had." She looked out over the dark water. "Maybe that's why I trust and expect more from you, more than your brother. I know that's not fair, but I feel we're connected in some way, similar to your mother and me, but different. Am I making sense?"

Her comments surprised me, but a security guard approached us before I could answer. It was the same guard from the night before.

"Excuse me, Mrs. Ronan. Don't you think it's time to go inside now? Mr. Ronan wants the beach secure at this time of night."

My aunt slowly turned her head and looked him up and down. "I will decide when it's time," she said, dismissing him.

He quickly moved away from us, a little stunned, and we both giggled.

Shortly after we had finished the wine, a crisp sea breeze began to blow, and we began to feel cold.

"I think it's time for this old girl to turn in. Thank you, darling, I needed this," she said and picked up the tray of dishes.

"Leave it. I'll clean up. You go to bed."

She stood up, kissed my cheek, and headed inside. I sat there for a bit longer, with the security guard not far away, enjoying the smell of the ocean on the evening breeze. Then I picked up the tray of dishes and took them into the kitchen.

I wandered around the house, watching the security guard from afar and observing the stillness around me. When Frank and Sean returned from their dinner, I needed to say something to improve the atmosphere.

"Did your meeting go well?" I asked.

Frank didn't answer.

"Auntie Ell and I had dinner on the beach," I said, trying to explain.

Frank turned away and went upstairs.

I decided to go to bed, but I waited until I heard his bedroom door close before going up.

* * *

I dreamt of walking on the beach hand in hand with Erick when I sensed a strange presence in my room. I woke with a start. Frank stood at the end of my bed, watching me with anger in his eyes.

"Frank, what are you doing?" I yelled as I sat up, grabbed my sheet, and held it to my chest, feeling very vulnerable in his presence.

"You're late," he said.

I checked my watch. "It's only six forty."

"If you didn't roam the house at all hours of the night and have beach parties till late, you would be up earlier," he said before turning and leaving my room.

As soon as he had gone, I leapt out of bed and ran to the door to make sure it was closed, then locked it and jammed a chair against it. Why was Frank in my room? Did he know why I was here, or was he trying to scare me? If that's what he was trying to do, he had been successful.

I sat on the floor, shaking. I wanted to phone Erick, but I knew he would rush over and cause a scene.

When I finally got to my feet, I was still trembling. I had to calm down and work out what to do. I couldn't tell my aunt as it could cause problems, and I would probably have to leave, and I would want my aunt to come with me. Frank was becoming unhinged and dangerous. Our safety was at risk.

I thought of something I hadn't in a long time: what would my mother do? I knew. My mother would protect her sister no matter what. Somehow, I had to get Auntie Ell out of here and away from this man. The operation wasn't my priority now. It was our safety.

I quickly dressed in my lightweight black summer pants and green sleeveless top, barely brushing my hair and teeth. I was trying to decide how to approach her about leaving when I heard shouting from her bedroom. I pressed my ear to my door, trying to hear what they were saying, but I couldn't.

Suddenly, I heard a door slam, and Frank's heavy footsteps along the corridor and down the stairs.

Slowly, I opened my door, crept to my aunt's room, and quietly knocked. I opened her door. "Auntie Ell, we need to talk."

She was pacing when I entered, and without even looking at me, she said, "Not now, Ally."

I wasn't going to be dismissed. "Auntie Ell, what's wrong?"

She stopped, put her hands on her hips, and stared at me. She looked like my mother. "Frank said you tried to break into his office. Did you?" she snapped at me.

All I could say was, "What? No, I never tried to break into Frank's office."

"He said you've been roaming the house at night, going where you shouldn't."

"Some nights I sit on the patio with a cup of herbal tea. I didn't know Frank expected me to stay in my room at night." I erupted. "Did he tell you he was in my room this morning while I slept?"

She didn't want to hear me. "Don't start turning things around, Alexandria. Did you or did you not try and break into his office?"

I wanted to tell her the truth but couldn't. "I'm insulted by Frank's accusations."

"He thinks you may need professional help. Maybe he's right," she said.

Her words hurt. "You can't be serious. You don't believe that, do you?"

"I don't know. I'm no longer sure about anything. Maybe we all need some professional help," she said as she put her hand up to her forehead.

It was then that I noticed the bruises.

I moved toward her, took her left hand, and pushed up her blue chiffon sleeve. There were fresh and old bruises on her arm. I checked her right arm, and there were more.

"He did this to you. Where else are you hurt?" I was horrified.

She pulled her arms away from me. "Don't change the subject."

"Me roaming the house at night is a little different from him physically hurting you, and you still haven't answered my question, which makes me believe he did." I was yelling.

Eloise turned her back on me.

"I'll kill him," I said.

"No, you won't," she replied. "Why do people think I'm helpless and can't care for myself? That I'm so frail I need my niece to protect me? Well, I don't," Auntie Ell sounded angry. "You wouldn't think of your mother as being helpless." She stopped talking.

"What are you saying?" I was confused.

"You judge Frank the same as you judged your mother." She was pacing around the bedroom again.

Again, I was stunned. "Auntie Ell, look at your arms. Frank is not the person we all thought he was. He's mean and dangerous and trying to drive a wedge between us. Look at the way he treats you. Look at the way he treats his brother," I pointed out.

She came up to my face as she had never done before. "You think you're the only one who knows this? You're quick to judge without stopping to think what others are going through, what your mother went through." Then she turned her back on me again. "I was lucky Frank forgave me. He could have left me, but didn't because he loves me," she said.

"Why would Frank leave you? You're the one who has to leave him. Leave him now," I pleaded.

"Because I was the one who had the affair."

It took me a moment to realize what she had said.

"What? When?" They were the only words I could get out.

She hesitated for a moment, then told me, "About eight months ago. Frank was working all the time, and Scott from the club was kind and caring, and one night …" She started to cry. "I told Frank, and he said he forgave me."

Trying to calm the situation, I softly said, "Auntie Ell, you having an affair is no reason for Frank to hurt you. You need to leave him. There is no excuse for what he is doing to you."

"I changed him. My actions made him this way. He doesn't trust me or you, and he said I was as deceitful as his mother and that he would never let me leave. It's all my fault," she blurted out. "I love Frank, and I love you. I haven't told anyone else about what's happened, so tell or don't tell people. I don't care. Life is too short, and you must go home and get on with yours." She turned her back on me, picked up her handbag, and walked off.

All this information was overwhelming, but I knew I had to go after her. "Wait, I'll come with you. We have to talk," I called out.

"No, I'm going alone. We've talked enough," she said firmly. She was practically running down the stairs with me not far behind her.

I didn't know what was happening. Frank had been driving a wedge between us, and Ell made statements I didn't understand. "Auntie Ell, please wait."

But she wasn't listening.

My aunt and I had hardly fought before, and it scared me. I ran down the stairs, trying to catch up with her when Ming stepped in between us.

"I think your aunt wants to be alone," she said.

"Get the hell out of my way," I growled as I pushed by her.

When I had Auntie Ell in my sights again, she was getting into her waiting car. Her driver had the door open, and he closed it behind her. As he was getting into the driver's seat, he stopped for a second and looked at me with a weird smile. I realized it wasn't her normal driver, Andrew. I had never seen this person before, and I was suddenly very afraid.

The car drove off, and I ran after it, calling her name, but it sped out of the gate, disappearing into the distance. The last thing I saw was Ell looking back at me.

I quickly ran into the house, noticing on the way that the guard at the gate was gone. Something was happening.

CHAPTER SEVENTY-ONE

As I made my way to the front door, I was frantic. Sean ran up to me.

"Ally, what's going on?"

"Ell got into her car, but I didn't know the driver. I called out, but the car wouldn't stop. I think he plans to hurt her even more," I said, trying hard to catch my breath. "I must go after her. I need your car."

Sean looked confused. "What do you mean 'hurt' her?"

"He's been hurting her, Sean. Your brother has been abusing her," I yelled.

"No, Frank loves her. He wouldn't hurt Ell."

"I saw the bruises, and she told me. I need to go after her. Please, Sean, your keys."

"Wait here in case she comes back. I'll go after her. It's going to be fine. I promise," Sean assured me.

"Sean, please hurry. I'm scared."

Sean headed straight for the garage. I felt relieved he was going after her. I was scared for my aunt's safety. I knew I needed to confront Frank. I had had enough.

I ran to Frank's office and barged in without knocking. He barely looked up as I entered, which angered me more.

"Where is she?" I demanded.

"Not now," he said.

"Does Eloise know who you are?" I asked.

He tried to brush me off again. "I don't know what you're talking about, Ally. You've been acting very strangely lately. But you've always been a little strange. You need professional help. I've told your aunt that," he said.

"Was it before you gave her more bruises?" I said, snarling at him.

He stopped moving papers on his desk and looked up at me. "I don't know what you're talking about."

I could see I was starting to annoy him.

"I know," I said. "I know about your illegal activities. I know people refer to you as Gemini." I was enraged. I moved closer to his desk. "I swear if you hurt her again, I'll make sure the full force of the law comes after you."

Before I knew what was happening, Frank leapt from his chair and grabbed my arms. I could feel his fingers dig into my flesh.

"Don't you threaten me. Who do you think you are? Your relationship with Erick is pitiful. As for my wife, who made a mockery of our marriage, she will never embarrass me again. And if she tries to leave me, I'll make her so miserable she will wish she were dead. She's as deceitful as your scum of a mother."

I broke free from his grasp and slapped him hard across his face.

But it didn't seem to affect him, and he laughed. "Is that the best you can do?" He put his face to mine. I could tell he was about to hit me when he saw something behind me that stopped him. "Get the hell out of here. I'll call you when I need you!" he shouted.

Before I could turn around to see who he was speaking to, I felt a sharp blow to the back of my head, and I fell to the floor unconscious.

CHAPTER SEVENTY-TWO

Lying unconscious on the cold stone floor, I thought I heard my father's voice saying. "Come on, my beautiful ballerina, get up now."

I quickly opened my eyes, but my dad wasn't there.

The smell of old dust hit me first, and when my eyes were fully open, I could see I was in the dimly lit wine cellar. The pain in my head made it difficult to lift it, but after hearing my father's voice, I knew I had to get up.

Slowly looking around, waiting for my eyesight to adjust, I noticed a man lying on his side in one corner of the cellar, not moving. I recognized his shoes and pants. It was Frank.

I crawled over to him, calling his name. When I got to him, I tried waking him. I continued to shout his name and shake him until his body rolled over. There was a bullet hole in the middle of his forehead. Someone had shot Frank.

I'll never forget the look on his face—one of complete surprise.

My head pounded, and I was terrified as I crawled into a corner of the cellar and stared at Frank's body. I was shaking, unable to take my eyes off him. Then I realized I didn't know where my aunt was. Fear took over. *Had she been shot as well?*

Then a voice came out of the shadows.

"He always thought he was smarter. Everyone assumed I was weak and incompetent, could only take instructions and abuse, and wasn't capable of doing anything else. And some, including you, felt sorry for me. Now Frank has learnt the hard way."

My eyes adjusted to the figure talking. It was Sean.

"Sean, Frank's dead."

Sean smiled at me. His demeanor had changed. "My brother wouldn't listen to me when I first wanted to 'expand' the business," he said.

"What? Frank's been shot!" I yelled, trying to get Sean to understand his brother was dead.

But he continued talking. "I set plans in motion years ago and continued to let my idiot brother think he was the one calling all the shots. When your cheating aunt came along, it made him weaker and easier to manipulate, and I could finally execute my plans."

My mind became clearer. "You shot Frank?"

"I noticed the tension between you and Frank when you moved in. I didn't know it would work to my advantage. I have to say, seeing you two at the sickening family dinner made my day. It took all my strength not to laugh," he said with delight. "My business deal is nearly complete, and I needed the perfect moment to catch Frank off-guard, so when you stormed into his office yelling at him about Eloise leaving, it allowed me to make my move. I had always planned that Frank would die sooner or later. I just had to wait for the perfect time." He spoke with no emotion at all.

"So, you murdered him?"

"Oh, dear, Ally, I don't like to call it murder. I think of it as putting him out of his misery," Sean said with a laugh.

"Where is my aunt?"

"By now, your aunt has joined her husband in the afterlife, thanks to my driver, who will say he was stopped and ambushed by masked men, which led to her unfortunate death," he said joyfully.

"The different driver in the car, you organized that." I was putting it all together.

"I know I promised you I'd find her, but I had no intention of chasing after her car, and no one was around to hear our conversation. All people will see on the security cameras is me on the beach. So, I have an alibi," he said, very proud of himself.

I yelled at him, "You bastard, she did nothing to you. She only showed you kindness." I tried to fight back the tears at the thought of my beautiful aunt being murdered.

"Maybe you should be more concerned about what's going to happen to you," he said as he pulled out a gun from his back waistband.

"You won't get away with this."

He moved closer. "I think I will. Nobody knows who I am. I've kept a low profile, stayed in the background all my life, and let Frank take the lead on everything, making it easy for people to think he was in charge." He laughed. "Playing with people's minds is entertainment to me, and I enjoy it greatly. After I shoot you, I'll tell the authorities I came down here looking for Frank and found you both dead. Any suspicion will lead to the housekeeper as she has also disappeared, never to be seen again," he stated.

"Ming? I don't understand."

"Ming was only a house manager, nothing more. However, the forged documents we created suggest she was working for a Chinese shipping company. When the negotiations failed, Ming was under orders to assassinate Frank, Eloise, and me, but she couldn't find me, and you happened to be in the wrong place at the wrong time.

"I will be heartbroken at losing my dear brother, sweet sister-in-law, and caring friend. It won't be hard for people to believe, as no one thinks I have the spine to orchestrate such an elaborate scheme, and I made sure there's no evidence to implicate me. I'll be free to run the company my way." He said all this with delight.

Sean's words made me outraged rather than scared. My mother was a spy and my father a firefighter; surely, I have some of their fearless genes. I used the stone wall behind me to stand up.

"If you're going to shoot me, the least you could do is tell Erick I was eating pizza the last time you saw me. He deserves that much, and it will give him some peace." If Erick heard our safe word, I hoped it would point to Sean.

"Pizza?" Sean laughed at me. "You're pathetic."

I was praying the planted bug in the cellar was active and that the agents next door had been listening in. Hopefully on their way to help me. For now, I needed to keep Sean talking.

"What about your family? Your kids?" I asked.

The question hit a nerve, and he became irritated, waving the gun around. "Those little brats and that whore of a wife. I filed for divorce before I left home, and with no prenuptial agreement, they won't get much."

My adrenaline kicked in, and I wanted to provoke him. "You won't get away with it, and you know why?"

"Go ahead. Amuse me before I put a bullet in your head." He was very smug.

"The government knows you're involved. They know you're Gemini, and they've known for some time."

He laughed. "Nice try. Everything leads to Frank."

"Go ahead, laugh. I've been working for them the whole time. When I arrived here one of the first things I did was plant listening devices in the office and here, so they've heard *everything*, and I passed on all the information I could get. Ask yourself, Sean, how did I know about Gemini?"

He looked at me in disbelief.

I leant forward and continued. "Why do you think I went paddleboarding all the time? It was to hand over information. Did you know the agency is next door? Your false documents leading to Frank won't work. *We* have evidence it was you. Poor Sean, so badly treated, won't be believed with what the agency has on you." I smiled at him. "Now, who's having the last laugh?"

Before he could reply, a noise came from the top of the stairs. As Sean turned his head, I lunged at him, hoping he would drop the gun and maybe I would have a chance to get away.

My efforts were in vain as we both fell to the ground, and Sean never lost control of the gun. He picked himself up, and as I tried to stand, he grabbed my arm and threw me back onto the floor.

"You're more stupid than I thought." Sean seemed unnerved, but he was still pointing the gun at me. "Too much talking, you lying bitch."

Terrified, I knew my time was up. I closed my eyes, and my whole body tensed, waiting for the bullet to hit me, then I heard the gunshot, but nothing happened.

I opened my eyes to see Sean with the same look of surprise on his face as his dead brother, as blood dripped from his head. Someone had shot Sean from behind.

CHAPTER SEVENTY-THREE

I was in shock and unable to move when I saw her. "Mom" was all I could manage to say as she stood over Sean's body with a gun in her hand.

She crouched down next to me. "Darling, are you alright?"

"Mom?" I said again.

"You need to get up, okay?"

I pointed to Frank.

"I know. Come on. Get up now," she said.

She helped me to my feet, and I threw my arms around her. I had never been so happy to see her.

"It was Sean. He's Gemini," I babbled.

"I know," she replied.

"He killed Auntie Ell."

"No. Ell's safe. I was able to intercept the car before anything happened, but I wasn't quick enough to save Frank," she explained.

I hugged my mother again. I didn't want to let her go.

CHAPTER SEVENTY-FOUR

Eva

As I led Ally out of the wine cellar with my arm tightly around her, she buried her face into my shoulder as we hit the bright sunlight.

The house was filled with agents and police. I turned and saw Agent Donaldson heading my way, but I kept walking. My only concern was to get my daughter outside.

Donaldson caught up to me. "Agent, a moment, please. We need to debrief."

I realized I was still holding the gun I used to shoot Sean, and I handed it to Donaldson and kept walking. "I'm taking my daughter to get checked out."

"Fine. There's an ambulance outside to check you both over, then you'll be taken to a safe house," he said.

I didn't even stop to listen. When I reached the ambulance near the front door, the paramedics took Ally, put her in the back, and placed her on a stretcher. I followed her.

Agent Donaldson came to the back of the door. "Agent, a word, now."

I bent over Ally as she lay on the stretcher and kissed her forehead.

"Don't go," she said.

"I'll be right outside. I won't take my eyes off you, I promise," I assured her. I stood at the back of the ambulance so she could still see me.

"You broke protocol," Donaldson said.

I was trying very hard not to lose my temper. "You told me my daughter would be safe. You said nothing would happen. So, yeah, I broke protocol, and you should be glad I did because if Sean had shot my daughter, I would have shot you next," I said. I hadn't blinked the whole time I had spoken.

Agent Donaldson shifted his weight, a little taken aback. "Agent, I know you're upset. I'll give you and Ally a moment, and we'll talk again when you're in the safe house."

One of the paramedics came out of the ambulance. "Your daughter is okay. She may have a concussion and will need to be watched."

"Is she right to travel?" Donaldson asked.

"Yes. Watch her for a few days for any symptoms of concussion."

Before the paramedic finished explaining, two agents went into the ambulance, ushered Ally out, and escorted the two of us into the back of a black van.

Ally placed her head on my shoulder. "What's happening?" she asked.

"We're going to a safe house. It's standard procedure," I tried to explain.

Ally started to panic. "What about Auntie Ell and Erick and …?"

"Shh, everyone's okay. Eloise is in a safe place, and we have a lot of people watching over the others. Erick has been notified, and he's also helping to watch the family," I reassured her.

"Erick knows what happened? Can I see him?" Ally asked.

"Not yet, honey, but soon."

Ally closed her eyes, and we rode in silence.

CHAPTER SEVENTY-FIVE

The safe house had one bedroom, a small kitchen with a table, and a bathroom. When we arrived, I put Ally on the double bed and reassured her that everyone, including us, was safe, then stood at the bedroom door and watched her sleep.

When Ally was born, I spent most of my time standing in her bedroom doorway, watching her. I didn't see a grown woman now. I saw my little girl.

"I've been informed Ally will be fine," Agent Donaldson said. He had arrived not long before and now stood next to me.

"Yeah, no thanks to you," I snapped.

"She knew all the risks."

"She's my daughter and should've never been approached." I was furious.

Donaldson looked tired and frustrated. "Your daughter wasn't our first choice, but you were off the grid. We had to reassess the situation and review every possible scenario before deciding Ally was our best option. If she hadn't got all the intel when she did, the body count would've been a lot higher. Did you ever stop and think why Ally was so eager to join us?"

His question made me uneasy, and I didn't want to think about the answer. "Let's get this debriefing over with," I said, sitting at the kitchen table. I told Donaldson everything from the beginning to now, how I discovered by accident that the agency had enlisted Ally for the Gemini operation, and how I was furious about it. When I questioned the agency, I was instructed that under no circumstances was I to interfere. However, I convinced them to keep me informed. I reviewed the recordings daily, waiting to step in if I felt my daughter and sister might be in danger.

When the last recording reached me, we realized Sean was Gemini, not to mention a psychopath. I begged the agency to step in, but they needed the final bit of information, a confession, so I knew I had to act.

A fellow agent, a friend, and I intercepted Eloise's car, hoping Eloise and Ally were together and could be taken to safety. When I found out Ally wasn't in the car, I tried to get to her and Frank. I wasn't quick enough to save Frank, but I got to Ally in time. I had chills every time I thought about how if I had been a second slower, I might have lost my daughter forever.

I didn't care about the repercussions of stepping in. I would do it again.

The debriefing went on through the night. Every hour I would stop to check on Ally.

Finally, Donaldson left. He said he would be back the next day for Ally's debriefing and that another agent would come with supplies.

I was exhausted and needed to lie down. *You're getting too old for this shit,* I told myself.

It was going to be a tough few days ahead. I would get Ally through her debriefing, then she would have to face her aunt.

I lay next to my daughter and put my hand on hers, watching every breath she took until I finally fell asleep.

CHAPTER SEVENTY-SIX

Ally

In the early hours of the morning, I woke with a start. My mother was asleep next to me with her hand on mine.

I lay there staring at her, studying her face. She looked a little older since the last time I saw her. There were a few more gray hairs and lines around her eyes, but she was still beautiful.

I had always imagined that Erick would be the one to come riding up on a white horse if I needed rescuing. But my mother didn't need a white horse, as many mothers don't. They appear at the precise moment to save their child. Mothers put their bodies, minds, and spirits between their child and a schoolyard bully or a crazed gunman.

As I lay there thinking about my childhood and my mother, I knew I didn't want to lose her again.

I was woken again later in the morning by Mom stroking my forehead. It helped soothe my headache.

"Donaldson will be here soon. Please answer all his questions truthfully and ask him anything you want. You'll need closure about what's happened."

After eating a little bit of breakfast, I showered and changed. I don't even know how my clothes got there.

When Agent Donaldson arrived, we sat at the kitchen table, relieved that my mother insisted on joining us. After he took my statement and I answered all his questions, I signed a confidential paper indicating that I would not talk to anyone about what had transpired.

Now it was my turn. And I needed answers.

Thanks to the listening devices I had planted, the agency had confirmed the day before that Sean was Gemini but waited to get more on him and Wang-Lei, the son-in-law of Mr. Ching, the owner of the Chinese shipping company being investigated. They also needed to ensure that Frank and Mr. Ching were not involved.

Sean and Wang-Lei had been working for many years together, using their businesses for illegal activity and planning to dispose of Frank and Mr. Ching at the right time. Two powerful men from powerful companies, so wrapped up in their importance that they didn't know members of their own families were manipulating them and planning their demise.

I asked Donaldson about the comment Sean made about Ming. He confirmed that, unfortunately, they had found Ming's body and that she was an innocent bystander. The agency found the forged documents. If they hadn't heard otherwise, everything would have been pointed to Ming for our deaths. I felt sorry for Ming and the mean things I thought about her while I was there.

As for the security guards, none were involved; they were only carrying out orders from Sean and Frank.

Wang-Lei fled before he could be arrested. However, the Ching family was "taking care" of him.

I had one more important question.

"When can we go home?" I asked Donaldson.

"Soon. There are a few things to check, and we need to finalize the cover story of what happened," he said.

My mother put her arm around me. "Honey, we need something to tell everyone about Frank and Sean."

"So, we have to lie to everyone?" I fired back.

"Yes," she said. "Of course, Eloise and Erick know what happened, but we all must be on the same page with our story."

In a quiet voice, I said I understood and turned to Agent Donaldson. "Does the agency agree I've fulfilled my part of the agreement? I did what I was instructed to do, and I'm now finished with the agency, right?" I wanted to go back to my boring life. I wanted to be back home with Erick, Blossom, and my family and friends, including my mother and aunt.

"Yes, you're released from any association with the agency. You've completed your assignment and fulfilled your agreement, and we won't be contacting you again," he said.

"What about my mother? You and I had a deal that my mother would also be permanently released from the agency if I did this assignment."

I heard my mother gasp.

Donaldson looked at her. "We intended to keep to the agreement; however, the rest is up to Eva." He got up and left.

"Ally, what did you do?" she asked.

"When they came to me about the assignment, my conditions were that I could tell Erick and that they would release you from all your future commitments."

She was speechless.

"If you want to. I can't make you come home. I guess I was hoping ..."

She looked stunned.

"Please, at least think about it. You have grandsons now. Don't you want to see them grow up?"

"Of course I do. I've wanted to for a long time. But, honey, you and I must clear things up before I can come home. We need to talk about the past," she said.

Mom was right. We had a lot to discuss before the two of us could move on. She stared into my eyes, and I shifted my weight in the chair.

"I know what I did in your mind is unforgivable," she said, "but, darling, I must explain. Ally, I didn't send Erick away. It wasn't me, but I didn't stop it either, and I'm sorry for that. All I could see was my daughter's romantic involvement with this man who hadn't told her the truth, and I thought if he left you would move on with your life. I didn't know how much in love you both were, and I didn't see it until after he was gone. I tried to find Erick and get him back to you, but the agency had shut all doors to me. Then when I saw how distraught you were, I couldn't bear to see the pain I had put you through. I felt I had failed you again and couldn't fix it, so my instinct was to run and stay away. I guess I got that from my mother. She ran from Eloise and me."

I sat in silence as I listened to her, then I asked, "Why didn't you give me Erick's message? Things could have been better if I had only known he might be coming back to me."

"I didn't want you to put your life on hold, waiting for someone who might come back. But I realize now it wasn't my decision, and I'm sorry," she said as she took hold of my hand. "When I eventually found Erick, I negotiated with the agency to release him early from his contract, hoping he would return to you. And before you ask, no, Erick doesn't know anything about it."

"What about you now? Do you still want to stay in the agency?" I asked.

"I'm tired, Ally. I want peace and to be with my children and sister."

"I'm also tired, Mom. I'm tired of being angry with you and I don't want to blame you for my problems anymore. That's unfair. I want you to come home. Please come home." I was begging her. It was something I thought I would never have the opportunity to do.

"That's what I want, to be with my family. Maybe we can talk Eloise into staying here with us," she said.

"Auntie Ell. I have to face her. Where is she? I must try to explain."

"She's been staying at Adam's. I saw them both yesterday while you were asleep," she said.

"How did you explain your sudden return?"

"I told Adam I heard about Eloise and Frank's situation and decided it was time for me to come home."

"What did Adam say when you saw him? Is he okay?" I asked.

"He hugged me and handed me my grandbabies," she replied with a smile. "Your aunt is coming here soon. She wants to talk to you. Please remember she's grieving over Frank and feels betrayed."

"I didn't betray her." I felt the need to defend myself.

"I know. No one understands the reasoning that's going through your head at the moment better than I do, so my advice to you is to let Eloise talk and get her feelings out. It was the mistake I made before with you and your brother, not accepting how you were feeling. I don't want you to make the same mistake," she explained.

It wasn't long before my aunt arrived at the safe house. She and my mother hugged, but Aunt Ell would only look at me with her arms crossed.

"Are you okay?" I asked her.

She didn't answer.

"I'm sorry about Frank, I—"

She put her hand up to stop me, and a sharp pain struck my chest.

"Are you? Are you sorry about Frank?" she asked.

"Yes, of course I am," I replied. "I never wanted it to end this way."

"Stop. Stop talking, Alexandria."

I paused and attempted to follow my mother's suggestion and acknowledge my aunt's feelings.

"I stupidly expect more from you, more than anyone else. How could you not tell me? After all you went through with your mother and Erick. I felt betrayed," she lashed out. "Was that the real reason you pretended to be caring toward me? So, you could get in the house to spy on us?"

I heaved a long sigh. "I didn't stay with you because of Frank. I would have stayed with you anyway. You know I would do anything for you. But you have to admit it wasn't a very safe situation he put you in. Part of you must have wanted me there for support." I paused. "I'm sorry you had to go through that. I know that awful feeling of being betrayed by someone you love. I'm sorry I hurt you and didn't tell you what was happening, and I'm sorry about Frank."

"You don't get to talk about Frank. He was innocent in this."

"Innocent? Frank was hurting you." I turned to my mother. "Did you know? Did you know he was physically abusing your sister?"

"She told me," my mother said quietly.

"That's no reason for him to die the way he did. When I think you"—she clenched her hands to hold back her tears—"we could have been burying you," she said. "I nearly lost you as well. How could you have put yourself and Frank in danger?"

I defended myself. "I didn't put Frank in danger. His brother did. I didn't kill Frank, his brother did, and if you hadn't left when you did, he would have killed you too," I said. "Did you know before they came to the island that Sean and his partner planned to get rid of Frank and Mr. Ching?"

"Alexandria, stop," my mother said.

I drew a breath and slowly released it before speaking again.

"What is the cover story?" I asked quietly.

We all sat at the kitchen table, then Mom started to explain. "The cover story is that Frank's business would have bankrupted a rival overseas organization, so they sent someone to stop Frank and Sean from continuing with the merger. Due to the involvement of an international firm, the government is conducting a thorough review of everything in the house, and you are both assisting them. You didn't see the shooting, but you found the bodies. After hearing of the deaths and your traumatic experiences, I rushed to help you both get through it. That's the story, and we must stick to it. You two must understand how important it is. Only Erick and the three of us know the truth apart from the agency," she said.

"What about Sean's family?"

"They told his wife the same story, and his body is being shipped back to her," she explained.

"I never thought Sean would be … he didn't seem to have a bad bone in his body," I said.

My aunt spoke up. "Sean acted beaten down by Frank. He reminded me of Uncle Mike, and I was too frightened to say anything because Frank was already furious with me about the affair."

My mother leant over to her sister and hugged her tightly.

"Auntie Ell, I love you. We will be okay, won't we? Please, can we be okay?" I asked.

"I'm angry, Alexandria. Not only with you, but with Frank, Sean, and myself. Sean didn't only make his brother look foolish," she said grimly. "Frank was so busy controlling me that he didn't see what was happening in front of his face. I want to scream. I want to scream at them, but you're the only one here." She paused. "I have to get through tomorrow first."

"Tomorrow? What's happening tomorrow?" I asked.

Auntie Ell let out a sigh. "I'm burying Frank. It will be private with only me and Eva there. I need to bury him and move on." she said.

I wanted to object and tell her I wanted to be there and support her, but I realized she had to do this by herself with my mother.

"I know you're mad at me now, but I'm here for you. I will always be here for you," I assured her.

CHAPTER SEVENTY-SEVEN

Ally

When I arrived home the next day, my house was quiet apart from the soft music coming from the back deck. Blossom was lying on the cool wooden floor, purring as if she hadn't noticed I had been away.

As I slowly moved toward the music, I saw Erick sitting in the sun, humming. I watched him for a moment. I loved this man more than I ever thought possible. How stupid I was to risk it all.

I walked up behind him and put my arms around his neck.

"Careful, my girlfriend will be home soon," he joked. He stood and hugged me. "At last, you're home. Blossom missed you."

We kissed.

"I don't ever want to leave again. I want to stay home."

Erick put me down but kept his arms around me. "Good, because I'm not going anywhere, and from what I hear, your mom's staying too."

"I know. It's good news. I told Mom she could stay with us until she's settled. I hope that's okay. I know I should have checked with you first," I said.

Erick put me at arm's length and looked into my eyes. I thought he might object to the plan, but all he said was, "That's fine. I get how important it is for her to come home. But your mom and I need to have a serious conversation alone at some point.

"It's going to be okay. You know Ell's been staying with Adam? She and I talked last night. I guess she wanted to talk to someone who knew what happened," he explained.

"I'm happy you two could talk. I hope one day she'll forgive me," I said.

"She will. At the moment, she's angry and disappointed with many people, including herself. She still loves you. Give her time," he told me.

"She said she loves me?"

A smile came over his face. "Well, I had to put her in a chokehold to say it," Erick said with a laugh, "but yes, she truly loves you. And a part of her understands why you got involved and was glad you were there. She's not ready yet to admit it."

"Thanks, I needed to hear that."

"So, tell me, my beautiful lady, are you all finished with the spy business?"

"Yes. Although it did make me think about my future … I've been thinking about returning to school and getting my certification to teach dance to disabled and underprivileged kids. Every child deserves the opportunity to dance if they want to, whatever their circumstances. I thought I might get Mom involved and get her to help me set up the dance studio and program. It'd be something we could do together. What do you think?"

"I think that's a great idea. You have my full support." He smiled but looked as though there was something else he needed to say.

"What is it? I know that look."

"I love you more than anything, Ally, but there are things we must discuss and agree on so we can move forward."

"Such as?" I asked.

"Such as we always tell each other the truth, no matter what. No more secrets and spying for either of us. I won't go through this again, Ally. Agreed?" he asked.

"Agreed."

"Also, I'm happy with the way things are, but I'm also happy to get married if you want to."

I was shocked. "Is this a proposal?"

"Do you want it to be? Either way, I'm fine as long as we're together."

I always thought I would say yes to marriage, but I told him I was content with how things were for the time being.

"Okay then, but if either of us changes our minds, we tell each other. Agreed?"

"Agreed." I threw my arms around his neck, and a wave of calmness washed over me.

Erick held me in his arms, and we kissed and started to dance to the music on the radio.

* * *

Months later, Erick and I adopted a little girl named Molly. She was an adorable three-year-old golden Labrador we rescued from the pound. She was excited to run with Erick or take slow walks on the beach with me, Mom, and Auntie Ell.

Neither Erick, Mom, nor I heard from the agency again. Donaldson kept his word.

I enjoyed returning to school, and my mom was looking forward to participating in the new dance program.

In front of our family and friends, Erick and I had a beach ceremony to exchange commitment rings with Molly and Blossom by our side. Neither of us felt the need to get married as our commitment to each other was as strong as it could be.

We had our fur babies, and the four of us were happy.

Maybe one day we will get married. Maybe.

CHAPTER SEVENTY-EIGHT

Eva

The sun was glistening on the water and a soft sea breeze gently swept over my sister Eloise and me as we sat on the back deck of Ally's house and watched our family playing on the beach. It was Eloise's and my birthday, and we were celebrating it with family and friends. It had been a long time since we had spent our birthday together, and I had missed it.

Eloise stayed on the island and moved her belongings, including our grandmother's piano, to the bungalow we purchased together, close to the kids. I was complete and content living with her again.

After Frank's funeral, Eloise never mentioned him, and she didn't want to be reminded of him or his brother. She only took enough money from Frank's estate to live comfortably and gave the rest to a shelter for abused women.

Eloise and Ally went through an emotional time, but it didn't take long for them to get back the special bond they once had.

Megan was sitting near us. She and Adam were expecting another baby. She got up from her chair and asked where Adam was.

"I am tired of feeling like a whale," she said.

Megan was very close to her due date, but though she may have been feeling like a whale, she looked radiant. She picked up my hand and placed it on her belly, and I felt my granddaughter kick.

I couldn't wait to meet her.

Megan saw Adam running up to her. "Come on, husband, we will walk until this baby comes out," she said.

"Whatever you want, my darling," he said and took her hand. Adam reminded me a lot of his father.

From inside the house, there was a tiny baby's cry. Cassie and Mitch had a two-month-old girl, Harper, in her travel cot. Harper settled herself and fell back to sleep.

Bernie and Michael were ecstatic as Kaloe and Nakeli's adoption had been finalized.

My amazing daughter and Donna were dancing on the beach with Cassie, showing Donna's and Bernie's little girls how to dance the hula. Memories came flooding back from when Ally was little, dancing and laughing on the beach with her friends. My daughter was still a beautiful dancer.

Erick was with Mitch, Michael, and Anton, playing with Adam's twins, competing to make the best sandcastle. I think the men were enjoying it more than the kids.

The sound of the laughter from the beach brought back wonderful memories of my sister and me playing with Dad and Uncle Mike. I watched all that was happening around me, feeling very blessed. I was back with my family for good, and the past was finally behind us.

My eyes filled with tears, and Eloise asked if I was okay.

"Yes. This is what Dad and Uncle Mike wanted for us. To be with family and friends we love and who love us."

With that, Eloise reached over and took hold of my hand, and we looked into each other's eyes and recited our twin chant.

"We were born together, and together we will always be."

THE END

www.ingramcontent.com/pod-product-compliance
Lightning Source LLC
Chambersburg PA
CBHW040517170726
48295CB00012B/234